KING

A Deep 8 novel

_____

KENZIE MACALLAN

KING
a Deep 8 novel

Praise for Kenzie Macallan

"This series keeps getting better. I thought book 1 was good but book two was even better." **Tonya Peterson, Goodreads ★★★★★**

"I was TOTALLY and COMPLETELY engrossed in this suspenseful, unique who-done-it. I couldn't flip the pages fast enough to get to the conclusion...and when I got there, I was so sad that it was over! I didn't want this book to end and for me, that makes this a definite 5 STAR read! Kenzie Macallan is a shining star in the Indie community, DEFINITELY an author who needs to be heard!!!"
   Jacquie, Goodreads ★★★★★

"It's the mystery of this story that 1st grabbed my attention and it's the way secrets and lies are discovered and unlocked that kept me enthralled." **Bren, Goodreads ★★★★★**

"...before I knew it I was sucked in to the world of Beck and Pippa. Y'all are just gonna have to read this awesome book that had me on the edge of my seat to find out what happens with ALLLL of that!!" **Michelle Van Mourik, Book Bub ★★★★★**

"This is the first book that I have read by Kenzie Macallan but hopefully it won't be the last, this is an unusual story but in a good way. This is an enjoyable action-packed story that twists and turns." **TrishAM, Goodreads ★★★★★**

"King is a thrilling story with danger around every corner. Kings mission takes him to a family he didn't remember. Their book is exciting and full of heat. You will definitely be left wanting more from the team and to find out if they will be able to get all their answers about deep 8 or not." **Tiffany Hannick, BookBub ★★★★★**

ONE

Beck

HIS WORDS HIT me like a freight train, slamming into my chest and knocking the air from my lungs. I drop into the chair behind me, my muscles weaken, and my vision tunnels. The words filter through the air, absurd yet undeniable. My mind rejects this unknown and ludicrous information, but my soul recognizes the possibility before I can process it.

This messenger of fate has kind, warm eyes, like polished onyx, but they hold power. He carries people's secrets, my secrets, and the power to unravel the life I've built.

Katoo Ole Kapiti, the esquire who has tilted my world on its axis, leans down. "Your Highness, you need to tie things up here," he says, his voice measured but urgent. He leans in, his presence formidable. "Meet me in Mubala, Zambia—your birthplace."

I flinch at the word. Mubala. A place I've never set foot in, yet it belongs to me.

Katoo slides a plane ticket from his jacket, placing it on the desk in front of me like a detonator. "Don't take too long. Matters are urgent. We must name you king within seven weeks of our ruler's passing. Your parents—our king and queen—died four weeks ago." He pauses, letting the weight of it settle in my gut. "If you do not accept the throne, other families will lay claim to it."

I nod, but my voice fails me. My brain short-circuits, scrambling for a response, but before I can form one, he turns and strides from the room, a blur of black and red. The door clicks shut, and the silence is deafening.

They are not my parents. They are two people who gave me life thirty-six years ago and then gave me away.

I'm the heir to the royal throne in the Sai tribe. I press my palms into my knees, trying to ground myself. I was adopted. I always knew that. But I never imagined my birth family was… royalty. The word tastes foreign, unreal. A kingdom? A throne? This isn't my story. It can't be.

The first thing I want to do is call my parents, but I shut that down. I don't want to hurt them. They gave me everything, and I won't disrespect them.

There are a few things I know for sure. A white couple, Albert and Ellen McKenzie, adopted me in England when I was three. I'm their only black child, and my siblings are their biological children.

They never made me feel less than, but I hated being part of family portraits. To say I stuck out like a sore thumb would be an understatement. I never questioned where I came from because it didn't matter… until now.

My teammates stare at me with expressions of shock and uncertainty. Sean Knight, one of my partners in MBK Global Security, breaks the silence. "Did he call you 'Your Highness'?"

A sharp breath rushes from my lips. "I need to get going," I murmur, pushing to my feet. "There are things I need to tend to before I leave." My voice is alien, and my legs are shaky. I don't recognize this place of insecurity and uncertainty.

Mac, a former MI-6 agent and teammate, steps forward and grips my shoulder. "If you need anything, please call us. You may need backup down there." He refers to the next mission given to us by our boss, Neil McFadden.

A smile forces its way to my lips in an attempt at reassurance. It's a punch in the gut, and I have trouble breathing. Life is full of gut punches, and I've dodged most of them, but this one hits me head-on.

My life was on track. I live with a beautiful woman who I will marry, and we'll have kids. The American dream wrapped with a neat little bow.

Katoo came along and put a bomb in my box, leaving nothing but chaos and a plane ticket to a past I never wanted to uncover.

The busy streets and crowds of people in New York City are a blur as I find my way back to my penthouse. The word "king" runs in a loop in my head like a broken record.

As if on autopilot, I pack a suitcase for a short trip. It shouldn't take more than a week to wrap things up and make it clear I'm not who they need as their leader.

Once inside, I shed my jacket and head straight for the bathroom. My fingers run over the bumpy surface on each side of my face near my temples and eyes that look like raised stars. I've always wondered where they came from, and I may get my answer. Are they tribal scarring? I can't imagine branding a baby, but I didn't imagine finding my birth family in Africa.

The penthouse is eerily quiet. Most days, I thrive in routine, mixing protein shakes, working out, or mulling over a case, but not today. Today, I sit and listen. The words of wisdom to guide me and my inner voice don't kick in, and no clarity emerges. I have no sense of calmness. Numbness replaces it.

The big-screen TV comes to life. Steve Harvey talks to the audience about taking the jump, having faith, and moving forward. I'm at a loss as to which way I should move, but his words resonate with me. My jaw clenches. This isn't a jump. It's a free fall off a goddamn cliff. Besides, I've never believed in faith.

I flip open my laptop, fingers flying over the keys as I search for the Sai Tribe. Nothing. I dig deeper. Still nothing. It's like they don't exist. But that's impossible. Every kingdom has a footprint, a trace in history. Why is mine erased?

My phone draws my attention with my parents' ringtone. I debate whether I should answer their call. My stomach knots, but curiosity gets the better of me.

"Hello, how are you two doing?" Answering on a video call, I force a light tone, but my throat tightens.

Their faces come into view, washed with worry. My mum tries to smile. "Hello, sweetheart. We were hoping you would make a trip home. We have something we need to discuss with you."

My pulse jumps. "I'm getting ready to go on assignment. Can it wait until I get back?"

They look at each other and frown. My dad responds, "We can wait. Let us know when you can make it."

Guilt churns in my gut. I resist the urge to ask my parents questions they don't have answers to. What would they know about a royal family in Africa thousands of miles away?

"I'll be in touch." My mum taps her nose and touches the screen. It's always been our way of saying goodbye.

Putting a protein shake together, I force myself into the gym, hoping to burn off the unease. It's a state-of-the-art gym. My circuit changes from day to day, hitting the major muscle groups to get the greatest benefit. There's no point in working out if you're not efficient and putting in maximum effort. I try to make the most out of every movement. Perfection doesn't just happen; it's created.

The weights feel like lead in my hands. My focus is shot. No endorphins, no clarity. Just more damn questions.

The day drags, and my mind spins. My life story has been shattered and replaced with what some would call a fairy tale.

Clouds float past the window as the sky darkens into dusk, and shadows swallow the light in the penthouse.

I leave my post in front of the TV to go to bed. I can't remember if I ate dinner, but Taylor isn't home yet, so she must be working late.

My mind spins in eighteen different directions, but I must have succumbed to sleep.

When I wake up, my body feels heavy. The sheets are twisted around my legs, trapping me. My hand stretches across the mattress—Taylor's side is untouched. Cool. Where the hell was she all night?

TWO

Beck

THEY SAY things always happen in threes. Number two is about to make itself known, and I can feel the weight of it pressing down on my chest. I roll over, my pulse quickening at the sight of the empty walk-in closet, minus designer dresses, suits, and shoes. The open doors mock me, a silent declaration that my world is shifting once again. The penthouse, once a sanctuary, feels hollow. Cold.

I swing my legs over the side of the bed. My body aches from taunt muscles after restless dreams, full of odd visions of my childhood I don't recognize. My mind reels, unable to piece together the fractured images haunting my subconscious. But I push those thoughts aside. Right now, there's a more immediate problem.

Pulling on my tracksuit, I follow the footprints in the ivory shag carpeting to the living room. She had to have carpet throughout the apartment done in ivory, a color that's impossible to clean.

A chill runs through me, the same feeling I get on a mission about to go sideways. Years of being in the field as a highly trained operative give me insight into the strangest moments.

Taylor.

She stands at the front door, dressed to the nines, even on a Saturday morning. With her purse hanging off her wrist, she looks at her nails with boredom. Mountains of Louis Vuitton luggage surround her. Boxes labeled with her precise, slanted handwriting complete the scene.

My gut tightens. "Going somewhere?" I know the answer. Maybe I even know why she's leaving, but I need to hear it.

The women in my life have left for various reasons, but it's never a shock. Somewhere in my gut, I know it's tied to when I lost Emelia. She was taken from me way too soon. I never got to tell her how I felt, and it's plagued me ever since.

Taylor barely glances up from inspecting her nails. Her soft brown eyes view me with sadness tinged with regret. "I'm leaving you and this." She waves her fingers between us. "It's not working for either of us. You're never home, and I'm about to make partner at the firm. We want different things."

She places her purse on top of the luggage and walks toward me with the grace of a runway model, her heels clicking on the marble floor. Her pink pearl jacket accents her ebony skin.

She could have been a high-end fashion model with her defined cheekbones and full lips, but God gave her a voracious appetite for the law, and she pursues it relentlessly.

Her well-manicured fingers touch my cheek, cooling it. I fight the urge to jerk away.

"We're going through the motions, Beck, and I'm about to embark on a different journey," she murmurs. "I love you, but I'm not in love with you. I want the kind of love that sets my soul on fire, an insatiable hunger. We're existing." Her hand falls away from my face, and my skin warms again.

My ego gets the better of me. "Is there someone else?"

She gives me a small, knowing smile. "No. That would be one more ball for me to juggle, and I wouldn't do that to you. Clean breaks are always better." She steps back, and the space between us feels cavernous. "Besides, you are an excellent lover," she adds, almost as an afterthought, her voice devoid of emotion

That stings.

Just like that, she ties it up in a neat little portfolio. Her job here is done. She's not wrong. We have been monotonous. I saw this coming but didn't want to face it.

At my age, I should be getting ready to settle down and have a family. Given the recent events, that will be put on hold. I don't even know where I came from. Maybe I don't even know who I am.

I nod, stuffing my hands into my pockets. "Did you say you're about to make partner? Why didn't you tell me?" I hang on to the rope that is slipping away.

She shrugs. "There wasn't much point."

A lump forms in my throat, but I swallow it down. "The furniture?"

"The movers will be here in a couple of hours to move most of it to my new apartment in Hackensack." She adjusts the strap on her handbag.

I nod, not surprised she's taking the furniture with her. She picked out every piece to match, from Natuzzi leather to Ethan Allan wood furnishings.

"I'm taking everything but the bedroom set." She scrunches her nose. "You can keep it." She doesn't want to be reminded of my love-making skills while in bed with a new man.

A bitter laugh escapes me. "How generous."

I hate change and crave consistency, yet my work at MI-6 had me living around the world like a nomad. Creating MBK with my partners gives me a place to lay my head at night, and my life has rhythm. As of late, having a bed to sleep in is the least of my problems.

What I don't understand is after a year of being together, this relationship dissolves in a couple of sentences. Maybe it was disintegrating before our eyes, and this was the final sinkhole. There's a piece of me that's angry because I didn't pick up on this sooner.

I lean down and kiss her on the forehead. "Be well, Taylor. Let me know if you ever need anything."

She nods, but we both know she won't call. As she turns back to her belongings, her attention already fixed on her phone, a knock at the door signals the arrival of the doorman.

I open it, and he tips his hat. His knowing smile twists something deep inside me. I help him haul her things onto the luggage cart. Her eyes never stray from her phone. As I'm about to shut the door, she looks up.

"Goodbye, Beck. Take care of yourself." That's all I get as she returns to the messages on her phone.

The door clicks shut, locking away everything we once were. I collapse onto her leather couch—soon to be gone, just like her—and let out a breath.

I want to say, "Oh, by the way, I'm going to be king of a tribe in Africa."

There's no point. I'm not sure I believe my own words.

I run a hand over my face, exhaustion pressing in from all sides. In less than twenty-four hours, my life has unraveled, and yet, something tells me this is just the beginning.

THREE

Beck
_____

THE LONG FLIGHT offers me nothing but time—time to read, to think, to wrestle with the reality that's closing in around me. I scroll through everything I can find on Mubala, searching again for any trace of the tribe I'm meant to lead. But the information is scarce and fragmented, like my own past. A past I never questioned—until now.

Uncertainty isn't new to me. As an operative, I've walked blind into missions, relying on instinct and training. But this is different. This isn't an assignment. This is my life unraveling in real-time, and for the first time, I have no strategy, no exit plan. I don't know what waits for me on the other side of this flight.

The unpredictability of any situation should be second nature, but this is different. This is emotional. I never questioned my adoptive parents about where I came from or who my birth parents were because I felt fortunate enough to have been chosen. This sheds new light on questions about my past. Why now? What is going on that they need me?

Sleep is fleeting, coming in waves between restless memories and unanswered questions. When we land in Dubai for a brief stopover, I barely register the opulence of the airport, too preoccupied with the storm inside my head. By the time we touch down in Lusaka, the weight of exhaustion clings to me like a second skin.

The moment I step off the plane, I'm met by a man waiting just beyond customs. He's tall and lean, dressed in a crisp linen shirt and dark slacks, his expression one of quiet respect. He bows deeply, his voice smooth and polished.

He stands in front of me and bows. "Your Highness Siwanda. It's an honor to serve you. My name is Jobi," he says in English.

I wave my hand down to get him to stop. "That's not necessary. Please, call me Beck."

He turns his head to the side. "Forgive me, but I thought your name was Dacari?"

I stare at him, remembering Katoo used that name when addressing me, and let out the breath I'd been holding. "Dacari is fine. New country, new name, right?" Another alias to add to the pile. He continues to stare at me with questions in his eyes.

Jobi nods but watches me as if trying to decipher something unspoken. He gestures toward the parking lot. "It is safer to drive to Mubala. The flight is long and unreliable. Sometimes, two engines are not better than one." He winks, but his words carry an edge of warning.

The fourteen-hour drive north begins. He suggests we stop along the way to break up the drive. I should be impatient, eager to get this over with. Instead, I welcome the time. I need to figure out my next move. I have a half-brother and half-sister waiting for me—people who could take the throne in my place.

He grabs my large duffle bag, but I grip my briefcase, unzipping it on the backseat of the car to get my weapon, tucking it into the back of my pants. He throws my luggage in the trunk of his beat-up car. He smiles often as if he doesn't know what to make of his passenger. The car is a small Mini Cooper and looks like a box on wheels with more dents than smooth surfaces.

"I promise, sir, she is tougher than she looks."

I've traveled in worse conditions. The real concern isn't the car—it's the rising tension in the city. As we pull out of the airport, the streets pulse with unrest. Smoke curls from burning debris in the distance. Protesters flood the sidewalks, their voices a collective roar of frustration.

He runs around the front of the car in a hurry and motions for me to get in. I curl into the back seat, placing my briefcase on the floor, and discover I must stretch my legs along the entire back seat. Otherwise, I'm not going to fit in.

Jobi's grip tightens on the wheel. "We must get out of the city quickly. It is not safe."

I glance at the chaos unfolding outside. "I can handle myself."

His jaw sets. "Perhaps. But my orders are to protect you."

The words sit between us, unchallenged. He doesn't know who I am or what I'm capable of, but I let it go. I've been in harm's way my entire life. My clock has been ticking for years. I know I'll run out of luck one day. I'm not depressed; it's just a fact of life. When you're an agent, death nips at your heels.

In the distance, I can hear a mortar go off, bringing my thoughts back to my time on the ground in Kuwait and how turbulence exists in war-torn countries. Sometimes the war goes on so long governments forget why they're fighting, and most are a losing battle. The innocent suffer as the powers in charge treat them with total disregard, a necessity for a perceived gain. Zambia seems to be no exception to this rule.

Lusaka is larger and busier than I thought it would be. The city soon fades behind us, swallowed by an expanse of rugged countryside. Lush green trees line the roads, standing tall like sentinels, but the earth beneath them is cracked and burnt, angry from the relentless sun. The reddish-brown color indicates it has a high clay content, not optimal for growing crops.

Heat steams off the pavement in waves. The air in the car is stifling. Without air conditioning, sweat clings to me, soaking into my shirt. It's going to be a long ride.

I'm blessed with the quiet of the scenery and the hum of the engine in the background. Jobi keeps his eyes in the rearview mirror, waiting for me to say something, but I don't. Instead, I watch the land shift around us—rolling hills, vast plains, pockets of dense jungle.

We climb into the mountainous area heading north. In the distance, I can hear the thunder of waterfalls. I've never been to the continent of Africa, and it seems full of contradictions. One minute it gives clues to its lack of resources, the next to its beauty and splendor.

"Please, sir. Would you like to go to the waterfalls? There are many along the way. People say they are some of the most beautiful in the world." Jobi's words rush out like he's unable to hold them in for one minute longer. I realize I need to give up on him calling me anything but sir or highness. I'm not going to win this round.

I nod. "Why not?"

We pull off at an overlook, stepping out into the heavy, humid air. The roar of the falls is deafening, a thunderous rush of water cascading into the depths below. A rainbow arcs across the mist, vibrant against the dark rock. I raise my phone to take a picture, then pause. Something about this moment feels... significant. A sign? Maybe.

A German couple is taking photos and inadvertently moves closer to me. Jobi jumps between us, his posture rigid. "You must keep your distance," he warns them.

The man blinks in confusion. "I'm sorry?"

I hold his arm. "That's not necessary."

"Sir, you are my king. I cannot let anyone threaten you." His lips draw a firm line.

I almost laugh at the absurdity. I'm about to tell him to the rest of the world, I'm a nobody, but he won't understand. They sent him to guard me. This is his world and what he knows. I doubt he's ever left the continent of Africa or even Zambia.

I exhale, nodding. "Alright."

As we drive deeper into the countryside, the land opens up, revealing herds of zebra and giraffes grazing in the distance. I haven't had the opportunity to go on safari, but observing these wild animals in their natural habitat, roaming free is something to envy. They claim it as their own, making me feel like an intruder in every sense of the word, maybe even to myself.

Women in vibrant clothing walk along the roadside, balancing impossibly large baskets on their heads, their laughter floating through the air. The stark contrast of joy against the backdrop of poverty unsettles me. Jobi waves to them and smiles. They wave back, talking in their native language.

My thoughts travel to where they might go, where they live, and if they have families. The poverty in Zambia is glaring. Shanties dot the countryside. They live to survive and survive to live, accepting their fate. The sight turns my stomach, given how much wealth there is in the rest of the world. I can't imagine what awaits me in the village of the Sai tribe in

Mubala. If this tribe needs help, I wouldn't know where to begin.

I lie back and use my jacket as a pillow. The rhythm of the car makes me sleepy as the pink and orange sun streaks the sky in a blaze beyond the treetops. An incredible peace comes over me as the land speaks to me, welcoming me home, a home I've never considered. I fight to keep my eyes open but succumb to the hours of travel to a place I'm not sure I want to visit.

When I wake up, night has fallen, and its blackness is all-consuming, coming at me from all sides. The headlights shine on the road, making it look like we're driving in a tunnel. The temperature has dropped, but I'm still sweating. I see the whites of Jobi's eyes in the rearview mirror, and the lower part of his face is lit up from the dashboard.

"Sir, I want to get as close to Mubala as possible before we stop for the night." His eyes beg for permission.

"Whatever you think is best. You know the lay of the land." His eyes widen. I'm not used to giving up control in any situation, but I don't have a choice. This is his territory, his country.

We turn off onto a small dirt road. The ruts and holes in the road bounce the car up and down violently, making me concerned about the damage to the suspension. He stops under a tree and kills the engine. I peer out the window but see nothing but darkness.

"Jobi, where are we, and why have we stopped?"

He turns his body toward me and puts his arm on the back of the seat. "We are spending the night here, off the road, where no one can find us."

I glance at my gun, reassured by its weight against my spine. "Right. No hotels out here, I take it?"

Jobi chuckles. "Not the kind you would want to stay in."

"We must stay in the car. There are many dangerous animals out here. Camping outside would not be a good idea." His voice is calm, but the warning is clear.

Silence falls between us as I take in the situation.

"Okay," is all I can say. I'm at the mercy of my destiny.

We settle in for the night, him in the front seat and me cramped in the back seat. The air is thick and heavy with the scent of earth and something wilder lurking beyond the reach of the headlights.

I stare out into the abyss, listening to the distant calls of unseen creatures. My entire life, I've lived with the certainty of who I was. Now, I'm heading toward a fate I never saw coming.

Somewhere in the heart of this land, my destiny waits.

I just don't know if I'm ready to meet it.

FOUR

Beck
___

DAWN BREAKS, and the sun filters through the broad-leaf trees. The air in the car becomes suffocating as I wake up in a pool of sweat. The tapping on the window catches my attention. It's not the tap of a finger but the sound of metal against the glass. I shade my eyes with my hand and notice two men standing outside the car.

Jobi startles at the sound. "Your Highness, there are two men with guns. I will take care of everything."

"No. Listen to me. Now would not be the time to call me Your Highness. Let me handle this. Watch for my signal." I put my hands in the air to show I'm unarmed.

"You get out first and talk to them and distract them."

Jobi nods.

My weapon is on the floor of the car, and I need to get to it without letting them see me. Jobi gets out with his hands in the air. They train their weapons on him. He closes the door and talks to them in a language I don't understand. As they talk to him, they keep pointing at me.

I reach down behind me and grab my weapon, stuffing it in my waistband. I pull the door handle to let myself out.

When I stand to my full height, I can see over their heads. They look up at me, and their mouths fall open.

One of them points his weapon at me. "You, I need your passport and anything else you have on you, and then I'm going to kill you." His accent is thick, and his mouth draws a taut line. The color of my skin is the same as theirs, but my clothes give me away as a foreigner.

I lower my hands, clasp them in front of me, and shrug. "My luggage is in the trunk." I nod toward the back of the car.

These two haven't done this often or very well because I have split them up without them paying attention to the circumstances.

The other one points his weapon at Jobi. "Give me the keys."

Jobi glances in my direction and digs in his pocket for the keys, handing them to the gunman. The man throws them to the guy at the trunk, and that's my cue to make a move. I reach for the gunman and twist his wrist as he releases his weapon, a Chinese-made NP-22, a SIG copy. Grabbing my Walther PPK 380 from behind my back, I pull him to me, using his body as a shield, and point my weapon at the guy behind the car.

"In case you're wondering, I'm an excellent shot. Put your gun down slowly and step away from the trunk." The man I'm holding has a grip on my forearm, which only makes me tighten my arm on his neck.

He places his weapon on the ground and stands up with his hands in the air. His eyes are wide.

"Get the keys and his gun." I motion to Jobi with my head.

He gets the items, moves next to me, and points his gun at the robber standing at the back of the car. He seems familiar with how to handle a gun, which is odd for a driver.

"Here's how this is going to go. You two stand over by the tree, and we'll be on our merry way. Got it?" They both nod. "Good."

They walk to the tree and make a mad dash for the dense forest. Smart move. I guess we don't need to worry about them returning.

Jobi and I get in the car with their weapons and drive back to the highway. Jobi is so busy staring at me; I worry he won't see what's ahead of him.

"Do you have something to say?" I ask as I look out the window.

"Sir, they were not there just to rob us. They were there to kill you. They thought they could get away with both."

"How did they know where we were?"

He shrugs.

"Pull the car over."

He jerks the car to the side of the road. I tell him to pop the bonnet and use my flashlight to look around the engine. Stuck inside the fender is the blinking red light of a GPS tracker. I yank it off and crush it with my boot.

"Jobi, who wants me dead?"

"I don't know, Your Highness."

"Does everyone in the village know I'm coming, and do they want me to be king?"

Jobi gives me the biggest smile I've seen since I've been here. "Village, sir? You will see what Mubala is about, and no, not everyone knows about you, but I am Wafiq's personal assistant. I have been assigned to you for the time you are here."

"Wafiq?" I don't enjoy being at a disadvantage.

He frowns. "Your brother."

Katoo has not returned any of my texts or calls, keeping me in the dark about the names of my half-brother and sister. I nod. "Forgive me. This is all new to me, and it's been a long trip. I must have forgotten." I don't want to give too much away, as I'm unsure of who the players are in this game.

We drive in silence for the next couple of hours, stopping at an open market to stretch our legs. The market is vast, with tents full of crafts and local produce. There are beautiful bowls carved in rich browns, some black and beige. Other tents have jewelry and tightly woven baskets from local artists.

I step up to a tent that grabs my interest and ask about the price of the popular wood-sculptured hippo. As I reach for my wallet, Jobi places his hand on my wrist to stop me.

He whispers, "He wants you to barter with him, give him a counteroffer. It's how things are done here." He smiles and nods.

My counteroffer is below his asking price. He counters with another offer, and I accept. He seems satisfied with the result, gracing me with a smile as I hand him several kwacha bills.

I continue to roam through the other tents and get stares from the natives. This isn't a tourist spot but a place where locals come to buy what they need. I learn the art of negotiation for the few things I want, like a hand-carved bowl, woven baskets, and a tribal mask to remind me of my trip to Zambia. As much as I want this to be a brief trip, I also want to savor everything about my homeland.

Homeland?

It's an odd thought to acknowledge this piece of earth as my homeland. I've only ever known England, but my recent move has me getting used to New York City, and I will stay there for the foreseeable future. This country is a far cry from where I come from, and I don't even know what awaits me in Mubala.

We drive for several more hours as we approach an enormous gate. It's made of dark wooden poles and stands at least ten meters high. The double doors appear to accommodate an eighteen-wheeler. Walls are attached to the wooden gates. They go on as far as the eye can see, with no end.

Jobi gets out of the car and walks to a small window in the wall. There is talking, laughter, and nodding. He comes back, and the gates open as we drive through to the other side.

He looks at me in the rearview mirror. "Welcome to Mubala." His eyes are warm as he beams.

What appears before me is nothing like I imagined.

FIVE

Beck

THIS IS ANYTHING BUT A VILLAGE. It's a full-on city behind a wall. The streets are clean, and every house looks the same with beige stucco and a terra-cotta tile roof. People mill about with baskets full of food or other things from the market. Along the way, we pass several schools, children playing on playgrounds, hospitals, libraries, and firehouses. The only thing missing from the picture is a police station. There are no police cars anywhere.

I feel as though I've stepped into the Disney movie *The Princess and the Frog.* My nieces watched the movie enough times that I could recite each song by heart. I keep waiting for everyone to break out in song and dance.

We drive to the outskirts of town and stop in front of an enormous three-story white palace that towers above the surrounding one-story buildings. A man stands at the top of the stairs with his arms behind his back, trying to look casual, but his raised shoulders give him away.

"Please, sir, that is Wafiq," Jobi turns and whispers.

I step out of the car and hold the man's stare. They are eyes I recognize as my own, but nothing else about him is familiar. I expected us to have more features in common, but it's early in this courtship.

"I gathered as much. Jobi, thank you for everything. I couldn't have done it without you." I extend my hand to him.

"Sir, I would like to show you the traditional Zambian handshake." He grabs my hand and starts with a traditional handshake, ending with an upward clasp of our thumbs.

Laughter bubbles up from my chest. "I need to honor your... or my traditions. I'll remember this. Thank you."

Jobi reaches for my luggage, and I grab my suitcase as we trudge upstairs to meet my brother.

When we make it to the top, we stare at each other for a beat, and he narrows his eyes, examining my facial scars. My fingertips skim the raised stars on my face as I notice he doesn't have the same markings. That is a question for later. I'm a head taller than him, and he is much leaner in stature. Years of working out have added muscle to my body. Otherwise, I would look like him.

He doesn't acknowledge the branding. "Dacari, I never thought I would see you or meet you. I never knew you. Mama and Papa said you died when you were three. This is truly a miracle."

My body stiffens, but I say nothing.

"When you sent me a message you were on your way here, I thought there had to be a mistake. Jobi sent me a photo. You are very real, indeed." He smiles, and his eyes turn glassy.

I never sent him a message. Katoo must have sent word, making it look like it came from me. Wafiq pulls me in for a hug, squeezing me and patting my back. He pulls away and holds me by my shoulders. I'm speechless. Much has been said in so few words, and the holes in my life I never knew existed come to light.

"Sabeen sends her regrets. She couldn't be here to greet you, but she's eager to meet you." Something passes in his eyes I can't decipher. I hoped she would be here so I could meet her. "Please come in. This is your home now." He waves his hand to the doorway.

The view of the chairs and furniture triggers a memory, but it passes. Sights and sounds of a home I don't remember bombard my mind. He moves ahead of me to show me around. I notice family photos of what I assume are my parents, Wafiq, and a young woman.

I hold the framed photo in my hand. "Who is this?" The woman's face is soft and welcoming.

"That is our younger sister, Sabeen. She's a gemologist and works for the company."

I cut him off. "The company?"

"Yes, Sai International Gems. We call it SIG. There is a lot we need to catch up on." His smile is tight.

I rub my thumb over the frame, and it catches on something sharp and rips the skin. A single drop of blood is accented against the cream color of my thumb.

"Are you okay? Let me get a bandage." Before I answer, he rushes out of the room.

I suck the blood off my thumb, and the metallic taste hits me. It's not a taste I've ever relished, but blood follows me wherever I go.

Having him out of the room gives me time to look around and make mental notes. I rub the middle of my chest with my palm as a reminder to breathe. I can add another brother and sister to my list of siblings.

Photos of the… my family cover the mantle above the fireplace. My mother holds a baby boy in one and a baby girl in another, but there are no photos of me. Even though I'm just beginning my journey to understanding my homeland, it breaks my heart knowing they forgot about me after they thought I had died. I don't even know the circumstances that surround my supposed death.

Wafiq hurries back into the room and hands me the bandage. "Here, you can wrap your thumb."

The bleeding has stopped, but I smile and take the bandage from him. "Thank you."

We continue to walk through the house as he points out the various rooms. The open floor plan downstairs flows from the kitchen through the living room to the dining room, great room, and outdoor patio. Upstairs, the master suite is at the end of the hall after we pass his and Sabeen's childhood rooms, along with several guest rooms. He doesn't give me a tour of the third floor.

I step into the master suite and can feel the ghosts of my past. The duvet is rumpled, makeup and jewelry cover the dresser, and a pair of shoes lie haphazardly on the floor. The pain in my chest intensifies like someone is taking a knife and twisting it. Thoughts of my adoptive parents come to my mind, and what it would feel like to lose them. I'm caught between two worlds and don't know which way to turn.

Wafiq stands behind me and says, "I haven't been here since they died. I couldn't bear how I would feel to know they are no longer in the world with us." His head hangs down, and he folds his hands in front of him.

"I'm so sorry for your loss. If you don't mind me asking, how did they die?" My voice is quiet, as if I were speaking to a scared animal. I'm not sure who's more afraid, me or him.

He looks out the window. "Papa was a pilot and an excellent one at that. They were flying to Nairobi to go on safari with friends. Not long after they took off, the plane had engine trouble and crashed into the brush." He stops to take a breath. "We did not recover the bodies, but we gave them a proper memorial."

He turns to look at me. "All of Mubala is still in mourning, even though it happened over four weeks ago." His tears never fall and dry up in his eyes. He walks toward me and stands face-to-face. "I thought you would have known. After all, you contacted me about wanting to come here. How did you find us? Why did you wait so long to come back?" Anger flashes in his eyes.

His chin tilts up as he glares into my eyes, looking for answers.

As a former MI6 agent, I'm trained to think fast on my feet. "I was notified through a correspondence that my biological parents had passed away. I knew nothing about them until now. My adoptive parents, who I consider my only parents, raised me in England. Curiosity brought me to Mubala."

He glares at me but seems satisfied with my answer, and his shoulders fall. "My sister and I would like you to stay here in their house. I hope you can make it your home for a while." His lips curl on the ends.

"Thank you. I would like that, although I don't plan on staying long. I'm not the king of a place I know nothing about. You would be the better fit."

He chuckles. "If only it were that easy. You must become the king to make decisions that affect the city and our family. Please join us for dinner at my house. I'll have Jobi pick you up." He puts his hand on my shoulder. "It's good to meet you, my brother."

Later that afternoon, there's a knock at the door. I see a female figure bouncing up and down through the frosted glass in the door. When I open it, I'm greeted with a wide smile.

"Dacari?" She beams.

"Yes?" Being at a disadvantage seems to be my new normal.

"I'm Sabeen." She jumps through the doorway to hug me.

She's only slightly shorter than me and hugs me tightly.

"I'm so happy to finally meet you. When Wafiq told me you were alive and coming here, I was overwhelmed with joy."

"Please, come in." I offer her something to drink, and we spend the next couple of hours sharing pieces of our lives apart.

Wafiq is two years younger than me, and she is four years my junior. They were brought up knowing about my existence but not much else. I share vague details about my life until I know who's who in this game. She gives me another hug before she leaves.

The door shuts with a click, and the house is quiet, but I feel like it wants to talk to me, to tell me things I should know. The voices are quiet and soft, reminding me I will know everything in due time. Either way, I will become king whether or not I want it.

SIX

Beck
_____

SLEEP DIDN'T COME to me last night. Images and memories I have no connections to swirl around in my head. This house must be triggering the past, bringing back memories of being here as a child. My parents remain as ghosts in my world. I remember faces I don't recognize.

Wafiq's reaction to me was mixed with ambivalence and concern, but Sabeen greeted me with open arms. She's warm and sincere, wearing her heart on her sleeve, unlike her brother. My biggest question remains: why did they give me up for adoption, and why has Katoo contacted me with an urgent matter?

My phone rings with Neil McFadden's ringtone from my secure line. I like to know who's calling before answering it to prepare for the unexpected.

"Neil, what can I do for you?" My former boss from Scotland Yard is working with my security company to track down a group called Deep 8.

"I see you made it to Mubala. I couldn't get a hold of you yesterday." His tone is edged with irritation.

I smile to myself. There's nothing worse than an agent

being in the wind, even though I work off-book for him. "Zambia isn't exactly known for its cell service. Besides having an interesting family reunion, what am I looking for here? You said this was our next mission."

"I'm sure you're aware of the Chinese presence in Zambia. Their influence and sale of military weapons to the Zambian government is not a secret. They make quite a spectacle."

"We encountered one of their imitation handguns during an unsuccessful assassination attempt." It's another day at the office with shop talk.

I hear him mumble, "Are you aware of the emerald and diamond trade in Zambia?" He doesn't ask about the assassination attempt because it's been foiled.

The word diamond brings my thoughts back to Taylor, but the sentiment evaporates quickly. For whatever reason, she wasn't the woman I needed. She was a season for a reason, and right now, I'm not interested in a lifetime. I need to get my shit together.

"Beck?" Neil's voice grabs my attention.

"Sorry. I've got a lot on my mind. No, I'm not aware of the emerald and diamond trade. Wafiq, my brother, mentioned their family company, SIG, Sai International Gems." I try to pull my attention back to the conversation.

There's silence on the other end, which is never a good sign. "I have a feeling I need to send you back up. You don't seem to have your wits about you."

My body stiffens. "That's not necessary. Everything is under control here. If I need backup, I'll let Sean know." I don't need to raise an alarm before I get to know the family that got rid of me. I want answers about my past here in Zambia.

"I'm emailing you the dossier on the Zambian gem industry. We think there's a connection between the Zambian gem industry and the funneling of money from billionaire accounts into digital accounts worldwide. We can't figure out how they are doing it. There may be a Deep 8 connection, but we know they operate in the dark. Our links are weak. I'm not sure you're going to find anything worth pursuing."

"Well, if Afghanistan was any indication of how they operate, I have my work cut out for me. I'll look around and see what I can find out."

Sean Knight was hired by his old friend, Isaad, from his time in the sandbox, only to find out Isaad was working with a group called Deep 8, stealing minerals from the Afghan mines. We also discovered a new mineral, stellarium, which may have Earth-changing properties. We're still investigating those properties.

"Stay in touch. Let me know what you find out." Neil clicks off without a goodbye.

What could diamonds and emeralds possibly have to do with stealing currency from billionaires? If the Chinese are involved, blood diamonds may be the result, funding rebel arms deals. War is money. I need to tread carefully. My new family deserves my attention.

The harsh light streams through an upper window as the air conditioner hums away, keeping the house cool. This city has more modern conveniences than some towns back in the UK. A sharp knock at the door draws my attention as I walk over to let them in.

Wafiq smiles. "Brother, I'll take you on a tour of Mubala. I thought you might like to see the place that you will rule over." He's dressed in a suit and tie as if he is going to a business meeting.

I'm exhausted from hearing about and refuting that I would soon be king and rule over my domain, a country I know nothing about. Resigned to the fact that I will hear about it for the rest of the trip, I give in, not denying his reference.

I nod. "That sounds great. I want to get to know you better and the city I was born in. I might have some questions for you if you don't mind."

His smile is tight as he walks down the front stairs leading to the street, and I walk beside him. "I'm not sure I'll have the answers you're looking for about how things came to be for you. That's more Katoo's department." His voice tightens, and he looks away. I'll save that information for later when I see Katoo. Considering Katoo didn't mention my brother's name, there must be tension between them.

On the street awaits a car that makes me stop and stare. I turn to Wafiq.

"Is that—" I don't even finish my sentence.

"The newest Tesla Roadster. The answer is yes. Please." He waves his hand.

His ride is a deep, metallic red with styling to die for. "How do you have this car? There were only a thousand made."

He smirks. "It's all in who you know. I snagged one and had it shipped here."

The price tag for this car is two hundred and fifty thousand dollars. The gem business must be quite lucrative, especially if the Chinese are footing the bill.

"Top on or off?" he says as he opens the door.

I use my hand to shield myself from the punishing sun. "Top on. I'm from the UK. We're not used to the sun."

He gets in and starts the engine without a sound. "I know about UK weather. It seems we went to rival universities. I went to Cambridge while you studied at Oxford." Sunglasses cover his eyes, and I can't read him.

He eases the car into the street. "You're interested in how I know. When I heard you were alive and coming here, I researched everything about you, but Katoo beat me to it. He has a lot of information on you." His grip tightens on the steering wheel.

The tension in the car kicks up a notch. "Well, it's a shame you had to go to the second-best school."

"It's too bad we kicked your ass in rowing. Light blue always outshines dark blue." His comeback is quick.

I laugh out loud. Cambridge wears light blue, while Oxford wears dark blue in the blue rowing boats. "You're right. Your crew is up in wins, but we're never too far behind."

He cracks a smile for the first time since we've been together. This would be a good time to ask about my scars.

"Wafiq, I have to ask about… my scars. How did I get them?" I don't remember a time when I didn't have them.

He looks out the window, contemplating his words. "The Sai tribe scars their firstborn son at birth. There is a special tool with the family symbol used to do the branding, so to speak." He turns his head in my direction. "The baby is never in pain. That's not the purpose. They numb the area beforehand. The tradition is passed down through the generations, symbolizing being a man and a possible leader." I notice he uses the word possible, so maybe my trip to the throne might not happen. He closes his eyes briefly, almost as a sign of respect.

His reaction takes me by surprise. He frowns and looks out the window. There are many things I could say, but I don't. I need to respect the place and people of my origin. I'm unsettled knowing they have marked me without knowing what the future would hold.

"There was an attempt on my life before I arrived here. Do you know anything about it?"

Confusion covers his face. "No, what happened?"

"They were going to make it look like a robbery, but Jobi and I took care of them." I let my ambiguous words hang.

"I'm glad nothing happened to you. You can't die twice." He smiles.

We tour the city as Wafiq shows me the town council building, a police station tucked away out of sight, and the offices of SIG, among other prominent spots.

"I notice there are no police on the streets. You have no crime?"

He sits up in his seat. "There's no need to have them out in the open. Everyone knows that if you commit a crime, you will be escorted from the city. We have a zero-tolerance policy for crime here."

"It seems rather harsh. Everyone makes a mistake or a wrong decision." I counter his belief system. Totalitarianism is not a new concept.

"This falls under 'the think before you do philosophy.' We've only had a couple of people leave over the years." His face remains neutral, like he's talking about the weather.

There is a gaping hole in the earth at the far end of the city. We drive down the spiral to the center in time to see them detonate a small bomb, shattering the surface of the earth.

He stops well away from where any debris could get on his sports car. "When we loosen the earth just below the surface, we have a better chance of finding emeralds. We call them green light. The workers can sift through the rubble and find the rough gems. They are one of the rarest minerals on earth." He recites the strategy as if he were at a board meeting.

"And how about your diamonds?" I lay the groundwork for my probing questions yet to come.

"Zambia has some of the highest quality diamonds in the world. Recently, we opened a mine over the mountain that produces a healthy number of carats per week." He lets out a breath through his nose.

"What part do the Chinese play in all of this?" I watch his body stiffen.

"The Chinese have no role in SIG. We are independent and plan to stay that way." His body turns toward me, shoulders squared.

I confront him with my nonverbal stance. "The Chinese have a foothold in Zambia, so I can't imagine they have not approached you."

"What do you know? You're *part* owner of a security firm. Leave the running of SIG to Sabeen and me. When you become king, you will be a figurehead, and we will make the decisions for you."

There's no hesitation. He has it planned out. I will be the puppet, and he will be the master. It's a bold statement, but I can see where I would be a threat to his world, a region he has been leading for a long time.

I don't correct his vision of me. I'll use it to my advantage later. He doesn't know my history, and that will come back to bite him in the ass.

SEVEN

Pippa

THE PHONE RINGS with the James Bond theme song, letting me know Neil is on the line. I smile every time, and I always answer the same way.

"Hello, Jane Bond here." Then I laugh.

There's a deep sigh on the other end. "Do you ever tire of answering the phone like that when I call?" Neil's dry voice holds no humor.

"Nope. Life is too short, and I plan to make the most of it. What's up?" I put him on speakerphone while I tap away on my keyboard, trying to crack the encrypted information we got from the assignment in Afghanistan.

"Can you make the most of it in Africa?"

This has my attention. "Africa? I thought Beck was in Africa?"

"He is, and I think he needs help. I haven't heard from him in three days. I'm worried this is a little much for him with his family. We're not sure what's going on, and Katoo is the only one to trust in Mubala. I need an objective set of eyes and ears down there. Your cover is his employee. You leave first thing tomorrow morning." His words are in hyperdrive.

I take in the deets he's giving me. This isn't a choice. "Why me?" My voice is small.

He waits for a beat. "In a digital age, we need your skills. You proved how strong you are on assignment in Afghanistan, and I think Beck needs someone like you. He's been in the spy game for a long time and might be losing sight of his objective. Your ticket is coming to you via courier. We want this to look legit. Otherwise, we would send one of our planes. You'll pick up your gear at the airport in Lusaka. Good luck." Neil clicks off.

What does that mean? Does Beck need someone like me?

His words get in my head as I doubt myself. This is only my second assignment with Neil. How can I help Beck? I haul a suitcase from the closet shelf and plop it on the bed.

The knock at the door pulls me out of my thoughts. The courier must be here with the ticket.

I open the door, and Jess stands there with two bags of groceries and a smile. She's my foster sister, and she knows me better than anyone else on the planet. I must have an odd look on my face.

"Hey, are you okay?" She holds up the bags. "I brought dinner and thought we could catch up."

I snap out of it long enough to invite her in. "I hope you brought a bag of peanut M&Ms."

"Why are you stressed? What's going on? I bought the fixings for pizza. We can use that fancy grill on top of the stove."

I nod.

"I'm glad you got to keep my apartment and didn't have to go into WITSEC," she says and continues to the kitchen.

My alter ego as Red Enigma, hacker extraordinaire and

expert on navigating the dark web, got me a job working for a warlord in Afghanistan. When I took the job, the SIS contacted me so I could come back with the information they needed, and that's how I met Neil. I uploaded a lot more than that when we had our first encounter with a group known as Deep 8.

We thought my real identity had been compromised, but from what we've uncovered, they only know me by my handle, Red Enigma. My actual identity is secure for now. I've directed my close contacts to my new handle, Red Bond. I laugh every time I type it to a contact.

Jess scurries into the kitchen and unpacks the ingredients. I stand at the island, watching her without a word. She stops, crosses her arms over her chest, and stares at me.

"Out with it." She smiles. Those are her boyfriend's favorite words. She and Sean were close friends who took it to the next level. They are sunshine, rainbows, and googly eyes, and I couldn't be happier for them.

I take a deep breath, running my nails up and down my thighs. She knows enough to wait for me to be ready to share.

"He chose me," I mumble.

Her arms fall to her sides, and she moves closer. "Who chose you?"

"Neil. He chose me to be Beck's partner in Africa."

Jess's eyes soften. She understands what it feels like to be an outsider, the loneliness of always looking in instead of being part of what's happening. We leaned on each other and made our own "in" group. She reaches over and grabs my hand.

I'm only capable of a whisper, afraid to say the words out loud. "I've never been chosen before. No one ever chooses me. That's why I turned to computers. My entire world revolves around people who can't see me. I reinvented myself the way I wanted to be seen. It's taken me thirty-three years, but this time, he chose me for me because he thinks I can help Beck."

She folds me in her arms and rubs my back. We can't always choose our family, but we can choose who we want our family to be. Growing up in foster care together strengthened us. We know each other's secrets, weaknesses, and doubts.

She was the biracial child no one wanted, and I was the spitfire redhead no one could handle. Together, we are the perfect team. Since she reconnected with Sean, we've drifted apart because we have to grow up eventually and make our way in the world, but our bond will never be broken.

She pulls back from me, and I stare at the floor as she holds me by the shoulders. I look up at her. "There's one teensy problem." I hold up my finger and thumb an inch away from each other.

"Oh, no. What?" She puts her hands on her hips and narrows her eyes.

"I kind of have a crush on Chocolate Thunder." I give her a big smile.

"Don't you think calling him Chocolate Thunder might be offensive?" She's spent years battling racism, so this doesn't sit well with her.

I give her the time-out sign. "Slow your roll. The chocolate is because I think he is delicious, and you know how much I love chocolate. The thunder part is because… well, have you seen how big he is?" That gets me a smack on the shoulder. "I would never in a million years say anything offensive. I know better than that. But do you see where I'm coming from?"

The knock at the front door makes our heads turn. Neither of us moves.

"Are you going to answer the door?" Jess asks.

I look at her as my heart beats in my ears. "This is going to be life-changing. I can feel it."

"Then you better go answer the door. I'll stay here and unpack the food and get dinner started. You should probably send whoever it is back out for peanut M&Ms." She turns to the bags sitting on the counter.

The messenger stands on the other side of the door with my ticket to Africa. I give him a tip and shut the door. Slipping the ticket out of the envelope, the words glare up at me: Dubai to Lusaka, Zambia. My travel experience is limited. However, in the last couple of months, I have traveled to four different continents. I'm holding my breath and blow it out as I make my way back to the kitchen.

I lay the ticket on the counter, and Jess picks it up for a closer look. "You'll have to find a way to uncrush on Beck because he might need you to understand whatever is happening down there." She crosses her arms and gives me the stink eye. "You might not want to call him Chocolate Thunder to his face. He might not take it well."

"He doesn't know how much I like chocolate." I stick my tongue out at her, and we laugh together.

Emotions run around my body, bumping into each other from excitement to holy shit, what am I doing? A piece of me thinks Neil has it all wrong. I'm not cut out for this. I need to stay in my lane and work on the dark web, encrypting code and hacking. I don't even know if Beck wants backup or if he's expecting me. A bigger piece of me screams with joy. I've got one shot at this and need to hit the bullseye. I need to be the one Neil picks again.

EIGHT

Pippa

ONE WOULD THINK I was traveling to the ends of the earth. The plane ride took forever, and I'm riding in the back of a fart car through the jungles of Africa. Sitting still for this long is painful for me.

My mind goes a mile a minute, and to calm myself, I visualize code in my head, but it doesn't work. I'm distracted by what might lie ahead of me. What I wouldn't give to be cruising on my Harley Davidson V Rod.

As I look out the window, Zambia offers a unique beauty with its lush landscape and exotic animals only found on this continent. However, the backdrop is a level of poverty I've never encountered before. Children go without shoes, and their shirts are ripped and torn. Some babies are lucky to have diapers, while others go naked.

I grew up poor and know what it feels like to go hungry and have holes in your clothes, but this is another definition of destitute. My heart breaks as I imagine how these people must struggle daily. I can't know for sure. I've never lived their life, never walked their path. Despite their circumstances, their eyes shine, and they smile and laugh. They seem to live in the moment, worrying about another day of survival tomorrow.

The long trip has me in my head, and I've convinced myself I'm out of my depth. I need to contact Beck as soon as possible so I can turn around and go home. Neil can find someone else from the team to complete the mission and provide backup. However, if I'm going undercover, I should probably make it worth my while. I've come up with a scheme to get closer to Beck. My plan will allow us to stay together without question. I might as well get some while I'm here.

We pull up to the gates of Mubala. Their sheer size is intimidating, and the wall is forbidding. The people of the city either have something to hide, or they don't like foreigners, or maybe both. Either way, I'm the outsider, not just a foreigner, but I might be the only white person in a fifty-mile radius. Keeping a low profile will be imperative and next to impossible.

The city is spotless, and there's unity in its configuration. Streets run north to south and east to west. The buildings are uniform, without room for personal touches. Things are too clean and too perfect.

The people walk around robotically without looking at each other. Some people on the street notice me in the car and glare with scowls on their faces. I must look like a ghost to them. I hold my arms across my body as a shiver grabs me, giving me a warning sign. How is it that the people living without luxury are happier than the people living within these walls?

I didn't know what I signed up for, and I'm not sure Beck knew either, but as I observe the surrounding landscape, there's a dichotomy that makes me rethink running away. The entire scene has piqued my curiosity. I text Beck from the car two minutes before we arrive at the house.

> Me: I'm almost there. Btw, I'm here as your girlfriend. Pucker up, big boy.

> Beck: Excuse me??

Okay, maybe that was a little over the top, but we have to be on the same page. The man could use some spice and loosen up a bit.

Jobi stops the car as I look up the stairs. He's been relatively quiet during the ride. I don't know if it's because he was told not to talk to me or some other reason, but it's put me on edge. Conversation helps me stay out of my head.

Beck stands at the top of the stairs with his hands behind his back and a stoic look on his face. That's not a deterrent for me. I lived with my foster father, who was a real bastard. My training in how to navigate unhappy men is extensive. I've learned to master most of them. I'll see how I can tame this beast.

I grab my suitcase stuffed with goodies and climb the stairs with Jobi in tow, carrying the rest of my luggage. My eyes focus on Beck's beautiful yet stern face, and I smile.

"Hello, darling. How are you?" Charm usually works.

His tight lips relax as he looks at me with questions I can't decipher. "I'm good." His eyes dart over to Jobi. "I'll take those. Thank you, Jobi." They do a weird handshake I'm not even going to ask about.

He waves his hand to the front door. "After you, love." His baritone voice does things to me that shouldn't be legal, especially the way he accents the word *love*.

The door shuts behind me with a click. His voice hits me from behind with increased volume. "No, I am not your boyfriend. I'm on a mission. I have a job to do despite meeting my family for the first time. This isn't an all-inclusive holiday. I know you're new at this, but do try to keep up. I'm not even sure why Neil sent you."

I whip around, and my face and ears grow warm. "Screw you. If you think for one minute I'm going to take your bullshit, you can guess again. I thought if my cover was your girlfriend, us being close wouldn't be questioned." I step closer and crane my neck. I'm about a foot from his face. He is so hot, and I am so screwed.

"This job is very serious for me. Despite what you think, I'm here to help in any way I can. I know I'm new to this, and I have a lot to learn, but you don't have all the answers either. By the way, there's no *I* in *we* because we are on a mission. Now, where's the bathroom? It's been a long trip."

His eyes widened minutely. "The restroom is down the hall, third door on the left. We have a dinner engagement with Wafiq and his girlfriend in a half hour. Dress appropriately. And for the record, I didn't ask for backup. *I* work alone, that means without a partner."

After his directions, I turn down the hall and flip him the bird over my shoulder, hoping he's watching my ass. Chocolate Thunder just downgraded to melted chocolate. Who am I kidding? I love melted chocolate, and the banter was a turn-on. He needs to see things my way, and this will go much easier. I've come up against his kind of attitude my whole life. The time has come for me to stand up and fight.

He shows me to my bedroom upstairs as I get the cold shoulder. I pull myself together and come downstairs dressed in burnt orange, my favorite color, from head to toe. The dress hugs my curves and dips in the front, showing cleavage to give Beck something to simmer about during dinner. He waits for me at the bottom of the stairs with his hands in his pockets.

His face is like stone and could break at any minute.

"The showerhead was amazing. It was just the release I needed after a long trip. As my boyfriend, I thought of you the entire time." I wink at him.

He remains unruffled. "I'm so glad you enjoyed yourself."

He points to my shoes. "What are those, and why are you wearing them? They don't go with the dress."

"They're Chucks, and what are you, the fashion police?" I give him one of my sideways glances as I narrow my eyes.

He gives me a smile that stretches across his face. "Yes, I am. My girlfriend trained me well, and I wear top designers. You need a pair of heels."

"Girlfriend? And I'm not wearing heels. I need comfort after being on the road for an eternity." I cross my arms in front of me.

His smile falters. "Ex-girlfriend. You're not going to change them, are you?"

I shake my head.

"The Chucks are an interesting touch. Let's go."

I've won one battle. I hope the entire mission isn't like this. "That's what I thought." I stick my chin up and walk past him. No one tells me what to wear, and my new mission is to investigate more about the ex-girlfriend. I didn't know there was a girlfriend, let alone an ex.

Jobi picks us up in a high-end black town car, and his eyes flash between us, questioning the tension. We sit apart from each other in the back seat. Beck pushes the button to put up the privacy shield so Jobi can't see or hear us, but words may not be a problem.

I take in the sights through the side window. "Who's Wafiq?"

"As a good agent, that should have been your first question. He's my brother. Didn't you read the dossier?"

"I was busy diving into the diamond industry. You didn't give me a chance to ask because you were too busy assessing my wardrobe. What's your vibe on him?" I look at his remarkable profile, with high cheekbones and full lips.

He shrugs. "No vibe. He showed me around and introduced me to the family gem business."

"That could be our in to get more intel." I scoot closer to him.

He turns his head in my direction. "What are you doing?"

"We need to look the part, like a couple." I don't touch him. He needs to feel like he's in control.

His phone buzzes in his pocket.

"Are you going to answer that?"

"No." He swipes left, sending it to voicemail.

He looks away and closes his eyes. "There's nothing to tell about Wafiq. The Chinese seem to be the problem. That's where our focus needs to be. Wafiq assured me he is not involved with the Chinese."

I nod. "Ummm."

"What's that supposed to mean?" Someone is touchy about his newfound family.

We pull up to a house almost as stunning and enormous as the palace. The outside is done in white stucco with a terracotta tile roof. Lighted sconces shine everywhere, making it look like something out of *Architectural Digest* in the wilds of Africa.

Beck offers me his arm as we climb the stairs to the front door. Black wrought iron scrolled bars cover two twenty-foot doors. Behind the bars, there's a man dressed in a white sports suit. He turns and makes eye contact with me but never smiles. This game just got interesting.

NINE

Beck
_____

MY GOD, what was Neil thinking when he assigned Pippa here? She is fierce and stubborn, two qualities where we will butt heads. The last thing I need is a female partner. After losing Emilia, I requested not to have another female partner. Neil must have missed the memo or ignored it.

There must not be too much to investigate on this mission. She is a green agent, and I'm not even sure what type of training she has had up to this point. She's one more piece for me to navigate while in the middle of getting to know my birth family. I must convince her I have everything under control. She needs to leave to go back to New York City.

I'm lost in thought as we enter the foyer. Wafiq wastes no time introducing himself to her as his eyes explore her from head to toe. Jealousy spikes, a feeling that's been dormant for quite some time. I ignore it, remembering she's a pretend girlfriend.

"Well, it looks like my brother and I have the same taste in women. You are uniquely beautiful, and your tattoos are something to be admired." He gushes over her, and his eyes never leave her cleavage. I don't let his comment bait me.

Her dress plunges in the front and back, reaching the top of her back dimples, putting her colorful artwork on display. She's making a statement. I'm just not sure who it's meant for.

A tall, thin woman sweeps into the room between Wafiq and Pippa to introduce herself and stake her claim. "Hello, I'm Zahara, Wafiq's girlfriend. It's nice to meet you." Her smile is tight, and her eyes assess Pippa to scope out what she perceives as the competition.

This will be an interesting catfight. Although I don't think Pippa is in it. She wants to stir the pot to see what comes to the surface. I step up and put my arm around Pippa's waist. My hand fits comfortably on her curve as a tingle runs up my arm that I try to dismiss.

"Zahara, I'd like you to meet my girlfriend, Pippa." I will never compromise a mission.

They shake hands as Pippa gives her a thousand-watt smile. Zahara forces a smile. I'll be interested to see how Pippa handles herself. Half the game is knowing how to read people and react to them. As a pro, people are an easy read for me, but Pippa is in deep waters.

We move to the dining room with a table big enough to seat fourteen people. Wafiq stands at the head of the table.

"Come, Pippa, please sit next to me. I want to get to know my brother's girlfriend. I'm sorry, Sabeen won't be joining us this evening. She has other plans."

Sabeen is absent a lot lately, as if he doesn't want me to get to know my sister. He doesn't know we've been spending time together over lunch.

Zahara's eyes throw Pippa daggers as she sits on the other

side of Wafiq. I sit to Pippa's right and let the show begin. Let's see what she gets out of him. Her approach will require finesse, which she doesn't have as a new agent.

Heads turn as Sabeen strolls through the door in a flowing turquoise dress. Her smile lights up the room.

"Did you think you could keep me from spending time with my brother and meeting his girlfriend? I got everything done you asked for so I could be here."

I stand to greet her and receive one of her tight bear hugs. "I'm so glad you could make it."

She has joy in her eyes and an innocence that can't be ignored. "This is Pippa. My girlfriend." I trip over my words.

Pippa stands as Sabeen goes in for a hug. The smile on Pippa's face does something to me, hitting me in the place I closed off years ago as I push it away. There seems to be an instant connection between the two of them. Sabeen sits on the other side of Zahara but doesn't greet her with the same fervor.

The small talk begins, and Pippa is flirty but not in a lascivious way. She compliments them on their house and Zahara on her choice of clothing, hair, and makeup. Her approach is effortless to calm the waters.

The conversation is light during a five-course meal. Pippa eats every single item set in front of her. Her appetite seems endless, a far cry from Taylor, who ate like a bird.

Sabeen leans on the table as we wait for dessert. "So, tell me, Pippa, how did you and Dacari meet? He hasn't mentioned you in the couple of days that he's been here. I'm sure he wanted to surprise us."

If my new name throws her, she doesn't show it. She laces her fingers with mine and looks lovingly into my eyes. The sun has darkened my skin, and she's the color of Paper-white flowers, but the twisted contrast is striking as we both look down at our hands. Her hand brings warmth and a connection I wasn't expecting.

She smiles. "I think I'll let him share the story." Turning back to Sabeen, she whispers, "It's quite beautiful. He's such a wonderful man."

Of course, she throws it back my way. I can tell a story with the best of them as I squeeze her hand and give her a smile that reads, "Payback is a bitch."

"We met in Central Park in New York City last spring. The flowers and trees were in full bloom, and I was stretching by the park bench after a long run. She was buying an ice cream from a vendor. Her beautiful red hair caught my attention. The breeze swirled it around her head, and it mesmerized me. There were some orange tulips and a bush with fragrant white flowers. I picked some of each and brought them to her. Of course, she couldn't resist, and we've been together ever since."

Her eyes never leave my face as she rests her chin on her palm. "I think it was very fortuitous he chose orange. As you can see, it's my favorite color." She kisses me on the cheek to complete the picture of relationship bliss.

Sabeen's eyes are dreamy as she gets caught up in the fantasy.

"You have excellent taste in women," Wafiq smirks.

Pippa doesn't miss a beat. "As do you. Zahara is so beautiful she could be a model."

Wafiq strokes Zahara's face. "She is much more than her looks, trust me."

"Beck tells me… I'm sorry. How disrespectful of me. Dacari tells me your family is in the gem business. Do you deal in diamonds, emeralds, or both?" She humbles herself to gain his trust. It's a good move, but is it enough?

Wafiq shifts in his seat. "Sai International Gem mines both diamonds and emeralds. Zambia has the highest quality diamonds in the world, and emeralds are very rare minerals. We have the benefit of both." He takes a sip of wine and looks over his glass at her. Sabeen glances in his direction but says nothing.

The server comes to ask which kind of ice cream we would like. Wafiq defers to Pippa.

"What flavors do you have?" Her eyes grow wide, like those of a child.

"We have strawberry, chocolate, and vanilla," he says without expression.

"I'm going to think it over. Come back to me." She waves him off.

I order my usual decaf green tea to stay clean and avoid sugar while Wafiq, Zahara, and Sabeen put in their orders.

Pippa saves hers for last. "I can't decide. I'll take a scoop of each with whipped cream. Thanks." I don't know where she puts it all.

Sabeen cuts in. "That's a great idea. Do you want to share?"

"Of course." Pippa's face lights up.

She picks up where Wafiq left off. "Are you worried about lab-created diamonds decreasing the value of mined diamonds? They are much cheaper, not only to make, but the sale price can be up to seventy-five percent less." She puts a spoonful of ice cream in her mouth as if she's talking about how to play cricket. Sabeen's eyes bounce between them as she digs into the sundae.

Wafiq wipes his mouth with his napkin and watches her. "You seem to know a lot about diamonds. But no, we aren't worried. They are two distinctly different markets. The demand for mined diamonds is very high and profitable throughout the world. Lab-created diamonds are a whole other clientele."

"But of those diamonds, can you guarantee they aren't blood diamonds? I know there have been strides made with the Kimberly Process, but many diamonds are smuggled through the Congo and then get certified." She's pushing him.

Wafiq steeples his fingers, rubbing his lips up and down between them. She might have pushed too far. I want to interrupt, but I also want to see where it goes. Wafiq is smart enough to get out of it.

He clears his throat. "There are no blood diamonds that come from SIG. We treat our people very well, compensating them for their work. Our diamonds don't go through the Congo. They get certified here by Sabeen." His words are tight.

Pippa puts on a sad face. "I'm sorry. I didn't mean to suggest that your company deals in blood diamonds. It was more of a general statement about the industry. Americans are your biggest consumers. They are more conscious about where the diamonds come from, labor practices, environmental impact, and the communities that benefit from them. When I came to Mubala, I could see that everything you say is true. I just wanted your opinion from a longtime expert in the business."

Wafiq's eyes narrow. "Why do you know so much about diamonds?"

"I saw an article on the plane ride here, and since Africa is known for its gemstones, I thought it would be a good idea to read up on it." She smiles and takes a sip of water.

Sabeen rearranges the napkin on her lap. "We're aware of everything you're talking about and are taking steps to increase our lab-created diamond production. It sounds like you might be interested in coming to my lab." She smiles, trying to calm the turbulent waters Pippa has stirred up.

Wafiq breathes out a sigh of relief. "Thank you, Sabeen. It's a touchy subject in the industry. We don't like to talk about it."

"Love, we don't want to overstay our welcome. You need a good night's sleep after your long trip." I grab Pippa's hand to get her attention.

Wafiq nods. "We enjoyed having both of you. It was a pleasure meeting you, Pippa. I look forward to getting to know you better."

I hold Pippa by the arm as we make our way to Jobi, waiting for us by the car. We slide into the back seat without saying a word, knowing nothing can be said in front of him.

As soon as we are in the house, the conversation begins.

"Your story lacked originality," Pippa says, as she takes off her Chucks and drops them on the floor, as if the story of how we met is the biggest concern of the evening.

"How do you know so much about diamonds? My story was simple yet elegant," I reply, while I take off my jacket.

She turns toward me. "Twenty-two hours is a long time for me to sit. I read everything I could about SIG and the diamond industry. I have to say, it was fascinating, and some of it isn't all that pleasant." She scrunches her nose. "You need to embellish your stories and make them more romantic and unique."

"What did you learn about SIG? My story was told from the male point of view," I say as I follow her upstairs, taking notice of her firm backside. She walks toward the master suite. "Where are you going?"

"To bed."

I grab her arm and feel her heat. "Your bedroom is across the hall. We won't be sharing a bed."

She smiles. "That's fine." She goes to the room across the hall and stands in the doorway. "It's not what I learned about SIG or diamonds. It's about what I learned tonight. Your brother is hiding something. Good night." She shuts the door.

"No, he's not," I whisper to myself. I've got to find a way to send her packing back to the States.

TEN

Beck

MY HEAD BEATS LIKE A DRUM. The last couple of mornings, I woke up with a headache. Each morning gets progressively worse. Today, I feel disoriented and dizzy. At first, I thought it was jet lag, but now I'm not sure what's causing these symptoms, especially since I'm not prone to headaches.

While I've been here, I've stayed on my routine of clean eating, regular meals, and light workouts. Whatever this is seems to be kicking my ass.

I sit on the side of the bed and hold my head in my hands as nausea rolls through me. Breathing through my mouth has helped in the past, but it doesn't touch the pain in my head. I lie back down and stare at the ceiling, thinking of how to get rid of my other headache, Pippa.

Convincing Pippa to leave will not be easy. She thinks she's on to something like perhaps my brother, running a gem company, is an international spy. During the time that I have spent with him, he has gone out of his way for me. I have a sense of belonging here, which is strange after spending my entire life as an outsider.

There's a deep connection I recognize when my brother laughs, and it sounds like my laugh. We share mannerisms like the wave of his hand. If there is a question of which wins, nature or nurture, I would say it's a fifty-fifty split, considering we've been raised on opposite sides of the world.

Then there's the fact that everyone here looks like me. We seem to share a similar body type and facial structure. The more comfortable I get, the harder it is for me to want to leave.

My parents keep calling, and I keep sending them to voicemail. I'm not ready to talk to them. I don't want to break their hearts. Maybe I'll stay longer, but I need to use a direct approach with Pippa and tell her she needs to go home.

Staggering to the bathroom, I splash cool water on my face and hold a cold washcloth to my head. The headache dissipates enough so I can function. I'm not a fan of painkillers, but I take two out of the bottle. I pull on a pair of khakis and a white T-shirt as I make my way to the kitchen.

Pippa has in her earbuds and is dancing and singing, if you want to call it that, while making breakfast. She's wearing short shorts and a tank top. They leave nothing to the imagination.

The sight hits me below the belt. I want to remove her clothes with my fingers, piece by piece, and look at every tattoo to read about her story, but I push it down. The mission comes first.

"Good morning," I say to her back, but she doesn't hear me.

I tap on her shoulder. She turns around, and I wave to her.

She takes out her earbuds as Luke Combs blares something about a hurricane. It's not what I expected, but it fits her. "Hey, handsome, how are you today?" She's a little too bubbly in the morning.

"Okay, I guess." I shove my hands in my pockets as my fingers brush the pills.

She steps closer. "What's wrong? Your eyes aren't right."

Her big green eyes examine mine, and I notice the smattering of freckles across her nose. "It's just a headache," I lie. I don't need to give her a reason to stay.

She hums. "Well, let me make you breakfast."

The kitchen looks as though a cyclone hit it. Pancake flour is everywhere, as cracked eggshells sit in a pile on the counter.

"It looks like you got started without me." I try to smile, but a dizzy spell hits me, and I grab the nearest chair.

She's by my side in a flash and slips under my arm to support my weight. I sit down as the wave passes. Beads of sweat form on my forehead.

"We need to monitor this. How long has it been going on?" She whispers, "And don't lie to me. I'll know."

I jerk away from her. "*We* don't need to do anything. I'm fine. I had a dizzy spell, that's it. It might be the altitude."

"Really? At twelve hundred feet, I doubt it's altitude sickness, but if you want to play it like that, fine.

She shrugs and moves to the stove, flipping the pancakes and making scrambled eggs. I hold my head in my hands as I see a pile of eggs slide onto my plate, and she places a cup of tea in front of me.

"Eat something. It might make you feel better." She doesn't make eye contact.

I take a couple of bites, and my stomach settles. She puts her earbuds back in, humming as she eats. Stony silence surrounds us. She shuts me out. I can't blame her. I haven't exactly been friendly.

Leaning over the counter, I pull out her earbuds. "Look, this isn't going to work with us. You're green and new to the game. I need someone here with experience, someone who knows the ropes. No one would think less of you if you went back to New York."

She stands up and leans on the counter. "Neil sent me here for a reason, and for as green…" she uses air quotes, "as I am, you're missing a lot. You're too close to what could be happening right under your nose."

I sit back and cross my arms over my chest. "Really? Do tell."

"How much do you know about the diamond industry? Because I'm here to tell you, it can be a dirty, ugly business."

"My brother has shown me around and has included me in some of the business meetings so I can get familiar with the family business. I haven't done a deep dive into the details," I say defensively.

She throws her hands up. "And there it is. Your brother. You don't know him from Adam, but you're willing to take him at face value. He's hiding something. I can feel it. He was squirrelly last night when I asked him sensitive questions about the business, and I didn't even hit him with the tough ones."

I stand up and place my hands on the counter, leaning toward her. At six foot six inches tall, most people at least back away, but she doesn't flinch. I admire her ability to stand up to me.

"I think it would be best if you leave and let me handle this on my own. Believe it or not, I've done a lot of solo missions. I run most of my missions by myself."

She has the audacity to round the counter and stand in front of me with her hands on her hips, staring up at me. "Maybe that's the problem. Just so we're clear, you are not my boss, and I'm staying. You can't see the forest from the trees. It's too emotional for you, and I get that. Believe me, I understand what it would be like to find your family after all this time, but you need an extra set of eyes that are objective. Let me shadow you. I can stay in the background and figure things out. It's what I do best."

There's a hint of sadness in her eyes. I'm not sure if it's from her background about her family or the fact that I'm rejecting her for this mission. As for staying in the background, I doubt that will happen. She's the hurricane who's entered my life and demands attention.

She stands back. "Why don't you give me a tour of the city, including the mines, and we'll go from there. It will give me a lay of the land."

A knock at the door interrupts our negotiations. I look at her and nod in agreement. "We'll see how it goes. One day at a time, but I'll make the final call on whether you stay or go."

"That's what you think," she mumbles.

I open the door, and Sabeen turns around, smiling in a loose-fitting white dress. "Hello, big brother. I'm here to take you and Pippa to the lab today. I thought she might find it interesting."

Pippa pops out from behind me. "You know I would love to see the lab. I'm very interested in seeing the complete process in action, from mine to jewelry."

Sabeen beams. "We're putting the final steps in place with help from a company out of China. They are helping us go from rough diamonds to finished pieces we can sell instead of relying on the sale of uncut gems. It's an exciting time for us right now."

This gets my full attention. Pippa turns to me slowly. "It sounds exciting, doesn't it, darling? I can't wait to see the lab and hear more about the Chinese."

Wafiq has denied any involvement with the Chinese. Sabeen is joyful about the prospect of them being part of the family business. These two are not on the same page. Pippa may be right. I might be too close to this and could get burned.

ELEVEN

Pippa
_____

A JEEP AWAITS us at the bottom of the stairs with the top down, fully exposing anyone who rides in it to the morning sun. The African sun blazes hot, even at this early hour.

Sabeen stops and turns to me. "I noticed how fair your skin is, and I love your freckles. Do you want me to put the top up? I don't mind."

I pull a New York Yankees baseball hat out of my bag. "I put on my sunscreen, and I am ready to roll. Don't put it up on my account. I've been a lobster before." I look over at Beck and smile. "He might need a hat, though."

"I only put the top down in the morning. I like the fresh air. Soon, it will be too hot, and it will have to go up." She holds on to the grab bar and launches into the driver's seat. I take shotgun, leaving Beck in the back.

We drive out of town, and Sabeen waves to almost everyone. They smile and wave back, wishing her a good day, but look at me with suspicion. Surely, they have had other white visitors, but this must not be a tourist stop.

Sabeen notices the looks aimed at me. "Don't mind them. They're not used to visitors."

I nod and avoid the obvious reason for their glares. "You're certainly very popular. Must be nice to know everyone." Living out of sight has its advantages, but I crave contact with people.

Sabeen is beautiful with high cheekbones and full lips, much more like Beck than Wafiq. Her hair is cut close, and she stands about six feet. Large diamond-shaped silver earrings with an emerald swaying in the middle dangle from her ears. Her long neck allows her to carry it off, making her look regal.

She doesn't answer right away. "I grew up in this neighborhood and lived in my parents' house until they…" she blows out a breath, "died. I would walk to the local shops and grew up with many of the people here. Some are like family to me, but I'm not here much. A lot has changed since they aren't here anymore. The people are not as happy as they used to be."

The sound of silence is deafening. I'm barely aware of the noise of the all-terrain tires gripping the pavement and the wind whipping around my head. I'm lost in my thoughts about losing my parents, the con artists who left their child behind, never to be heard from again.

"I'm sorry for your loss. I lost my parents when I was very young. You won't think so, but it's a gift that you got to spend this much time with them. If you and your brother are a reflection of them, then they were wonderful people." The lie about losing them, as if they died, is easier than the truth and numbs the pain.

She nods as a single tear slides down her cheek in a familiar path and drips off her cheek. "Thank you."

I glance back at Beck as he sits stoically behind his Ray-Bans. He doesn't acknowledge that he's even heard the conversation. I face forward and try to brush off that he may be of little use on this outing. He tends to hold onto his anger.

As we drive to the outskirts of the city, industrial parks and buildings replace residential homes. Three warehouses are painted in a distinct green and have the black and white SIG logo. Others are a bisque color with the logo.

"I notice the SIG buildings. What are they used for?" I try to act nonchalant.

"We have various uses for them: storing rough gems and repair shops for equipment. Wafiq has personal warehouses. Those are the ones in green." She shrugs.

"Why does Wafiq have his separate warehouses? What does he use them for?" My questions come out quickly.

She smiles. "You have a lot of questions, but that's good."

I try to backtrack. "I'm sorry. Your country and city are new to me and fascinating. I've never been to Africa. It's easy for me to get caught up and excited about everything, and then it tumbles out in the form of questions. I feel like a kid sometimes." I scrunch my nose.

She turns to me and laughs. "It's fine. I like that you're not too serious. As much as I love my brother, he can get pretty intense. I don't know what Wafiq does in those warehouses. He hasn't given me access to them." She frowns.

Beck speaks up. "I thought both of you ran SIG. It seems you should have access to everything."

She shrugs. "He and Zahara must be working on something in them. Being the gemologist of the family, I'm in another part of the business."

She pulls up to a modern office building and shuts off the engine. "Now, you get to see what I do." She beams.

I stand between her and Beck on the sidewalk and need to look up to engage in the conversation. "What do you do as a gemologist?"

"You're about to find out. It will be good for Dacari to see what I do. Soon, he will be part of the family and our leader as king." She strides ahead of us.

I lean over to Beck. "I wonder if that makes me queen."

"I wouldn't count on it," he replies dryly and lengthens his steps to catch up to Sabeen.

He makes me smile. He's intelligent, funny when he wants to be, and kind, the triple threat. Despite my lust for him, I know I belong here. But something is off, and I need to find out what it is and protect him at the same time. Looking out for his health will be added to my duties.

I catch up to them in the elevator that whisks us to the top floor. Beck and Sabeen talk in low voices as I stand in awe of the landscape outside the glass windows of the elevator. On one side is the gaping mouth of one of the mines, and on the other is a pristine city, a perfect place with everything in order.

Sabeen ushers us into a darkened room that's only accessible using her fingerprint and retinal scan. On the far wall is a glass case full of things that sparkle under the right lighting.

I'm not into jewelry, but I'm drawn to the sparkle behind the glass. Different-sized diamonds and emeralds are scattered on black velvet, making them look like the most beautiful night sky.

"These are beautiful, and I'm not a diamond girl, but I can't look away either," I say as I look down at the case.

Sabeen stands next to me. "That's why they are so popular. People can't look away. With the right cut, you can see them across a room. They are tiny gifts of light."

I point to an emerald that's caught my eye. "That's stunning."

She leans into me. "You have an excellent eye. That is a top-grade emerald or green light, as we like to call it. Zambia is known for its emeralds. It was only a few years ago we discovered an emerald over five thousand carats."

"What is your job at SIG?" Beck cuts in, ignoring our conversation about the gems. He's been quiet until now, and that makes me wonder how he's feeling.

"I determine the gems' make, value, and authenticity. Recently, I've started cutting and creating jewelry so we can sell directly to customers. That's why we are consulting with the Chinese." She steps behind the counter to a safe behind a wall panel.

Beck stands next to me. "It's dangerous to get involved with the Chinese. They are rarely on the up-and-up. You and Wafiq need to be careful."

She smiles at him and holds a tray with jewelry containing earrings, necklaces, and bracelets. They are in some configuration of diamonds and emeralds with a flair of tribal design.

I hear myself gasp. They are unique and a once-in-a-life-time purchase. My eyes lock on a pair of earrings with emeralds surrounded by diamonds. Sabeen picks up the earrings.

"These match your eyes. Are you sure you don't know something about gems? You gravitate toward the finest in our collection." She smiles and hands me the earrings.

I hold them in my hand as if I'm holding a baby.

"Put them on. They will look splendid on you." She looks at Beck, who stares at me.

I pull my hair back over my shoulder and put them on. "They are exquisite. One day, I hope to afford something like this for myself." My secret is I can afford them, but there is a part to be played here.

Beck reaches over and uses his fingertips to push my hair behind my ear. A current runs through me at his touch. Few men have had that effect on me, but I noticed it last night when he held my hand.

"Sabeen is right. They match your eyes perfectly." His lips curl up on one side.

I bask in the attention but take off the earrings, handing them back to Sabeen. That much bling at that price makes me nervous, and Beck's touch has me scattered.

"Since I'm not a gem expert, I'm curious how you tell the difference between a fake and the real thing." I change the subject and deflect the focus.

Sabeen plucks one of the loose diamonds from the display case. "It's easier than you think."

She places the diamond with the flat side down on a black dot and hands me a magnifier. "Look through it. What do you see?"

As I look through the pointed end. "Nothing." I look up at her.

"You don't see the dot?" she smirks.

"Nope." I pass the magnifier to Beck to let him have a look.

"Then it's a genuine diamond. If you see the dot or the reflection of the dot, then it's a fake. You should work with me once we crown Dacari as king." She nudges me with her shoulder, and her smile is warm and genuine.

I hope she's as innocent as she appears. I'm warming up to her and want to keep her as a friend. Friends are hard to come by for me.

We look at some more stones, cut and uncut, as Sabeen explains their value based on cut, clarity, color, and carat. I absorb the information she shares with us in her area of expertise, and she explains it seamlessly.

The sun settles in the sky as we drive back to the house. Beck is still quiet, and I can't help but imagine what must be going through his mind. The first part of his coronation ceremony is tonight, and he must be nervous.

The two of us lumber up the stairs to the front door. There is a package wrapped with a green ribbon. As he approaches it, I grab his arm.

"Be careful," I mumble.

"Really? I don't think it's a bomb." He pulls his arm out of my grasp.

He reaches down and slips the card out.

It reads,

Welcome to Mubala, Your Highness.

I hope you make fine memories.

There's no signature.

TWELVE

Beck
_____

I FLIP THE CARD OVER. There's no signature. I pull my knife from its sheath and cut the tape at the top of the box. A lime green mesh bag contains tea bags. The label says, "Decaf Green Tea from Mubala."

"That was thoughtful. It looks handmade. I'll put it in the kitchen for you." She grabs the bag and walks away.

There's something about her that stirs me. She's a mix of puzzle pieces and not like any woman I've ever encountered. I walk behind her, which isn't an unpleasant view. "So much for staying in the background."

She places the bag on the counter and whips around. "You weren't exactly a ball of fire today. You still don't feel good, do you?"

"I feel fine. It's been a long couple of days and a lot to process." I'm not about to admit that I haven't felt right since this morning. Things are off. I can't grab onto things I should remember.

She cocks her hip out and stares at me. "I think you should go lie down before we go to your ceremony this evening."

"Who said you're going? You need to pack your bags for your trip home. By the way, I got you a parting gift." I pull a plane ticket from my pocket and set it on the counter. I haven't given up hope I can wear her down, and she'll go home, but I think it will be a long battle.

"First, as your girlfriend, I should be at your ceremony. It won't look right if I'm not there. Second, I don't have to prove myself to you because I don't work for you, so suck it up, buttercup. And third, you can take your plane ticket and shove it where the sun don't shine." She crosses her arms across her chest, lifting her ample breasts. I make the mistake of looking down.

"See something you like? Take a snapshot, it lasts longer." She smiles and doesn't change her position.

"Maybe I should hire you to work for MBK just so I can fire you," I say through gritted teeth. The petty statement leaves my mouth before I can stop it.

"I wouldn't work for you if you paid me a million dollars, and I'm worth a helluva lot more." She stares at me as electricity snaps between us. The hardness between my legs takes me by surprise. She's a worthy opponent and gives as good as she gets.

She smiles to let me know she's aware I felt it and walks away. "I have work to do since I'm the only one looking for answers."

I won't admit there's another reason I want her gone. She has awakened something in me I never thought I could feel for a woman again. She's fierce and tenacious, which are great attributes in an agent, but I don't think she knows how dangerous it can be in the field. I'm concerned about her impulsive side. My last partner was a highly trained agent, and she lost her life anyway.

After hearing her comment about losing her parents at a

young age, I had the urge to hold her to me, knowing her pain, which is not my usual reaction. Missing information about our parents seems to be the thread that ties us together. Since she's been here, she's tried to stand next to me as I push her away, but she always smiles like she has a secret I know nothing about. Maybe a nap would do me good.

I amble up the stairs, looking forward to lying down. Napping is not something I do, ever. Today, it feels like the only thing to do to regenerate and recuperate for the big ceremony tonight.

I WAKE up to Pippa smoothing her hand along my arm. Her fingers trace the muscles in my tricep, making their way up to the tribal tattoo on my shoulder. She's watching her fingers run along my skin, unaware I'm watching her. Her lips curve, and serenity glows from her.

"See something you like?" I throw her words back at her. She smiles before she looks over at me.

"I do. I wish you wouldn't spend so much time trying to get rid of me." Her voice is gentle.

I avoid her comment, wanting to focus on the evening ahead. "How long did I sleep?"

"Three hours. I brought my laptop in here to work to watch over you." She moves back.

I suck in a breath. "Three hours? I never sleep that long." My chest warms when she shares that she watched me while I slept.

"Do we need to see a medic? Do you think you have a bug?" She frowns, something I haven't seen her do since she's been here.

"No. It's just a cold or a virus. Nothing to worry about. What are you working on?" I raise my chin to her laptop. The top-of-the-line computer allows her to hack from any place in the world.

She removes her hand from my arm, and her warmth leaves me. "I'll let you know if I find anything. We got a lot of information from Sabeen on the Chinese involvement with the company, but I want the deets. As a hacker, curious minds want to know." She wiggles her brows.

I need the details. I'm just not sure I'm ready for them. A ceremony awaits me as I move closer to becoming king, another thing I'm not ready for. Wafiq mentioned something about being able to make decisions after I'm crowned. There's conflict within me about what my next move will be. Will I stay or go?

"I left a package in the walk-in closet for you. It's your attire for this evening and is definitely bold. Can't wait to see you in it."

She walks to the door with more sway to her hips than usual, and it gets my body's attention. This woman knows exactly what she's doing, and I won't cave to her overtures.

I sit up as a wave of dizziness hits me, and I hold my head. Standing up, I move and then stop, unable to remember where I'm going or what I'm doing. I sit back down as panic hits me I never felt before. Sweat beads on my forehead.

My working memory is shorting out. Taking breaths in through my mouth, I try to calm myself down. What is happening to me? My first instinct is to call for Pippa, but I push it away. I don't need her.

A package sits on the counter in the closet, and it jogs my memory. The ceremony tonight requires the attire contained in the box.

As I strip out of my clothes, I take a closer look at the intricate tattoo on my shoulder in the mirror. I remember when I chose it, or maybe it chose me. I knew without a doubt that it was the tattoo I had to have on my body. Pippa's tattoos tell a story. Maybe my tribal tells a story I don't even know about. The recent events make me question destiny.

I open the box. Inside are a red shirt, a black skirt, a long red and black checkered cloth, and several beaded collars. Taking each item out, I examine them. As I put them on, it's as if they were tailor-made for my body.

The mirror reflects an image of me I don't recognize. The red-and-black checkered cloth is a mystery to me, and I'm not sure how to wear it. This requires a woman's touch, and, unfortunately, there is only one woman I can call on to help me.

Pippa floats across the room in an emerald green dress that ties at the neck, exposing her back, and puts her artwork on display. She is fearless about showing who she is.

"You rang, Your Highness?" she says in her best British accent, which is pretty good.

"I don't think I'll ever get used to that title." The red-and-black checkered cloth lays across my arm. "I'm having trouble figuring out how to put this on."

"This is called a *shuka*. Men wear this during many different ceremonies."

She sweeps the cloth across my chest diagonally and grabs a pin I didn't see in the box. The pin carries what looks like the family crest. A lion is set in the middle with green emeralds in the shape of leaves. Diamonds are the eyes of the lion. The Siwanda family crest sits above the lion's head with the family name at the top.

She holds it in her hand as I examine it. "You have a rich family history." Something passes in her eyes I can't decipher as longing or regret.

"Everyone has a family story. I must be destined to be

attached to royalty. My family in England are from royalty as well."

She gathers the cloth and pins it at my waist. "Really? That's an interesting coincidence, don't you think?"

"I hadn't thought about it until now." An odd sensation travels through me. Is this a coincidence or something more? I dismiss the idea based on how far away my parents are from this part of the world.

She reaches up on her tiptoes to put the beaded collar around my neck. Red, black, and blue beads adorn it, detailed around the diamonds and emeralds set in gold. One goes around my neck; two others go around my wrists, and there are two more for my ankles. They feel heavy with the gems in them, reminding me of the heaviness of this ceremony.

The throne shouldn't be going to me. Wafiq should be the one to be crowned king. I'm here simply by default and the fact I'm the oldest. Some traditions are made to be broken, and I'm about to turn this one on its head.

Her eyes meet mine, and are the most brilliant green eyes I have ever seen. She doesn't cover the freckles across her nose with makeup. Her red hair cascades down her back in waves. She looks like one of those Irish wood nymphs. Her eyes convey a softness, but I know she's also sharp as a tack. I want to reach out and touch her, but then I remember I want her gone, and she's a pretend girlfriend.

She steps back from our intimate moment. "You look very handsome. Good looking enough to be king." Her smile doesn't reach her eyes. "I want to talk to you about going out tonight and looking at those green warehouses, see if we can't get in somehow." She holds my gaze.

"I was wondering about those myself. Although, I'm sure it's nothing. Wafiq and Zahara may use the warehouse to hold various stones for safekeeping."

She doesn't say anything and nods with half a smile. "We need to contact Katoo. I haven't seen him since I arrived. Have you?"

"Katoo?" I stop and watch as her eyes search mine. I should know that name, but it escapes me and scares me at the same time. Parts of my memory have vanished. I try to cover it up. "Oh, right. Katoo. Let's contact him tomorrow."

My mouth goes dry. My memory is like a sieve, barely holding onto things I should know. If this keeps up, I won't be able to fake it for long. Tonight is going to be a rough road.

THIRTEEN

Beck

MY MIND IS PLAYING tricks on me. Things I should remember escape me as if they are just out of reach, hovering at the edges. Recently, people and places are hard for me to remember, and my memory has never been a problem.

Fear crawls in my chest, rendering me immobile. Could this be early-onset dementia? The memory loss combined with the headaches points to something more significant, but I can't leave until we find out what's happening here. *Did I use the word 'we'?*

Pippa intrigues me, and she thinks that she's necessary to complete this mission. I'll let her play spy for a while longer and then send her packing. Watching her in action has piqued my curiosity about what may be happening in Mubala. She seems to have a keen awareness of when to question things.

Jobi picks us up and drives us to a banquet hall. We're quiet in the car, each in our heads about what the evening will bring. She rubs her hands up and down her thighs, looking out the window.

We pull up to the hall, and behind it stands an enormous outdoor straw hut with a concrete floor. Everyone streams in the front door dressed in formal attire for Mubala. There are no tuxes or formal evening gowns. Instead, they dress in brightly colored dresses, shawls, and skirts for both men and women. Red seems to be the color of choice. Some wear beaded collars, wristbands, and anklets.

The doorman stops us at the entrance. "I'm sorry, sir. No shoes allowed. You may store them over there." He's unaware of who I am and points to a closet filled with shoes on racks.

"This is my kind of party." Pippa rips off her heels and tosses them in the closet. "If I never wear those things again, it will be too soon.

Her toenails are orange, of course. Being barefoot feels strange in this forum, but oddly, it puts everyone on the same playing field, so to speak. The only thing to focus on is each other and our clothing. No one is looking down, and maybe that's the point. My feet cool on the floor as Pippa takes my hand and leads me across the hall. I like holding hands with her a little too much.

We make our way to the straw pavilion. Wafiq waves to us from the other end. He stands on an elevated platform that extends the length of the hut with several chairs, tables, and what appears to be a throne. Along the entire side of the pavilion are tables filled with enough food to feed an army. Carved decorative fruits accent the greens and some foods I don't recognize. The middle of the floor is empty, and people are milling around outside the hut, eating at tables encircled with torches.

"Ah, my brother. I see you are wearing your ceremonial garments, the *shuka*. You look splendid. The colors are striking on you. Come and sit down. What can I get for you to eat and drink before we get started?" His garment is similar to mine, but his collar is different.

He snaps his fingers and motions with his hand for a server.

"How about a bit of everything, and I'll take it from there? Oh, and some green tea. Thank you."

I sit down, feeling exhausted even after my nap. Pippa comes to the table with her plate loaded with mostly meat and vegetables. I thought my metabolism was high.

"Are you eating for two?" The snide comment is meant to fluster her.

"Not unless you jumped my bones last night, and I slept through it. I seriously doubt that happened because I would want to be awake for every minute of you naked." Her lips wrap around a spear of cucumber as she sucks it into her mouth.

Okay, so that backfired, and my groin hardens, which is not a good sign. The king can't walk around with a hard-on in front of everyone.

Sabeen comes by, and there is something about her that makes me smile, besides the fact that she is my sister.

She gives me a big hug. "How are you doing, my brother the king?"

"I'm not king yet, but I'm doing fine. You look beautiful this evening." Her dress is a deep red, and her diamond and emerald jewelry would be the envy of anyone in the world.

"Thank you, Your Highness. I'm going to go dancing. I'll see you later." She waves and smiles as she jumps into the crowd of people.

As the evening progresses, many people introduce themselves to me and offer gifts, which are set at the foot of the throne. Some are expensive gifts, and some are handmade. There seems to be a steady stream of people.

I lean over to Wafiq. "Where are all these people coming from?"

"We invited the entire city of Mubala to celebrate this initiation ceremony with us. As we introduce you as the next in line, they must honor you with something they value."

I nod and look over at the growing pile of gifts. One little girl bends over and places a stuffed monkey on the pile. She looks up at me and smiles with tears in her eyes. I grab the stuffed monkey and give it back to her. Her mother snatches her away.

"No, she mustn't take it back. It is a gift for you as our new king." She bows and leaves with her child in tow. As soon as this is over, I'm going to make sure the gifts are returned. Seeing the little girl cry breaks my heart.

A man from across the hall catches my eye, and it takes me a minute to remember him as Katoo. His eyes shift, giving me a silent message that he needs to talk to me. I make eye contact with him briefly and nod, excusing myself to go to the restroom.

The hallway off the banquet hall gets darker the farther I travel toward the restroom. Someone grabs my arm. I turn around in defense, grabbing hold of their wrist, and realize it's Katoo.

"Katoo, where have you been? You haven't attended any of the dinners with Wafiq." I need answers, and there are too many questions.

He nods. "There are many reasons I keep my distance from Wafiq, none of which I can talk about now. We need to meet tomorrow. There is much I need to share with you. I will text you the time later."

He looks down the hall from where we came from. "There are eyes on me. I must go." He takes both my hands in his. "Please, be safe."

Before I can ask why, he turns and leaves, disappearing farther into the darkness. Not once have I felt like I was in danger while inside the walls of Mubala. A wave of dizziness hits me as I grab the wall and lean against it.

I pull myself together and head back to the ceremony in hopes it will be short. Wafiq stands tall toward the back of the room, overseeing the festivities. I join him on stage.

He takes a large staff and bangs it several times on the riser. Everyone stops and stares. In an instant, it's quiet, and I can hear the crickets sing.

"We are here to celebrate our new king. Let me introduce my brother, Dacari Touré Siwanda."

Everyone stomps twice, hits their chest twice, and kneels with their head down and left fist on their forehead, right arm out to the side.

When people kneel and show surrender to you, the feeling is overwhelming. I'm humbled by it, and I stand up straighter, trying to look the part of a leader. They are about to make this man from a foreign land their new king. The ceremony is an out-of-body experience, one that should be happening to someone else.

My mouth goes dry, and it's hard to swallow as I figure out what to do next.

My brother whispers, "You can tell them to rise."

"You may rise." My deep voice cracks and doesn't sound as confident as Wafiq's, who has way more practice at this than me.

Wafiq raises his hands. "Let the celebration begin."

A group of men and women dressed in colorful clothing and wearing beaded collars arrange themselves in the middle of the hut. They stomp their feet in rhythm and clap their hands. There are no instruments to accompany them. The men grunt as the women sing. Low-toned grunts mixed with the high-pitched voices of the women create a beautiful song.

They dance in circles, bobbing and weaving around each

other. Warriors come to the center and begin jumping, some as high as five feet off the ground. As if on cue, they stop, arms out to the side, and look up to the sky. Everyone's head turns in my direction, waiting for my approval.

I stand up and start clapping as everyone follows me in appreciation of the performance.

An older woman approaches me. "You must take a woman to the center of the group and dance with her. She will be part of your destiny." Her skin has cracks like leather, but her eyes are intelligent and warm.

I gaze out over the crowd as Pippa takes my hand and leads me to the center of the dance troupe. The glare of the other women is cold and harsh. She is more of an outsider than me because of the milky color of her skin. If she's aware of it, she doesn't show it.

Her focus is on me like I'm the only man in the room. Taylor never looked at me with such adoration, and yet I don't deserve Pippa's warmth. I've pushed Pippa away at every turn, trying to get her to leave, but she's stubborn and yet forgiving.

The circle of dancers shows us how to do some of the dance moves. At one point, Pippa flies around me, and her hair looks like a red blur. She's magnetic. The men laugh with her as she quickly learns the steps, and I stand there and watch. Even the women who looked at her with disdain are smiling and dancing with her. Her energy flows from everyone she meets as a beacon of life and happiness.

She reaches up on tiptoe and gives me a chaste kiss on the mouth. The young girls laugh and giggle, covering their smiles with their hands.

The place in the center of my chest I try to keep from her cracks a bit, letting in some of her warmth. I can't ignore it. Life, love, and laughter bubble from her, and I can't help but get caught up in the moment. I've walked on the dark side of life for far too long.

I take her hand in mine and walk to the riser as I hear the engines of motorcycles in the distance. What's strange is I haven't seen any motorcycles in the city. The sound of the engines gets louder, and the back of my neck tingles. I turn around in time to see two riders pull out semi-automatic weapons and open fire.

I push Pippa to the ground and overturn a table for cover. "If you have your weapon, don't fire. Stay down." I can't have history repeat itself with Pippa.

Drawing my weapon, I fire toward the shooters. They stop shooting immediately, are caught by surprise, and ride away. Wafiq and Zahara are crouched in the corner.

I yell over to them. "Have you been hit?"

They shake their heads as I head to the carnage in the middle of the dance floor. I can't locate Katoo or Sabeen from my vantage point. As I assess the crowd, there are many injuries and deaths, which angers me because I'm sure those bullets were meant for me.

FOURTEEN

Beck

THE PEOPLE on the dance floor in front and on each side of me lie with bullets in them. Pippa finds me with her gun drawn, but the shooting is over, replaced by cries of agony over loved ones who are hurt or dead.

I've danced with death before, but never on this scale and not with people hugging loved ones to their chests. The scene guts me.

Wafiq and Zahara don't seem too shaken up. They dust themselves off as they look over the crowd. Zahara's face is emotionless, while Wafiq's face is grim and angry, but I'm not sure it's genuine. Katoo is nowhere to be found.

I don't let on that I think the gunshots were meant for me. "Do you have shootings here often?" I say to Wafiq.

"Actually, no. It's a rare occurrence. If we find out who it is, they will be exiled from the city. Sometimes the family leaves with them." He says it as if it's no big deal for these people.

I catch the word if. "Don't worry, I'll find them. That's what I do for a living."

Something passes in his eyes I can't unravel as doubt or fear that I might find something.

As I scan the floor, my eye catches Sabeen lying on her back with her hand on her shoulder. I jump down from the riser and run to her. Grabbing several cloth napkins, I hold them to her wound. Her eyes flutter open. My heart races in my chest, and I pray her injury isn't fatal.

I cradle her face in my hand. "You're going to be okay. It's a shoulder wound."

She covers her hand with mine and smiles. "I know. You're here now. Thank you for coming back."

Her eyes shut, and something flips inside of me. She views me as a savior, like I have the answers to the problems that live in Mubala. Problems I didn't know existed. I can only rely on my background as an agent and medical student to provide any help. I'm not a savior but rather a pawn in this game.

I can hear the wail of ambulances in the distance, getting louder as they approach. We hold cloth napkins and parts of skirts and shirts on the gunshot wounds for those on the ground. I keep the pressure applied to her wound and view the carnage as faces stare up at me in a plea for help.

My reassuring words are a small comfort as I tell them to keep holding a cloth over the wounds to stop the bleeding. Pippa tries to console the injured with friends and family who try to help. She doesn't hesitate to jump into the action.

The emergency medical teams make quick work of loading up the wounded and heading out into the night. We're left standing there with the bitter taste of a celebration scarred by violence.

Pippa and I watch as they take away Sabeen, and Wafiq rushes toward me.

"Was that Sabeen?" Tears crest in his eyes.

"Yes, it's a shoulder wound. She should be fine." My words are tight as I wonder where he's been during this time.

He holds his head up. "They will give her top priority because she's royalty. We will go to be with her when she gets out of surgery." He grabs Zahara's hand and heads for the door.

I hold Pippa's hand, which serves as an anchor and, in an odd way, comforts me. My other hand stops Wafiq from leaving.

"Wafiq, do you have any idea who those bullets were for?" I get close, so he has to look at me. His eyes will tell the real story.

"No. Usually, people are upset over things going on at the mine. Maybe it has something to do with that." His mouth makes a hard line as if he's said something he didn't mean to say.

Pippa steps up. "What's going on at the mine?"

He waves his hand at her. "Nothing. You know people always want more or something they can't have." He turns to Zahara. "Let's go. It's been an awful night."

They turn and leave, stepping over toppled furniture. They never asked how we were or if we needed anything. Something inside me deflates, a puncture to my overinflated expectation of my newfound family. I haven't given up hope that they are who they seem to be, but I find their reaction strange and unsettling.

Pippa grips my hand tightly. "We need to go to the hospital and be there when Sabeen wakes up. By the way, those were Ducati bikes."

"Did you get a look at them?"

"No, but I know what they sound like. My point is that they are high-end bikes. This wasn't some random act. I think they were hired."

The question, in my eyes, leads her to continue. "I ride a Harley. I know bikes." She shrugs.

I pull my hand away, forgetting I want Pippa gone so I can deal with this situation on my own without her distraction. My emotions are bouncing around, torn between my head and my heart. For the first time, there's disappointment in her eyes from the loss of touch or my reaction; I can't tell.

Jobi leans against the front of the car at the curb, waiting for us. "Where to, sir?" He missed the shooting.

"The hospital."

"What? Why?" His mouth hangs open.

"Sabeen got hit by a bullet in her shoulder. She'll need surgery, and we want to be there when she wakes up."

He nods as we pile into the car. The ride is filled with worry, and Pippa keeps glancing in my direction. I stare out the window, trying to piece together why someone wants me dead. This is the second attempt on my life. The third time may be the charm.

We step into the lobby of the hospital. Wafiq paces at the other end, smoothing his hands over his hair. Zahara sits stone-faced in a chair, watching him.

Pippa grabs my arm and pulls me aside. "I think you've already figured out those bullets were meant for you."

"How do you know that?" I say in a low growl.

"If you look at the entry point of the gunmen and where they shot, those paths lead back to you. The injured were in front of you and on the side of you. If you hadn't fired back, they would have kept shooting until they got to you. They weren't expecting you to have a weapon or to fire back. How's that for an analysis?" She stands back.

"I see why Neil hired you. You have a very analytical mind that sees things differently, but you're only going to get in the way." I want to add, "And a curvy, sexy body to go with it, which turns me on," but I leave that part off.

As if she hasn't heard me, she says, "The question is who wants you dead and why?"

"You read my mind. My guess is it has something to do with becoming king. I hate to admit it, but everyone is a suspect except for my brother. He wouldn't shoot his own sister." I nod my chin in his direction. "Look at him, he is out of his mind with worry."

"Maybe your sister got in the way and is a casualty he didn't expect." She looks away from Wafiq and turns toward me.

We have a stare-off without words, a war of theories on what exactly happened to put Sabeen in danger. I don't want her theory to be correct because that would mean I can't trust my brother.

A couple of hours go by until a doctor in scrubs covered in blood enters the waiting room.

"Who is here for Sabeen Siwanda?"

Wafiq and I walked toward him. My peripheral vision picks up a scowl on Wafiq's face as he glances my way. "How is she?" Wafiq asks as worry covers his face.

"She's going to be fine. We removed the bullet that nicked her lung, but she'll make a full recovery. You can see her briefly, and then she needs to rest. The nurse will show you to her room."

He turns to leave. "Wait. Do you have the bullet? I want to take a look at it."

The surgeon turns back toward us and glances at Wafiq. "Yes, it's going to the police so they can analyze it."

Wafiq shoots me a look. "What do you want with the bullet? This is a police matter. You need to stay out of it."

If I examine the bullet, I'll be able to tell what weapon it came from. I shrug. "Just curious. I own a security firm for a reason."

He nods. "You can check in with the police. We're going in to see Sabeen."

He takes Zahara by the hand. It's the first sign of affection between these two, and they head for the nurse, who shows them to Sabeen's room.

Pippa stands next to me and doesn't say a word. "What, you have nothing to say?"

"I think you're going to have to figure this one out on your own. I just hope you're not too late."

I look down and hold her warm hand in mine, closing my eyes. Her touch brings me comfort in a stormy sea of emotions and questions without answers. I might succumb to her undertow after all. I'm conflicted between wanting her for my carnal pleasures and knowing I work best as a loner. The pull to her is stronger than I realized.

I keep her hand in mine as we peek in to see Sabeen lying quietly in bed. Wafiq and Zahara are gone. Her eyes are closed until we get closer.

"Hey, you came to see me. I'm so glad you're a part of my life. I hope you plan on staying for a while." She smiles. "I like you."

She reaches out her hands to me and Pippa. They look at each other like sisters.

"Shhh, you need to get some sleep. I wouldn't want to be anywhere else right now. We'll be back tomorrow," I whisper.

She closes her eyes, and the fragility of life hits me. My existence has impacted no one else's life until now. No one close to me ever knew of my battle wounds, missions, or near-death experiences. My presence here has harmed someone else's life, which makes me think this coronation needs to be over soon so I can leave and save those I've come to know. Whoever is trying to kill me can follow me home, away from these innocent people.

The air is heavy on the ride back to the house as Pippa stares out the window, away from me. I want her to ask me questions and provide theories. Part of me doesn't want to carry this on my own. The events have snowballed into something too big and weighs too much. Her tenacity reminds me of Emilia. She may be a valuable partner.

As we move to the kitchen, Pippa offers to make my favorite decaf green tea from the gift left on the doorstep. She fixes herself warm lemon water and stands across from me in the kitchen without saying a word.

"I don't like the silent treatment," I say as I sip my tea.

She sighs. "It's not meant as punishment. Maybe you need less of my voice and more of your own thoughts. Things here are not as they appear, and I'll leave it at that. I'll see you in the morning, and we can go back to the scene and analyze it. Good night, Beck."

"Good night, Pippa. Thank you for being there this evening. You were very helpful." I throw her a bone, hoping tonight scared her enough to leave.

I finish my tea, and exhaustion sets in as a heavy blanket covers me and weighs me down, forcing me to sleep. My last thoughts before I fall asleep are the worries of everything I'm not seeing or acknowledging. I hate to admit I need Pippa to get through this otherwise, I'm flying blind, and it could bite me in the ass.

FIFTEEN

Pippa

GOD, that man is stubborn. Tonight, he was all over the place. One minute he's holding my hand, the next he's ripping it away. He keeps telling me how he wants me to leave, but I think he feels the pull we have toward one another.

I won't leave him with everything going on in his new world, from a newfound family to his health. My worry rattles me, but I won't let Beck see me like this.

I wash my face and view my reflection in the mirror. The freckle-faced skinny kid, who had no friends, has left and been replaced by a woman who has something to prove to everyone around her. I know I can do this job and figure out who wants Beck dead, but I've got to get him on board with treating everyone like a suspect, including his brother. My sixth sense is strong on this one.

My warm body hits the soft, cool sheets, and sleep should come easily, but it doesn't. This was my first shooting. If I stay in this job, it won't be my last. I have flashes of bullets hitting people as they jerked back and hit the floor until Beck told me to hide. I shouldn't have listened to him. My instincts were to pull my weapon and fire back alongside him. My mind couldn't catch up to what was happening, and I froze. Rookie mistake number one, and it won't happen again.

I toss and turn, trying to rid my mind of the images until sleep finally finds me. The sun streams down on my face from a top window, and the time on the clock says late morning. I spring out of bed, knowing I'll hear about it from Beck, who is probably already up, had breakfast, and ready to go back to the banquet hall.

The brush gets stuck in my hair, but I untangle it and put my red mane up in a ponytail. I throw on shorts and a racerback T-shirt and run downstairs. The house is usually quiet, but this silence has the hair standing on my neck. Something is wrong, but I can't put my finger on it.

"Beck?" I call out to try and find him somewhere in the house.

"Beck," I say, louder this time.

A thud comes from his room as I race back up the stairs to his bedroom. I open the door to find him face down on the floor.

Even though I lift heavy weights, trying to flip over a two-hundred-plus man is not an effortless task. I get him on his back, and his eyes pop open. They are the color of obsidian, which makes them mysterious and sexy, but this isn't the time for my hormones.

He looks at me with a frown. "Who are you?" The heaviness of his deep voice softens.

"Ha-ha. You're hilarious. I know you wanted me to leave, but you've got to be joking," I say as I stand up.

He gets up slowly and falters several times. I grab his arm and get him upright as he sways and reaches for the bed.

He leans back. "Where am I? What is this place?" The tension in his voice could break into panic at any minute.

I stare at him for a second and realize he's not joking. "You're in Africa, Zambia, to be more exact, visiting your birth family. I'm Pippa. Is any of this ringing any bells?"

He shakes his head, and I notice the beads of sweat on his forehead. "My head is pounding. Excuse me."

He bolts up with his hand covering his mouth and runs for the bathroom, not before hitting the wall first. Kneeling in front of the toilet, he dry-heaves. The floor is littered with dirty towels and washcloths.

I grab him by the arm and lead him back to the bed. He's like carrying dead weight. His feet drag across the floor as if he doesn't know where to put them. He lies flat on his back and breathes through his mouth.

"What did you say your name is again? Should I know you?" Sheer terror is written on his face with a plea for help.

Panic sets in, and my heart rate kicks up. I'm in a foreign country with a killer on the loose and a partner who's sick with memory loss. Neil's words come to me that the only person I can trust is Katoo.

"My name is Pippa. I'm going to write it down for you."

I place a trash can next to the bed and write my name on a piece of paper. So much for getting rid of me, especially when he can't remember who I am.

I run downstairs, yanking open the kitchen cabinets to search for a bucket and put ice in it. Then I run back upstairs to wrap some ice in a washcloth and apply it to his forehead.

"Thank you, Pip. That feels good." His hand covers mine as I hold the cloth to his head, and I don't correct him. When he calls me Pip, I melt on the inside.

The mineral water I brought with me will do him good. I pour him a glass and have him take a sip.

"I need you to keep taking small sips while I get help.

Don't get up for any reason other than to puke." I try to smile to lighten the mood.

His eyes widen. "Something is terribly wrong, isn't it?"

"I know you don't remember who I am, but you need to trust me. I'll get you help." I squeeze his hand.

I leave the door open to his room and walk downstairs to find Jobi's number.

He picks up on the second ring. "Jobi, I need a favor."

"Yes, madam. Anything."

"You need to get Katoo to come to the house. Dacari is sick, and I don't know what's wrong." By some miracle, I remember his new name. My hand holding the phone shakes while I try to still it with my other hand.

"Right away. I know where he is. Stay there, and I'll come back with him."

My words come out with a sob. "Please hurry."

I click off and notice the marks on my hand from gripping the phone. Tears stream down my face. I usually don't break down, but the cards are stacked against us.

At every turn, there is something else happening to him. I'm scared for both of us. He's sick and remembers nothing, and I'm new to the job. I have some leads, but I can't do it without him.

I swipe at my saltwater tears with the back of my hand and take a deep breath. A yellow wrapper peeks out from a drawer. I snatch open the drawer to find my stress relievers, peanut M&Ms. I brought them with me just in case, and right now, I'm having a just-in-case moment. Stuffing a handful in my mouth helps calm me down. The crunch of salty and sweet are the perfect combination to take my mind away from the turmoil and regroup.

Whatever is going on with Beck will not stop me from

finding out who tried to kill him. When I find them, they will wish they never crossed me. I'm fiercely loyal and protective. In other words, I can be one badass bitch.

I don't know how long I zoned out in the kitchen when a knock at the door startles me, and I rush to open it in hopes it's Katoo.

"Katoo, thank God you're here." He steps inside the door with Jobi behind him.

"Thank you, Jobi. We can take it from here." My protective side takes over.

He looks over at Katoo.

"He can stay. He works for me and can be trusted. I'll explain more later." His face is expressionless as he asks, "What are his symptoms? I'm sure he has caught a bug of some sort. We have lots of them in this part of the world. Since his body is not used to it, he will have a more serious reaction."

I let him drone on as I wave my hand to follow me upstairs and nod so he knows I'm listening. If this is a bug, I pray he has the cure.

The three of us stand at the foot of his bed and watch as he moans in pain. He's drenched in sweat, and there is vomit in the trashcan.

"I think there's more going on here than a bug. He woke up and doesn't remember who I am or where he is." My voice cracks.

He opens his eyes and says my name. "Pip, you're back. Every time I drink water, it comes back up. You brought friends. Who are they?"

I sit on the bed next to him and look up at Katoo. His face drops, and there's fear in his eyes.

"I've seen this before. It's not a bug. Dacari has been

poisoned. We need to act quickly. Jobi, come with me. I'll be back. Make sure he stays hydrated, and give him ice chips."

This day has gone from bad to worse. I prop him up on a pillow and feed him ice chips. There's no doubt in my mind that someone doesn't want Beck here and wants to erase any memories he may have of any part of his life.

SIXTEEN

Pippa

LYING next to him in bed, I fight to keep from falling apart. The ice chips seem to be the remedy to prevent him from throwing up. He sweats through his clothes, and I sit him up to help him change. The man is built like a tank. I would guess he has about four percent body fat. I check him out from head to toe as he stands in his underwear.

My hormones have horrible timing as my lady parts scream at the top of their lungs. For as big and strong as he is, he seems so fragile and helpless. He looks at me with bewilderment swimming in his eyes.

The painkillers he keeps down seem to help his migraine as he sleeps on and off for the next couple of hours. While he sleeps, I go to my bedroom and call Neil to find out what my next steps should be.

"We've got a problem" is never a good way to start a conversation. My hand shakes again.

"What's going on?" Neil says casually.

I tell him about Beck's condition in graphic detail and that Katoo is going to help. He's quiet on the other end, taking in the information.

"I'm going to need a blood sample. You can have Katoo send it out to me here in London." There's an immediacy in his voice that makes me think we're in deep shit.

"How do you want me to do that?" Irritation laces my voice since my only concern is Beck.

"I'll contact Katoo, and he'll bring the syringe and bottle. Pippa, do everything Katoo tells you to do, to the letter. This is serious. I can't give you the details now, but have your guard up and take good care of Beck. He needs you more than ever. We'll talk soon." He clicks off before I can ask more questions.

I throw the phone on the bed and growl with frustration. Years ago, I had a boyfriend who pumped steroids to grow muscle mass. He had me shoot him in the ass, where it's all muscle, but now I have to find a vein. Finding a vein in an arm will be trickier.

I open the door to Beck's bedroom to find him sitting up in bed in just a pair of shorts.

"Hi," he says with a smile.

"Hi, yourself. How are you feeling?" I sit at the foot of the bed, facing him.

"My head still hurts, and I'm exhausted. I'm glad you're here, even if I don't know who you are from my past." His eyes are sad and bloodshot. "Do you know who poisoned me and if my memory will come back?"

I move up the side of the bed and take his hand in mine. "I honestly don't know. Katoo, the man that was here before, he's going to help you."

"Tell me about you. How do I know you?" The curiosity in his eyes is genuine as he checks out my artwork.

"Well, you know my name."

"Pip."

"Pippa."

"I like Pip better. You have a lot of energy, and I like the freckles on your nose." He taps my nose with his finger. I haven't seen his playful side. That seems to have been buried deep under his need for structure and righteousness. This version of Beck makes me want to take advantage of our sleeping situation.

"Pip, it is. You're here to meet your new family, and we're undercover on a mission to find out what's going on here in Mubala."

"Mission?" His mouth hangs open.

"You're an ex-MI6 agent. You own a security company with two other men, Sean Knight and Peter Bryan. Do you remember them?" I'm crossing my fingers that something clicks in.

He shakes his head and looks down at his hands. "I don't remember anything. There are fragments at the outer edges of my mind that I need to put together."

Tears crest in his eyes but never fall as he wipes them away. My heart breaks. His vulnerability is raw, without his ego to cover it up.

"So much for being an MI-6 agent with tears. I've never felt fear like this. At least, I don't think I've felt fear like this before. It's like looking over a cliff, praying you don't fall." His eyes are vacant.

I have to do something to change the mood. "The good news is, I'm here as your girlfriend." I throw my hands in the air and smile. My snarky comments have taken a holiday for now.

He laughs. "Now, I would remember that for sure cuz, girl, you're hot."

A knock comes from the front door. I race down to open it as Katoo and Jobi push their way in, carrying paper bags. They hurry to the kitchen and unload the bags.

Katoo turns to me. "Jobi has been sworn to secrecy. No one can know about Dacari. You will let no one in to see him until he gets better. I have prepared several herbal remedies for you to give him throughout the day. We need to cleanse his liver and get rid of the poison." His words are rushed as I try to keep up with him.

He lays out rows of herbs like milk thistle, dandelion, and marshmallow root. The second bag contains fresh food that must be prepared a certain way each day. The timeline is exact, and Beck must drink a lot of water with lemon in it.

The last bag contains the syringe and collection bottle for a sample of Beck's blood. I turn to him with a plea in my eyes.

"Do you know how to do this? I have limited experience." I hold the items in my hand.

He shakes his head, which means I'm stuck doing the deed.

"Tell me, does Dacari drink or eat anything regularly that we could trace the poison back to?" Intensity washes Katoo's face.

I stop to think about my limited exposure to his routine. "He drinks green tea every day, sometimes more than once a day. As a matter of fact, he got a gift bag of green tea."

Reaching for the bag, I hand it to Katoo. He smells it and pulls it away.

"Panther's claw. My guess is that's not all that's in it. If anyone asks, you are to tell them Dacari has food poisoning." He is in command mode.

"Roger that."

"Who's Roger?"

"Never mind. It's just a saying. What can he eat? He needs to keep something down because the way he works out, he's burning through calories like crazy."

Katoo's calm until I look at his hands that are balled into fists. "He must have a high metabolism, which explains why the poison hit him so quickly."

He maps out the schedule for the herbs and the menu, which includes rice, garlic, parsley, and beetroot, among other ingredients.

"The fresh vegetables will come directly from my garden, and Jobi will deliver them daily. Dacari's meals will have basmati rice as a base, and everything else will work into the rice. As he feels better, we will introduce red meat and goat's milk to his diet." He speaks as if he's had experience with this type of poison.

He is firm about keeping a schedule with the herbs and how the food is prepared.

"Dacari is to have twenty-four-hour care, drinking water through the night. He needs to get rid of the poison as quickly as possible."

I write everything down, taking copious notes. Beck needs to get better soon, so we can figure out what's going on around here and who's trying to kill him. I need his expertise.

Katoo turns to leave, and I stop him. "Can you stay while I take his blood? I have to give it to you anyway to send out."

"Yes, it would be best if you got the sample before we give him the herbs."

Jobi elects to stay in the kitchen while Katoo and I trudge upstairs to take the blood sample. Beck sits up and directs his smile at me. Maybe this loss of memory thing isn't so bad. He seems to like me more without his previous agenda getting in the way. I'm growing fond of this side of him.

"Hi, Pip. Katoo. Hey, I remembered your names. That's a start. I still don't feel good, though." He wipes sweat from his forehead.

I'm digging the new nickname he has for me. It makes me

feel special, and it's endearing. I sit next to him, and his smile fades as he reads my grim face.

"I have to take a blood sample, which probably won't be pretty. I might have to jab you a couple of times. Katoo has to take it with him before we give you the herbs." His huge hand covers mine.

He squeezes my hand. "It's not a problem. I used to get injections all the time when I was younger."

My body stiffens, and Katoo narrows his eyes.

"How old do you think you were?" He watches Beck with interest.

"I would say I was very young. Maybe even still in this house. But how is it possible that I can't remember anything else? A vision popped into my head that I can't explain." His voice softens.

Katoo's clasped hands tighten, the knuckles strained. He puts his head down. When he looks up, he's somewhere else.

"You're right. When you were a little boy, you had to get shots. You never cried and were so brave." His Adam's apple moves as he swallows hard to keep his tears at bay.

He knows way more than he lets on, and I intend to find out what it is. Beck's family gave him up for a reason, and we need to get to the bottom of it to find his killer.

Katoo changes his tone. "Pippa, you need to get the blood sample so I can get it out today."

I nod and wrap a tourniquet around Beck's arm, feeling for a vein. He points to one on the inside of his elbow. "This is a good one. You should have no problem. I have faith in you. You can do this."

This is a one-eighty from the man I met several days ago. He's kind, considerate, and compliant. The combination is a total turn-on, and I'm falling into the deep end with him.

He makes a fist before I tell him to as I tap his arm to find the vein. The syringe goes right in, drawing blood. As he releases his fist, the blood draws fast, filling the bottle. I untie the band, pull out the syringe, and bandage his puncture wound.

He smiles at me with the most beautiful smile I've ever seen. Without his memory to rely on, he has to trust us to take care of him. He looks at me with no judgment, preconceived notions, or criticism.

The world would be a different place if people could live in the moment without judgment of any kind. At this moment, I know he sees me as I am, not who he thought I was when I came here. There's a pure honesty between us that is hard to come by between people.

We're lost in each other when Katoo clears his throat. I hand him the bottle of the poisoned blood in a paper bag, and I follow him downstairs. Before he reaches the door, I put my hand across it.

"Spill it."

"Excuse me?" He steps back, holding the bag in front of him, stone-faced.

"You know Beck's story, and you knew him when he was here. You know why they gave him away. Also, you said you've seen this kind of poisoning before. Where?" I'm curious to see what he does under pressure.

He sighs heavily. "Yes, I know his story, but it's not for me to tell now. He must get well and find his way. This is how it must be. He's strong and will get his memory back, maybe more than he bargained for, but he will have the complete story of his journey, just not right now."

He goes around me, reaches for the handle, and is out the door before I have time to process his cryptic answer. The web of Beck's life gets stickier and stickier, gluing us tightly together.

SEVENTEEN

Beck

MY SMILE on the outside covers the sheer terror I'm experiencing on the inside. I'm afraid to share half of what is going on in my mind because while I have few memories of my recent past, my long-term memory is roaring back to life. Pippa shared her limited knowledge about my background up until this point, but some things don't match up.

Each time I wake up with a dream from my past, there is a pain in my chest that radiates throughout my entire body. This sense of loss cuts me to my core and is like nothing I've ever experienced before.

The memories are part of my soul as I grieve for two people who gave me away and who I never knew. Something ticks in the back of my brain that their grief may have been more devastating than mine. I'm not sure they had a choice when they gave me away. I don't know why I think that, but some things are not adding up.

There's a soft knock on the door, and I know it's Pip. She is the soft glow I reach for amidst my barren desert of dark memories. She woke me several times during the night to make sure I drank water to flush out my body and took herbs.

"Hey, how's it going?" She peeks around the door.

Her red hair frames her petite face. Sharp green eyes look at me with concern. My body wants her as my groin grows in appreciation of her beauty, but this isn't the time.

Although, I can't think of a better distraction. I need to focus on ridding my body of the poison and capturing my memories piece by piece. Losing your short-term memory is a scary and frustrating experience.

"It's a little better." I give her one of my full-on smiles.

She sits next to me on the bed. I feel weak as a kitten as I try to harness some of the energy she brings with her.

"Stop doing that." She takes my hand in hers. Her warmth radiates into my body.

"What?" There's no outthinking this woman.

"Stop smiling when you're scared. I can't imagine what you must be going through. You know the basics about yourself, but it's like a broken blank slate. It would terrify me not to have my memories, even though my memories aren't all that great." She looks at me with sympathy in her eyes as if she understands a tortured past.

I'm reluctant to share what's been going on with me. "It's not all bad. I have been having memories about my childhood here in this house."

Her eyes grow big. "Do you want to tell me about them?"

"Yes. They weigh on me, and I need to talk about them. Sharing them with you may help with whatever is going on now." I rub the center of my chest. Relief blows out of me to tell someone about the distant past.

"I have a few vivid memories of when I was here as a child. My mum and I would play hide-and-seek around the house. Screams and laughter echoed in the rooms, or my giggles were muffled behind curtains. There are other disturbing occurrences in my dreams. I see myself in this house with my parents in rooms I don't recognize. In the dream, I'm looking up as if I'm small. If these are dreams of when I was here, why am I having them now? The dreams always end when I am in the dark of night going somewhere, but I don't know where, and I'm terrified."

I need to feel connected to her. "Come here." I motion for her to lie in my arms so I can hold onto her.

"You don't need to ask twice." Her body molds to mine as she throws her toned leg over my thigh. "I can imagine you must be terrified trying to piece everything together. I won't leave you."

I can breathe again. She grounds me, and the energy flows between us. We're on the same wavelength. My lips meet the top of her head on instinct, like I'm supposed to do it. Her milky white hand makes circles on my chest and around my nipples. I grab her hand.

"You need to stop that. I won't be able to control myself, and right now, we need to focus on what I remember and getting this poison out of my system." I kiss the tip of her finger.

Her giggle goes straight to my groin as it stands at attention. I try to push it away, but she has me by the balls. I can't seem to get enough of her, loving her muscular frame. She could take the raw, brutal side of me, the one that wants to own her. *Whoa. Where did that come from?*

We spend the next couple of hours discussing my dreams of being in the house when I was younger, but neither of us can figure out why I was given away to a family in the UK. She insists I call my parents to find out what they know, but I disagree. I'm not sure why, but I know I don't want to call them. Thank God they are part of my distant past, and I remember them.

She leaves our cocoon to make dinner for me and the

herbal concoction that has me in the bathroom most of the time. According to her, I need to get my memories back as soon as possible.

Everything hinges on putting together the memories of this house and my recent past. Part of me doesn't want to find out what haunts me. I want us to stay cocooned from the rest of the world. She tells me about my road to royalty, and I laugh as she remains serious. I don't feel like royalty. I feel like a pauper.

I drift off to sleep and wake up to loud voices coming from downstairs. Making it to the door requires me to sit up and walk across the room. I attempt to listen by holding my ear to the crack between the door and the frame, leaning against the wall.

Pip talks loudly to a woman whose voice I don't recognize. She refuses to let the woman come to see me.

"I am a doctor, a microbiologist. I might be able to help, and I want to see if he's getting everything he needs." The woman's voice is firm.

There is a brief silence. "Fine. You can see him, but not without me there. He's probably sleeping."

I close the door and get back in bed, taking my cue from what Pip said about being asleep. I pull the covers up to my shoulders and close my eyes.

The door opens with a creak, and they step inside.

"See, I told you he would be asleep," Pip says.

"Does he sleep a lot?" the other woman asks.

"Yes, and he's in the bathroom a lot, too. Now, it's time for you to go." Pip wants her gone, but I can't figure out why.

"And he has no other symptoms?" I can feel her breath, so she must be close to my face.

"No. I told you, it's food poisoning. You need to leave so he can get some rest and recover."

The woman sighs. "Okay, let me know if he shows any other symptoms."

The door to the bedroom shuts, followed by the click of the front door locking, and I hear Pip making her way up the stairs.

She opens the door. "You can stop pretending to be asleep."

"How did you know I wasn't asleep?" I sit up in bed.

"Because your breath was too fast for you to be asleep. Miss I Am a Doctor didn't catch on to that." She's holding my dinner.

"Who was that?"

She looks at me. "Your brother's girlfriend, Zahara. I have a wonky feeling about her, doctor or not."

"Wonky?" I laugh.

She shrugs and puts the tray down. The meal is the same as I had this morning, but with different herbs.

"How much longer until I can have real food?" I push the rice around with my fork.

"Until you get your memory back. Move over." She pats my thigh.

She scoots in beside me, but when I try to feed her, she puts her hand up. "No, thank you. That's like dog food. Actually, dog food tastes better than that." She looks away from me.

Is she looking away because she had to eat dog food at some point, or doesn't want it in her face?

"You know, you could season it a little." I make a face of disgust.

"Nope. Katoo was specific that I make it exactly the way it is. Otherwise, everything won't work together."

I choke down the last of the rice meal, and Pip puts the tray on the dresser. She sits and stares at me.

"I need to tell you why you need your memory back and why we are on this mission. Maybe it will bring back some memories for you." Tired, dark circles surround her worried eyes.

I pull back the covers and invite her in, which is not the wisest choice. She accepts without hesitation.

She tells me everything, and I'm blown away. She falls asleep in my arms. I comb her hair with my fingers, hoping my memory comes back soon so I can help her. She needs a partner to get through this, not a guy with no memory of what's most important. I fall asleep thinking about what she is to me in my life.

EIGHTEEN

Beck

OVER THE NEXT couple of days, memories trickle back into my brain, but they aren't the ones I need to figure out what's going on in Mubala. Some of my flashbacks go back to when I was a child in this house. I don't think they are memories I had before I was poisoned. I have no recollection of my life here in Africa since I didn't know I came from Mubala.

In other dreams, I recall some of my missions as an agent. They are graphic, disturbing, and some are sexy as hell. There are many places I've been in the world; most were beautiful, and some were terrifying. Through it all, I know what I am doing and have a sense of confidence and service. I served the Queen, the highest honor you can have as a soldier. Laying down my life to end evil would have been my privilege.

My recall of my security company is fuzzy. I haven't put the pieces together. The last bit of memory is of three men. One is in a wheelchair. Happiness surrounds us with a sense of duty to help others, but I'm not sure who they are yet.

My headaches have become less severe, and I've been

trying to move around the house. I wander downstairs to the kitchen and follow the smell of bacon and eggs.

Pip sways back and forth in front of the stove with her earbuds tucked in her ears. Her backside holds my attention, and my fingers curl to stop myself from grabbing her. When was the last time I had sex, anyway? Taylor. A vision comes as I look down on her face, and she looks distracted and disinterested, but nothing else comes to me. I want to erase it from my mind.

I tap Pip on the shoulder. "Good morning."

She jumps. "Hey, how are you doing today?" She sees something in my eyes. "What's wrong?"

"Do I have a girlfriend named Taylor?" I asked her, hoping she'll say no.

She hangs her head. "I think she's your ex-girlfriend, but I'm not sure." She turns back to the food cooking on the stove. "Maybe you should call one of your friends back home."

"No. I'll take your word for it." I want to hold her to me, try to reassure her there's no one else. There can't be anyone else because I want her.

My impulse grabs hold of me, and I can't stop myself. I turn Pip toward me and run my fingers down her creamy, smooth cheeks. Everything from fear to lust swims in her eyes. There's a second when I question what she's afraid of, but it passes with an overwhelming desire for her.

My lips capture hers as my tongue glides past her lips to take the first taste of her cherry-colored mouth. She grabs the back of my head and devours my lips, sucking and nipping as if she's waited forever for this kiss.

We spar with our tongues, feeling the intensity of every-thing that's led up to this moment. A searing heat moves through my body, seeking an outlet. There's no doubt that she is as wet as I am hard. My hands start to explore the curves that I crave. I don't want it to end when she breaks away and looks at me with guilt in her eyes.

"I'm sorry." It occurs to me that I might have taken things too far.

"Trust me, there's nothing to be sorry for." She gives me a weak smile.

She motions for me to sit down and plates up the food. I'm gleeful when I see she's added red meat to my usual fare. Her plate has bacon, eggs, and pancakes.

"Are you getting ready for a marathon? That's a lot of food," I laugh.

She shrugs. "Something like that." Her eyes focus on her food, not what I expected after our kiss.

I take my first forkful of food, and the flavors hit my mouth. I can't wait to eat the rest. Pip pushes the food around her plate and nibbles.

She laces her fingers together and rests her head on them. "There's something I need to tell you."

I put my fork down. "That doesn't sound good."

"Before you lost your memory, you weren't happy I was here. You did everything to get me to leave and go back to New York. I'm new to the field, and you wanted someone with experience like Sean, Mac, or Dean, and the list goes on of people that work for your security firm. Neil specifically asked for me to be your partner. I'm sorry if you feel like I was deceiving you."

I sit back in my chair and admire the compassionate woman before me. "Must be mind over matter because my body wants you like crazy." I lean forward and take her hands in mine. "I need you next to me. You ground me and calm me down when I'm about to snap. My lack of memory makes me crazy. You are an incredible woman, and you have been by my side through all of this. What else could I ask for in another human being?"

"You realize when you get your memory back, you'll be singing a different tune." She pulls her hands out of mine and attempts to eat the food on her plate.

I don't know what to say. In no world would I want to be without her. She has saved my life. I owe her so much that I can never repay. I need to find a way to get her to believe me.

She gives up eating and pushes her plate away. "Katoo is coming over today to talk to us about what's been going on. I have many questions for him, and maybe some of what he tells us will jog your memory."

The rift between us happens in an instant, and loneliness sets in. I miss her already. I don't want to be away from her and can't let it show. There's security in knowing she's on my side. She's proven herself to be trustworthy and reliable, which is hard to come by in this world. I need to close the gap.

"How about we work out together? You can show me some of your routine, and I can show you mine, from what I remember. Hopefully, my physical memory isn't fried."

This garners a smile from ear to ear. Her defined body gives me a clue to her routine. She gets her hard muscles from working out regularly. Even a guy without a memory could figure it out.

"That sounds fantastic. Right now, I could use some stress relief. I love going to the gym because it requires all my focus, pulling me away from the everyday crap. I'll meet you in the hall in a couple of minutes." She jumps up and hurries to the stairs.

I hope being in the gym will help me recall things I used to know and do. The smile that it brings to her face is enough for me. She needs to understand I will not change my mind about wanting her here.

Jobi drives us to a state-of-the-art gym in the center of the city. He questions if going is a good idea, but I have to get out of the house. There may be repercussions to my recovery, but I think working out will do me good.

We walk in, and heads turn as eyes fall to where our hands lock together. Pip jerks her hand away and puts her head down. She walks to the far corner of the gym, out of sight of prying eyes, and sits on the bench. I kneel in front of her.

"I don't belong here. Maybe you should work out by yourself. I can watch from here." Disappointment radiates off her.

"Ignore them. You're here with me, and that's enough. Let's focus on the workout." I hold out my hand.

The sadness in her eyes breaks me. "I've always been an outsider, but this is beyond my comfort zone. Maybe I can go for a jog and have Jobi follow me. I don't feel safe here."

"No. Stay here with me. I need you here in case something happens. I don't have my strength back yet. Focus on us and what we're doing." I stand up and look behind me at the faces wearing scowls.

An older man approaches me. "You are Dacari Touré Siwanda, soon to be our king. How can you be with someone outside your tribe?"

I look to Pip as she silently pleads with me to let it go, but I can't.

My voice is loud. "I am going to be your king and must set an example everyone can follow." I'm a head taller and tower over him. "Don't be so quick to paint everyone with the same brush. What you really want to ask is why I would want to be with a white woman? This woman saved my life and may become part of this tribe. She is why I'm standing here. As humans, we have no color on the inside. We bleed the same, breathe the same, and are born the same way. Funny how we don't think the same or see the same things. Color should mean nothing, but we have a long way to go. You would do well to apologize to her."

He gets down on one knee and puts his hand on his forehead. His arm is out straight as everyone in the gym follows him by posing in the same way. I am dumbfounded, humbled, and relieved, but I've also shocked the hell out of myself. I don't know where my words came from.

He apologizes and wanders off. The others who kneel, stand up and walk away without making eye contact with me or Pip.

She smiles. "I think you are going to make a great king. After that speech, I almost kneeled."

I put my hands on my hips. "Something tells me I didn't want to be king. Am I right?"

She shrugs, puts her gloves on, and picks up a set of weights. "I'll never tell."

"Well, if I can make changes, then it feels good to be king." I hope I haven't jinxed myself.

NINETEEN

Pippa
___

WE GO THROUGH THE CIRCUIT, and I can't wait to return to the house. My emotions are everywhere as I try to get a hold of them. When he finally remembers everything, he won't want me here. I need to create space between us so when he rejects me, it won't be so painful.

My fondness for him has grown stronger, especially after the kiss that made my knees buckle. We bonded, but it won't be enough. There's no future for us. He may decide to stay here and remain the king of Mubala.

The people have made it clear I'm not a welcome addition. Saving his life isn't enough to gain their approval. I'm used to being the outcast, the observer. This isn't about being an outcast. This is about exile. His people will never accept me.

While he naps, I grab a bag of peanut M&M's, my go-to feel-good remedy. They're probably not the best choice, but damn they're good, and I head to the third-floor loft with a triangular window that overlooks the city.

I curl up in the nook and hug my knees to my chest. The late afternoon darkens with stormy clouds, which reflects my mood. Maybe it's time to bail, but I don't think Neil will let me out of this assignment. I've made more right moves than wrong ones, and Beck needs me more than ever.

We need to get into that warehouse that belongs to Wafiq and find out what's going on. I've started digging into his mainframe. The firewall and encryption look familiar but only lead to more questions.

My thoughts blend into dreams until I hear the knock at the door, and Beck peeks his head into the room. The afternoon has succumbed to the night, and he reaches to flip on the light.

"There you are. I've been looking everywhere for you." He closes the door and leans against it with his hands in his pockets.

I try to smile but fail. "Yeah, just needed some space to think things through."

He nods, and there's something different in his eyes. "Pippa—"

In an instant, I realize his memory is back, and he's going to lower the axe. "You have your memory back. That was quick."

"Yes, and unexpected," he says, as his shoulders relax. "I think we need to talk."

"I'm listening." I know what's coming, the different tune he's about to sing.

"We need to focus on this mission and find out what's going on with my brother. I have to let Wafiq know I am on board with becoming king and see if it ruffles some feathers." He moves from one foot to the other. "We need to put whatever this is on pause. Agents should never get involved during an assignment. You have a lot to learn, and I need to stay on my toes without distraction." His stern face says it all.

I unfold myself from the bench by the window and walk

toward him, invading his personal space. This large man moves back into the doorway and hits the door.

"That's what this is about. Your need to stay in control because I don't have enough experience to be an asset to you. What about what you said yesterday? You said you need me by your side. Were you lying?" I press him. I know what's between us and what could be, but something else is going on with him.

Conflict swims in his eyes. "We need to stay focused. Unfortunately, I need you as my partner. At least I'm not trying to send you back to New York City."

I put my hand on his bare chest, where his shirt is open, and he gasps. The heat searing through my fingertips is undeniable. We have mad chemistry. My lips are inches from his.

"The heat in our kiss can't be denied as hard as you try."

His eyelids lower as he whispers, "Pip."

We freeze as we hear a loud pounding, coming from downstairs as if someone has been knocking for a while. Our eyes lock.

"We'll pick this up later, Big Boy." I smile. As soon as my hand leaves his skin, it cools, missing his warmth.

We trudge downstairs in silence.

I open the door. "You have impeccable timing. Please come in."

Katoo looks between us, knowing he has interrupted something. He steps inside, locks the door, and walks to the dining room. I almost run into the back of him as he stops at the end of the dining room table. Beck is behind me and moves around us to see what's going on.

Tears well in Katoo's eyes. "We had many joyful dinners here—full of laughter. Some meetings were serious, but most were filled with love and friendship. I will always miss your parents for the rest of my time on this earth."

He puts his briefcase on the table and pulls out a device. "This is a scrambler. I don't know if they bugged the house, but we can't take any chances. We need to talk."

"I swept for bugs, and there are none, but we can't be too careful." Beck gives me a sideways glance.

"Dacari has his memory back," I pipe in.

"Yes, I know." Katoo continues to set up the scrambler.

"How?"

"Based on his height and weight, I determined he would be free of the poison by today."

Beck and I stare at each other, and I put my hands up. Who knew?

Katoo sits at the head of the table and closes his eyes. "I can feel him, your father. He sat in this chair for every dinner, a king among kings." His eyes pop open. "You need to know he was an honorable man and had the best of intentions for this city, but fate had a different plan for him."

Beck nods. "You need to start at the beginning. Why did they give me up for adoption?"

"You need to understand the history of the Sai tribe. Your great-great grandfather left the Maasai tribe, along with a group of people who didn't agree with everything the Maasai demanded of their people. They moved west and settled in Zambia. At first, they lived off the land, but then your family discovered an emerald mine. This changed everything for the Sai people. They made him king and your great-great grandmother queen. The tribe could stay in one place and make a living from the mine, but it wasn't easy. There were a lot of hardships and deaths."

He stops to take a moment to gather his thoughts. "The royal line has been in your family since then. The title is passed down to the eldest son."

"Much like the British monarchy," Beck adds.

"Yes. If something happens to the eldest son, it goes to the next in the family line. Right around the time you were born, your father discovered several diamonds in the area to the north by the lake. They started mining for diamonds, but another tribe claimed they owned them, and a war ensued. By this time, the city was large enough to withstand the battle, but the other tribe threatened to kill you, their firstborn, as revenge."

"That explains the walls. But they had Wafiq, so the crown would go to him," Beck says.

"In this world, a firstborn holds more weight than a second born, or a female. It's the way things are. They gave you away to save your life." He grabs Beck's hand. "They loved you so much, but the grief of never seeing you again was a slow death for them. I've been keeping track of you almost your entire life."

A shroud of quiet blankets the room as we take a moment to understand everything Katoo has explained about Beck's past.

Beck's face is impassive. "All my memories of being here were of love and joy, which is why none of it made sense until now. Why did I get shots as a child?"

"They wanted you as far away as from here as possible, and that meant out of the country. Your shots were what you needed to travel. When I finally found you, I never told them. I didn't want to cause them any more pain." Telling the story seems to age Katoo. The creases in his face are pronounced, especially the worry lines on his forehead. He's lived through more than his fair share of tragedy.

"Why did you wait so long to contact me?"

"I wanted to see what Wafiq would do with his power. He's going in the wrong direction from your father's vision. This also gives the coronation a sense of urgency he can't stop." He stares at Beck with intensity. "I don't think your father's death was an accident. He showed the same symptoms of memory loss you did before he left on his last flight. I don't think anyone has visited the crash site since it's considered sacred ground. I think—"

"There are answers at the crash site that we need. Pippa and I can go first thing tomorrow morning." Energy comes back to Beck's face. He has a new mission, which is exactly what the doctor ordered.

"There's something else you should know. Since your father's death, Wafiq has taken over the city, but not for the better. It's one of the reasons we haven't heard anything about the shooters who tried to kill you. I can't prove it, but I think he's in with the wrong people. This is why I needed you to be the rightful heir."

I give credence to his theory. "Oh, trust me. He's in with some bad people. I've been trying to hack into his security system and mainframe. Parts of the encryption I've seen before, and I can't get into it. I need to find a back door."

Beck frowns. "Where have you seen it before?"

"Afghanistan working for Isaad. This has Deep 8 written all over it, but I can't be sure."

Beck's eyes widen.

TWENTY

Beck

"WHY DIDN'T you tell me? This changes everything." Neil had to have a clue as to what we were walking into with this situation.

Pippa spins a loose dried petal on the table. "I couldn't tell you because you had no memory, and I didn't want to add to what was going on with you."

Katoo clears his throat. "What is a Deep 8?"

Pippa and I look at each other. "For now, we'll keep that on a need-to-know basis. You can claim plausible deniability. They came onto our radar during a mission in Afghanistan. Keep sharp eyes and ears around Wafiq."

"I've never been close to Wafiq. He keeps me at a distance like he's hiding secrets. You must get into his warehouse. I think there are answers in there." Katoo doesn't seem annoyed that we won't tell him what's going on with Deep 8. I take it as a sign of trust.

"That's what we intend to do." I pinch the bridge of my nose with my fingers and take a deep breath.

"Please stay in touch. Depending on your questions, I may have answers," Katoo says cryptically and stands up to leave.

"Before you go, I need to thank you for everything you did and have done for me. I couldn't have made it without you. I will do everything in my power to find out what's going on here in Mubala." I reach out my hand to him, and he takes it, nodding slightly.

My words are loaded with so much meaning. His face tells me he's read between the lines.

Pippa walks him to the door. She comes back into the dining room and sits across from me.

"You got bombarded with a lot of information," she mumbles.

"So, do you think Wafiq is part of Deep 8?" I don't want to dive into my childhood, and I look away from her.

"I don't know, and I won't know until I can hack his computer or Peter breaks the encrypted hard drive we found in Afghanistan."

"If his tech is encrypted, doesn't it make sense that he's part of Deep 8?" My anger boils to the surface.

"Deep 8 may know we're here and is hiding everything under his nose. He may not even know his tech is encrypted. Technology today is developing at a faster rate than what humans can keep up with."

"I want to get into that warehouse." I sit back in the chair as exhaustion takes over. This time, it's from emotions rather than physical. "I have to get to the crash site and check out Tadashi's plane."

"Don't you mean 'we'?"

I don't respond.

"That's the first time I've heard you use your father's name." She sounds so small, but powerful things come in small packages. I'm thankful she's here with me, but I don't tell her. My mindset needs to alter into a *we* instead of *I* mode.

"I won't call him my father. Albert McKenzie is my father, the one who raised me. He deserves the credit. I understand they had to give me up to save my life. It must have devastated them, but it doesn't change the fact they never really knew me."

Bitterness comes through. My head understands why they gave me away, but my heart is playing catch-up. I never thought much about my birth parents because I didn't want to know the truth about the circumstances surrounding my adoption. The pain might be too much.

They took something from me I'll never get back, getting to know my brother and sister. My heart is heavy for everything they lost and the things I didn't even know I had to lose. Their story is not what I expected. While some things have become clearer, other things are muddier than ever.

"I want to know what caused that plane to crash. The crash site may have some answers I'm looking for. Everything seems to be a series of events that are strung together. We need to undo the knots."

Pippa reaches for my hands and then pulls back. I've done that to her, made her second-guess herself by pushing her away.

She holds my gaze. "We need to focus on what's going on here first. You and I have to come up with a plan to hit the warehouse and find out what Wafiq is up to. Then we can go to the crash site. I don't think the crash site will be pretty," Pippa says.

Her green eyes pierce me, looking into my soul as I try to resist showing my hand. My feelings for her are at war. I know what we had when I was regaining my memory, but I can't let it cloud the things I need to get done.

At every turn, she's been my savior and guide. She's stayed strong, and I wouldn't be here without her. She is selfless, and I'm selfish.

"How far in do you think Wafiq is with Deep 8?" I'm afraid of the answer.

"I don't know. Peter has been working on breaking the encryption so I can get in and see what's going on." Peter Bryan is the tech wizard at MBK Global Security. "I'm going to be brutally honest with you."

"I would expect nothing less. Fire away." As my mind has come out of the fog, I'm committed to discovering the truth about my birth parents, Wafiq, and Deep 8. Honesty is what I need to keep the emotions out of the picture.

"I know you want to save him, but he may be in deeper than we think. You may not be able to convince him otherwise." There's a crease in her brow.

"Somehow, I knew you were going to say that. What about Sabeen?"

"I hacked her laptop. She's clean and is probably unaware of her brother's involvement with any deep state group." This makes her smile. "We might need her help, and I don't get the sense she's very close with Wafiq."

Pippa pushes back from the table. "Let's get something to eat. I think you can have some real food tonight." She gives me a weak smile.

As I walk around the table, she reaches up to give me a tight hug. I want to stay this way forever. This embrace brings me back to when we lay in bed, her warm body snuggled up against mine. The thought gets the attention of my groin, and I pull back. Her face says it all: disappointment. But this isn't the time.

She whispers, "By the way, we're in this together."

Once we get the answers, it may come tumbling down. I know I'm going to have to call the team for support. Pippa and I can't do this alone.

Pippa moves around the kitchen, cooking a delicious dinner of filet mignon, baked potatoes, and greens. She makes my steak rare, just the way I like it. I notice a serving of beets on my plate.

"I think I've had enough beets to last me a lifetime." I laugh, but she doesn't respond.

"Katoo wants you to continue with the herbs and the beets. He wants to make sure we...you clean everything out of your system, and the poison is completely gone," she says without looking at me and continues to eat.

I choke down the beets. "He's an amazing man, and he's been through a lot. I'm glad he's on our side. Wafiq could have used him as a weapon against us."

She nods as I savor every bite on my plate. Her plate is spotless, like she needs energy to keep up with me now that I have most of my strength back. I pick up the dishes, place them in the sink, and wash them.

She turns off the running water. "Ah, no. We have more important things to do."

"It'll only take a minute." I turn the water back on.

We're painfully quiet except for the running water and an occasional clink of the dishes as I put them in the drying rack. I've created the distance between us, and I don't know how to change it, even if I wanted to.

I turn around and find her sitting at the island, staring at me with her phone in front of her. Her eyes are a dark, stormy green.

"We need to come up with a plan for tomorrow. I think our best plan of attack will be at night," she says without emotion. The woman who took care of me is gone, and the agent is back, trying to find answers.

"I agree. We'll get Jobi to drive us around town a bit and then drop us off at the warehouse. It can't be that hard to get into. I doubt Wafiq expects anyone will even pay attention to it." I lean against the sink with my arms across my chest.

"I have a plan that may be far more effective for an alibi. We'll have Jobi pick us up and plan to have dinner with Wafiq and Zahara. They are going to want to see you now that you're better. Jobi can drop us off back here so we can get into night gear and then pick us up and drop us off at the warehouse." Her shoulders are square, waiting for my counterplan.

"Sounds good to me." I smile, trying to break the ice between us.

She stands up. "Great. I'll see you tomorrow." Her arctic breeze hits me full-on.

She's anything but great, and she's not even trying to hide it. Her door closes with a thud upstairs, and I'm left standing in the kitchen, confused about where I went wrong with her.

Ever since I was poisoned, I haven't been on my game. My head and body struggle to take control when it comes to this woman. She's fire and ice, but at the root of it, she took care of me at my lowest point, and I can't ignore that. Her agent skills are impressive, but I don't know if she has the instincts in a tough situation. I'll see what tomorrow night brings.

TWENTY-ONE

Pippa

CRUSHED, but not defeated. If he thinks I'm giving up that easily, he's got another thing coming he didn't expect. I have what it takes to be a valuable agent. Neil wouldn't send me out here if he didn't think I could do the job. He sent me to keep Beck's head on straight.

My entire life has been a series of events to prove myself to other people. The anonymity on the dark web is a blessing. People operating on the web only know me as Red Bond. Other hackers come to me for advice, and I have nothing to prove to them. The dark web community is my safe place, a place for me to escape and hide.

I have nowhere to hide in the field. Even though this is unfamiliar territory, they have trained me for this. I have honed the skills necessary to get the job done. The only thing that gets Beck's attention is evidence. If he wants proof, he's going to get it.

My gut tells me Wafiq is up to his neck with Deep 8, and he might have had something to do with his father's plane crash.

There is a list of calls I need to make before I strike out to the crash site.

"Hi, Jobi. I need another favor."

"Hello, madam. Anything you want, I can get for you." Jobi's response is cheery. He won't be so cheery in a minute.

"I need to get to the crash site of Tadashi and Aafia Siwanda." Dead silence greets me on the other end of the call.

"It's not possible. It's sacred ground. You cannot go. You will be cursed." His voice is frantic and tight.

"Calm down and listen to me. I need to get there to find out what happened. Someone may have tampered with his plane. Beck, I mean, Dacari was shot at and poisoned. Someone or some group is trying to stop him from becoming king. There may be clues at the site to help find out what happened. You are the only one who can help me. Please."

There's a deep sigh on the other end. "Madam, we must go to the *Laibon*, and he must bless us with protection before we go."

Bless me, don't bless me. Let's get this show on the road. "What's a *Laibon*?"

"A shaman of sorts. He's part of the elder council and a medicine man. Engai is a god that can be a good omen or a bad omen. We need him on our side. I won't go until we see him."

"Can you pick me up in thirty minutes?" I ask.

"Yes, madam." He's not happy to be going to the jungle to see dead people.

"Jobi, no one can know about this. Please don't tell Katoo."

"It is done. I'll see you soon, but it's an eight-hour ride to the site."

"Perfect. That will be all the time I need. What kind of plane was Tadashi flying?"

"A Cessna Caravan. I flew with him many times. He was an excellent pilot. I'm very sad he's no longer here." Jobi's voice drops.

"I need to get there to find answers. Thank you." I click off to make my second call.

"Hello, Red, and why are you calling me at this ungodly hour?" Peter answers my call, annoyed.

"What? Were you sleeping or rolling around with one of your pickups from the local bar?" I laugh.

His Southern twang comes through. "That was a low blow, even for you. What can I do for you, sugar?"

"Have you made any headway in cracking the encryption of the Deep 8 data? I've run into it here in Zambia and was hoping for a break so I can do some hacking." I smile even though he can't see me and turn on my sexy, deep voice for what I say next. "You know how much I love it when you break encryption."

"Aw, sweetheart, are you trying to get in my pants with sweet talk about hacking? You know how it gets me hot when you talk dirty about coding, hacking, and anything encrypted." His voice is low and sexy, but he's not my type.

I laugh out loud. He's such a schmoozer and smooth with the ladies. "Just give me the 411, smooth talker."

"Unfortunately, I have not decoded the encryption. It's some high-level shit, that's for sure. I have a couple of guys working on it, so it may be soon, but you'll be the first to know. How are things over there?"

I debate about telling him everything that's going on and not going on.

"Okay, I guess. Beck is better, and the poison seems to have left his system, but he's hardheaded."

"Yeah, he's a tad wound up. If anyone can loosen him up, it's you." There's no joke in his words.

"It doesn't look like that's going to happen. I gotta go. Talk soon."

If I had stayed on the phone much longer, I would have burst into tears. I'm not sure if the tears are from frustration or hurt. Beck is a hard nut to crack, but my determination may win out. Once I prove someone tampered with the plane, he will have to listen to me.

A couple of things get thrown in my backpack as I download the documents I need to study the parts and mechanics of the Cessna Caravan. Eight hours will give me plenty of time to memorize everything I need to assess the crash site and the plane.

I wear black from head to toe as I slip out the door and into the street. Jobi pulls up in a Range Rover and waits long enough for me to throw my bag in the trunk and slide into the front seat.

We drive to the outskirts of town, where the buildings are not so close together, and the streetlights are few and far between. Jobi puts the car in park and sits there.

"What are we waiting for?" My impatience comes through.

"We must ground and center ourselves before we go in. Take off your shoes." He turns to look at me, and all I can see are the whites of his eyes.

I step out of the car and take off my shoes as Jobi grabs my hand, leading me to a grassy area.

He lets go of my hand, stands with his eyes closed, and hands out to the side. "Feel the energy of the earth. Center and calm your core. Then we will be ready to enter."

Going barefoot in the grass reminds me of when I was a child. The coolness tickles my toes as I try to focus on being calm and centering my energy.

Behind my eyelids are memories filled with sprinklers,

slip-and-slides, and squirt guns. My childhood wasn't all bad. The good parts are just hard to find. A smile forms on my lips at the playback, and I open my eyes to see Jobi staring at me.

"Ready?"

I nod, and we walk into a spotless high-end building with granite and gold accents. The elevator takes us to the top floor and opens to a magnificent modern penthouse I didn't even know existed in Mubala.

A man dressed in a cream-colored robe stands at the window with a spectacular view of the city. The horizon is lost in the dark as the few city lights blend with the stars in the sky.

Without turning around, he says, "Please sit down. I'm only doing this because I think you can find answers to the death of our king. His crash has bothered me since it happened."

He turns around and puts his hands on Jobi's head, neck, and shoulders, speaking to him in a language I don't understand. He ends it by hitting him hard on the top of his shoulders. He turns to me. His hands are like silk as they skim my head, face, neck, and shoulders. I look up at him, and he smiles. His hands cradle my face.

"You are a special gift. Very strong. You can withstand our new king. He is a powerful force. Much more powerful than he knows, but everything is not black-and-white. Go to him with an open heart."

Two tears trail down my cheeks, one for me and one for Beck. We can heal each other. He needs to believe in what we can give and take from one another.

He finishes giving me his blessing and protection. Jobi and I get in the car with me riding shotgun, my favorite seat.

"No," Jobi says abruptly.

"What do you mean, no?"

"You must get in the back seat. You will require sleep on this trip. I need to make sure you're able to use your gifts." There's no argument.

I get out and move to the back seat. Jobi stares at me through the rearview mirror. "He never smiles, and he said you were a gift. I must take excellent care of you, even if I have to sacrifice myself."

I reach out and put my hand on his shoulder. "No one will need to sacrifice themselves, but thank you."

The clear night makes the stars sparkle brightly. My impulsivity gets me into trouble, but my determination carries me through.

Beck and I need to be on the same page. Together, we can find the answers we need and prevent someone from killing him. I hope this journey won't get anyone else killed. We've lost too much already.

TWENTY-TWO

Beck

RESTLESSNESS ATTACHES TO ME, preventing me from sleeping as I wrestle with the various threads that string my life together. My dreams of being a child in this house feel real. The one constant is love. My parents loved me very much, so giving me away must have killed a part of them. I can't imagine giving up a child to keep them safe, but some things make no sense and never will.

My questions are why they didn't get me sooner, if not as a child, then contact me as a young adult. I'm a grown man, and finding out now isn't helpful; it's confusing. Did Katoo bring me here just to become king, or is there more to this? These are questions I have for Katoo. If he has the answers, I have a feeling he will not give them to me freely.

The house is quiet, and the energy has changed as if something is missing. I call out to Pippa, but she doesn't respond. The door to her bedroom is closed. I knock as I enter. Her room is neat, but her backpack, gear, and laptop are missing. My heart rate elevates. What has she done, and where has she gone? I've got to find her before she gets herself into trouble.

My feet pound down the stairs, and I'm out the door, headed toward Katoo's house. My first call is to Jobi, but it keeps going to voicemail after the first ring. I dial Katoo's number, and he picks up right away.

"Good morning, Dacari." His voice is even as he answers.

"Good morning. I can't get a hold of Jobi, and Pippa is missing with her gear. Do you know anything about where they might be?" I've broken into a run.

"We'll talk when you get here." He hangs up.

I shouldn't care so much about a woman I didn't want here, but her warm smile and love of life hold me to her. She's beautiful, smart, and a touch impulsive, but she never backs down from a challenge. Her determination is remarkable. My need to find her and keep her safe overrides everything else.

Katoo opens his front door before I make it to the top stair. I'm out of breath. It's been a while since I've jogged anywhere. Staying in shape has always been one of my top priorities, but with the poisoning, my priorities have changed. There is a wild redhead who has thrown me off balance, making me examine the missing pieces of my life.

"Welcome." Katoo waves me inside and locks the door behind me. "Where do you think Pippa went that would require Jobi to go with her?"

He moves to the living room on silent steps, sits down, and sips his tea. I'm about to crawl out of my skin from anticipation. It dawns on me where she has gone, and she needs Jobi to get there.

"No." I shake my head.

"Yes. They've gone to the crash site." He places his teacup on the table. "She's gone to great lengths to prove herself to you, and she saved your life. It would be in your best interest to acknowledge her abilities. You need her more than she needs you."

His honesty hits me hard. "I know, but I'm used to working alone. My life has been about being alone. Ever since my parents shipped me off to boarding school, I've had to fend for myself. It wasn't enough that a white family adopted me and then got rid of me. I've been a castaway my entire life. You learn to survive on your own pretty quickly."

He nods. "I think you need to dive deeper. You should feel fortunate that anyone adopted you. Do you think they had their reasons for sending you to boarding school? Have you ever asked them why they sent you away?" His hands are folded in his lap, and he cocks his head to the side, waiting for my response as he plays therapist.

My cell phone buzzes in my pocket, and I ignore it. I know who it is, and I'm not ready to talk to them. I need to find the answers here first.

"That's not what I meant. The color of my skin will never change, and it comes with certain restrictions. Maybe if a black family adopted me, I would have felt more accepted. I haven't talked to them out of respect. I don't want it to look like I'm ungrateful for everything they've done for me. That boarding school is the reason I got into Oxford."

"Maybe you are the reason you got into Oxford. Don't doubt your ability or strengths. As king, you will need to look confident all the time, regardless of whether you feel confident."

"Speaking of time, we're running out of it. We only have a week until the coronation, and we still need answers to many questions before someone tries to kill me again." My head aches, but not from the poison. The tension starts at my shoulders and snakes its way into the back of my skull.

The doorbell rings, and Katoo goes to answer it. A

muffled male and female voice come from the foyer. Sabeen peeks her head around the corner with her arm in a sling.

"Oh, Dacari, how are you feeling?" She rushes to me for a hug.

"Much better. I need to watch what I eat." I hug her, careful to avoid her shoulder, and continue the ruse of food poisoning. "How does your shoulder feel?"

"It's okay. The sling is inconvenient but necessary for me to heal properly. Where's Pippa?" She looks around the room as if Pippa is hiding from her.

Wafiq enters the room with Katoo behind him. "Brother, how are you feeling?"

Know an opportunity when it's presented to you. "Good. Sabeen was asking about Pippa. I was about to tell her she went to the crash site." I let my new information hang there to be digested.

Wafiq and Sabeen's eyes grow large, and their bodies stiffen. The air feels like it's closing in on us, suffocating our words. They are the words no one wants to say.

"Why would she go to sacred ground? She doesn't belong there." Wafiq raises his voice in anger.

Sabeen holds her hand over her mouth and utters the word. "Why?"

I focus my eyes on Wafiq. "Because we think someone tampered with the plane before they took off. We need proof, and that's the only place to get it."

Wafiq's Adam's apple moves down and back up again. He fixes his eyes on me, but his face is emotionless. Sabeen's eyes well up.

"That's impossible. No one was allowed near his plane, and he always went through an extensive pre-flight check. Accidents happen, and we need to accept that. There's no proof to be found." He becomes defensive. He knows something, confirming Pippa's instincts are correct.

"Well, accept it or not, I've got to go out there to find her and make sure she isn't in trouble. We should make this a brotherly trip. You know your way around the countryside. What do you say?" I put my hands on my hips and smile at him.

Katoo smiles behind Wafiq as everyone's eyes shift to him for an answer.

"I don't have time for this. There's an entire city I need to run. Can't someone else take you? What about Katoo?" He's flustered.

I step closer into his space. "If we find evidence someone sabotaged the plane, you could come back a hero."

His eyes scan my face, waiting for me to reveal some ulterior motive, but I have none that he can see. I'm appealing to his ego. He wants to be king so badly, he can taste it. This would allow me to find out more about him and his reaction if we find a problem with the plane.

"Okay. I see where you're coming from. Even if we find evidence, I'm not sure we'll be able to link it back to the person who did it, but it's worth a shot."

Katoo nods from over his shoulder.

"I can't believe someone would want to harm them. Everyone loved them. I think you two should leave right away. It's a long trip, and she's ahead of you," Sabeen says.

"I'll meet you back here in twenty minutes. Bring the Range Rover. I'm guessing we need it for the rough terrain."

Wafiq turns to Katoo. "Since you're a Laibon, we'll need a blessing before we go. The ground is sacred, and we don't want to upset Engai." His words are quiet but above a whisper. He leaves without looking back.

I turn to Katoo for answers to what Wafiq referred to

about the blessing. Sabeen takes my arm and leads me to the couch to explain their god and beliefs.

For as modern as this city is, it's steeped in old-world traditions brought by our ancestors. *Our?* The winds have changed, and I can feel the rhythm of the tribe. I need to keep moving forward with my goals in sight.

I turn to Katoo. "You called them, didn't you?"

He smiles. "Good luck out there."

I walk back to my birth parents' house, and Wafiq is on my suspect list, even if I don't want him to be.

TWENTY-THREE

Beck

WE ARE on our way out of the city and into the unknown. Wafiq is none too happy about going to the place of his parent's death. He grumbles about the sacred ground, and we must leave well enough alone.

We don't know what waits for us at the crash site. Katoo may be wrong. This might have been an accident, but given that Tadashi was such an expert pilot, it's unlikely. I'll be able to assess the wreckage.

I've had a fascination with anything that could fly from a young age. This may be sheer genetics at work. No one in my family was ever interested in airplanes and helicopters. I would take apart remote control and model airplanes and put them back together to see how they worked. My understanding of the mechanisms of aero engineering is extensive, but I didn't get that from anyone in my adoptive family.

I'm guessing Pippa has studied and memorized the schematics of the Cessna Caravan so she can do a full inspection. She's impressive in her ability to learn things quickly and with such clarity. At every turn, she amazes me. I misjudged her based on her inexperience, but she's making up for it in tenacity. I try to tamp down the wave of lust that comes over me for a woman with beauty and brains.

Wafiq grips the steering wheel tightly, with his eyes straight ahead. He hasn't spoken since we got in the SUV. His nervous energy started the minute I recommended he drive with me to the crash site. Even though Katoo's blessing, he remained stoic. I try to make small talk to ease the tension.

"So, tell me about Zahara." I throw him a softball.

"What's there to tell? She's my girlfriend and has been for the last two years. We're inseparable. She's also my partner." He bristles.

"Partner in what?"

"We're business partners. We make decisions about various things happening in the city and with SIG. She's a brilliant doctor." For the first time, I see light in his eyes as he talks about her.

"I understand she's a microbiologist. What exactly does she do?" I push him a little.

"She was the head of a medical nanotechnology department in Germany for a biotech company. Soon after we met, she left the company to stay here. She's fluent in many languages, including Chinese, so she helps me navigate business negotiations."

That's an interesting tidbit I'll keep tucked away. I don't follow up with any more questions and let the quiet seep in between us. From the moment I got to Mubala, he's been kind and welcoming, but there's tension between us, and I'm not sure where it's coming from. I can pinpoint it to after the shooting that injured Sabeen. Pippa suggested that Wafiq knows way more than he's letting on, and she may be right.

We switch seats, and I drive for the next several hours. The savanna is mostly flat, but we climb into the denser areas of the forest. The Range Rover uses everything in the suspension to navigate rough terrain.

His curiosity gets to him. "What about you? How interested are you in becoming king of our tribe? As the oldest, you automatically get the position." There's curiosity in his tone, with a strain in his voice.

Is that what this tension is about? The throne? "I have a life waiting for me back home in the States and my family in the UK. I will become king to appoint someone else to the position."

He stares out the side window as if contemplating something. "Who are you going to pick?" he says behind his hand.

"Well, it should be obvious. I would like to stay on for a while and then hand it over to you. You would be my only choice. Sabeen doesn't seem interested in everything that comes with being the head of the tribe." I keep my face neutral.

This information doesn't make him smile. "How long do you plan on staying?" He turns his head to look at me.

"I don't know yet. Maybe a couple of months. I want to stick around long enough to get to know you, Sabeen, and Katoo."

His jaw muscles flex at the mention of Katoo's name.

"What's the problem between you and Katoo? I thought he was close with our family?"

"Our family? You've been here five minutes. What do you know about our family?" His anger spikes and then dissipates. "Katoo is an old man and a pain in the ass. He thinks he has the answers to every problem. He's too old-school. We need to move forward with the company and plan for the future. He gets in the way."

The animosity between him and Katoo goes deeper than the old world versus the new world. As generous as he's been, he doesn't see me as part of the family, and that's the biggest problem. I am a part of the family whether or not he likes it. He doesn't realize he's leaving a trail of crumbs. Each one gets added to the mix, leading to more clues.

Up ahead, as we climb the side of the mountain, we see pieces of wreckage from the plane. The way the pieces are scattered looks as though Tadashi tried to avoid hitting the mountain straight on. The front perches precariously on a ledge. An unmistakable wave of red hair flies in the wind as Pippa stands next to it. She must have had Jobi get her a toolbox because some of the plane's engine has been taken apart. She's risking everything to get answers that may lead nowhere.

We find a semi-flat place to park and climb up the embankment where the plane balances on and in between several trees.

Pippa and Jobi have set up a tent next to their Range Rover to protect them from the sun. Jobi holds an umbrella over her so she doesn't burn.

Wafiq and I make it to where she's working to take the engine apart near the fuselage.

I lean over her. "Need any help in there?"

She lifts and bangs her head on the cowling covering the engine. "Well, it didn't take you long to figure out where I was." She stands up, and I offer my hand to pull her up to the ledge. She brushes herself off. "We looked inside the cockpit, but the bodies are gone." She focuses on Wafiq.

"It doesn't matter. They are no longer with us. It's just their bodies," Wafiq says. He's wearing sunglasses, and I can't read his face.

I turn to her. "You needed to come and get me so we could do this together. This plane is a balancing act about to go wrong."

She shrugs. Her actions suggest she's used to operating alone. As much as she claims to want to be part of a partnership, she's done everything from hacking to coming out here on her own. The warrior in me recognizes her. She understands what it means to be outside the circle. My protective side takes over. I don't want her to get hurt. I've been down this road before.

"What have you come up with so far?" I'm interested in her evaluation.

She's covered in sweat, dirt, oil, and grime but is unfazed by it. "I took part of the engine apart. If someone sabotaged the plane, they had to do it so it couldn't be detected during the pre-flight check. They had to have done something within the engine itself."

"You've done your homework. Let me take a look. Little known fact: I'm a pilot." I flash her a smile.

I purposely left that fact out of my conversation with Wafiq as his lips form a thin line.

"Oh, really? Well, you could have mentioned that before, like yesterday." Pippa puts her hands on her hips.

I point to a yellow wrapper hanging out of her pocket. "What's that?"

She sighs. "A peanut M&M wrapper. I eat them when I get stressed." She stuffs it deeper into her pocket.

"You bought them on your way out of the city?" I question with a smirk.

"No." She stares at me for a beat. "I brought some with me from home. I anticipated being stressed out." Her eyes avoid my gaze.

I laugh long and hard. If she only knew my weakness for Reese's Pieces, but I don't want to give her any ammo.

Part of the plane is on the ledge, and there's enough room for two of us to examine the engine. Wafiq and Jobi stay standing on the ledge. We take it apart piece by piece and examine each part, but we can't find anything wrong until we come across the air mixing valve. It's stuck and not able to move like it should. I hold the valve in my palm as if I hold their lives in my hand. We're both quiet.

"What's wrong?" she breathes.

"I need to check something in the cockpit." My heart is in my stomach.

We move to the window and look through it. The mixture control knob has been broken off. Tadashi probably struggled to move it. Pippa is to my left, looking in, and sees what I see. The plane shifts, a warning it's about to move because we've redistributed the weight.

Before it slides down the embankment, I pull Pippa into my arms and roll us out of its way. The plane crashes down the mountain with ruffled sounds as it hits the foliage.

I rarely subscribe to the notion that we get messages from souls on the other side, but I can't help but feel Tadashi wanted us to find this evidence. May he rest in peace.

Pippa and I get up as Jobi and Wafiq stare at us in disbelief.

"You could have gone down the mountain with the plane," Jobi says with his eyes as big as saucers.

Pippa looks up at me with a smile on her face. "Thank you. You saved my life. I guess we're even."

"You're welcome, but we have a bigger problem. Someone sabotaged the plane before they took off and wanted them dead."

Wafiq asks, "How do you know?"

"They tampered with the air mixing valve, and he couldn't get the mixture control knob to work. He broke it off as if he struggled with it."

Wafiq shrugs.

"At higher altitudes, the air pressure declines, so the amount of fuel must also be reduced to give the correct air-fuel mixture. Without the proper mixture, you run out of fuel. They must have been in sheer panic before they hit. We'll take the valve back as evidence."

I watch Wafiq as he takes off his glasses and wipes his eyes.

"Do you know anyone who would want your parents dead?" I make a point of using the word "your."

Something passes in his eyes, an acknowledgment. He looks down and rubs his glasses with his shirt to clean them. "No. Everyone in the city and within the company loved them. I can't imagine anyone would want to kill them."

I step closer to him. "You better think long and hard. Not only was the plane tampered with, but we have two missing bodies. You were the closest one to them."

TWENTY-FOUR

Pippa

"I'LL SEE what I can find out." Wafiq's words are ice-cold. "Jobi and I will ride back together." He turns to leave with his hands curled by his sides.

Jobi glances toward us and nods, following him without a word. He knows where his bread is buttered, and going against his boss's wishes wouldn't be wise.

Beck takes me by the elbow. "Let's get back home. I think we have much to talk about."

I nod and lift myself into the vehicle. Dusk settles in, streaking the sky in beautiful shades of burnt orange. My reward for a job well done, even if Mr. Moody doesn't want to acknowledge it.

This Range Rover is the Mac Daddy of SUVs with high-end creature comforts. I've been up for twenty-four hours straight, and sleep is catching up with me. I snuggle into the fine-grain leather seats and turn on the hot stone massage. The only thing better than this would be if Beck were giving me a massage. The seat reclines almost horizontally, and the cabin air ionization kicks in.

I'm a car and bike geek, so this ride is right up my alley.

Beck reaches for a bottle of water from the refrigerator in the console and hands it to me. A bathroom is the only thing missing from this SUV for the price tag.

"You good over there?" Beck tucks me in with a blanket from the back seat.

"I'm going to sleep if you don't mind. It's been a long day. We'll talk later."

I don't want to hear his reasons why we can't be together. I've given up on the two of us. We're not going to happen, no matter how hard I try. He will never see me as his equal, something I have to accept. That's the last thing I remember before I drift off to sleep.

My eyes open as I look through the sunroof at a diamond-scattered sky. The stars glitter and shine brighter than I've ever seen them, unmoving as we speed down the dirt road. I lift my hand to touch them, knowing something that beautiful will always be out of my reach.

"They're amazing in this part of the world," Beck says without taking his eyes off the road.

I move the seat to a sitting position and curl my legs under me, wrapped in the blanket.

"I've never seen them so bright." I yawn.

"I owe you an apology." I can barely make out his eyes, but they're dark and full of regret.

I turn my body toward him and pull the blanket up to my chin. "For what?" I'm breathy with anticipation.

"For not believing in you and for wanting you to leave. You saved my life. As soon as I got my memory back, I pushed you away. You have proven that you are an excellent agent. It would be my honor to be your partner so we can find out what the hell is going on in this place." His hands shift on the wheel. "I need you to be careful and watch your back."

"You have fear in your eyes. What happened?"

"Emelia. Emelia happened." His fingers grip the steering wheel as he shifts his body in his seat. "She was my partner. Things went south on a mission where she was undercover. I tried to stop her from getting in a car with our mark, but I was too late. The car blew up in front of me. We were beginning to realize there was more to our relationship than just partners getting a quickie. He blows out a breath. Tears form in his eyes as he bites his lower lip. "I've never told anyone how it affected me, but I was devastated for a long time. I always requested a male partner, never a female partner. Most of the time, I end up working alone."

"That's what Neil meant when he said you needed me," I say softly.

His head swivels in my direction. "Neil always reads his agents very well."

I point out the obvious. "You can lose someone at any time. You happened to lose her on a mission, but you could have lost her just as easily while she crossed the road at the wrong time. Sometimes you need to live in the moment, hold on to those precious times, and make the most of them." I stare out the front window as we race down the road, which looks like a tunnel guided by our headlights.

"I should have gotten to her to save her. That's what a good partner does. They have each other's backs," he says through gritted teeth.

"Sometimes things happen for a reason. I know, it's cliche. But who knows what waits for you in your future?" *I'm hoping it's me.*

"You seem to have mastered a view of life that only focuses on the present." He glances in my direction, curious as to what I'm going to do with that piece of information.

"You can only ever put one foot in front of the other. When you get to the next place, you decide where and how to take the next step. Life is a lot like coding. One piece leads to the next as you build a program."

He sighs deeply. We stop talking to absorb everything that's come to light, but as usual, I get restless. He's shown a side of himself he's kept locked away. An iridescent thread of hope has found its way into my heart, and I don't want to cut it.

I stroke his forearm resting on the console. My white skin is a stark contrast to his beautiful ebony tone, which has deepened in the African sun. My fingers seem to float across his skin. I can't get enough of him. Warmth flares through my fingertips and rushes to the area between my legs.

My hormones won't take a holiday when it comes to this man and are demanding I pay attention to them. If I can get this horny with the touch of his skin, would full-on body contact make me incinerate?

Goosebumps rise under my fingertips. He clears his throat. "I might have failed to mention that I am wildly attracted to you. I've been battling with myself from the minute you arrived. You have a kick-ass body that's strong and lean and a brain the size of... Africa. If you keep stroking my arm like that with your nails, I'll have to pull this car over." His eyes devour me, and his voice drops lower, making me pant.

On the inside, I'm giving myself a high five. On the outside, I try to look cool and composed.

"No worries. That's what all the boys say." I laugh. Flipping his hand over, I stroke his palm using my fingernails. "I always knew you couldn't resist me. I've been crushin' on Chocolate Thunder since Afghanistan."

"Chocolate Thunder?" He laughs. "No one has ever called me Chocolate Thunder. I'm afraid to ask where that came from."

"Well, as you figured out, my favorite candy is chocolate with nuts." I smile. "Jess will have a fit when I tell her I shared that with you. She was afraid you might be offended."

"I like it because I know where it comes from. I've been called worse."

I don't want to focus on the horrible names he's been called. He needs a distraction.

"Are you going to tell me what you're sporting in your pants right now is a kielbasa you packed away for a snack?" I bite my lip to keep from laughing.

Beck jerks the car to the side of the road and throws it into park. He unbuckles the seat belt and moves the seat back.

"Come here so I can give you a lesson in how kielbasa is made," he growls.

He lifts me onto his lap and holds my face as his thumbs stroke my cheeks. His eyes study the features of my face, making me squirm. I can't rid my mind of wanting to kiss his full lips that resemble an exotic fruit I want to taste again and again.

My resistance to this man is nonexistent. I don't put up a fight as my hormones take over. I don't want to fight anymore. I want him.

"I swore I wasn't going to do this, but you are irresistible and selfless, a hot combination."

He leans down and kisses me softly at first, but then takes over my mouth, lips, and tongue. I've entered the rabbit hole headfirst, and I don't want out anytime soon. I grab him by the back of the head as we give in to a scorching kiss, full of passion that's been on hold for a second time. He's ferocious with me as we sink deeper into each other. Our bodies take over, recognizing the need we have been denying.

He grabs my ass and positions my wet core over his groin. Our lips collide as we explore each other's mouths with our tongues. There's no domination, just want. There's a need to find each other and accept who we are, the outcasts. As my tongue memorizes his mouth, I imagine what it would be like on my sex. I bet he has a talented tongue.

He finds my diamond-tipped nipples as he strokes and pinches them with the right amount of pressure to make me detonate. I grind down on him, panting in between kisses. High school was the last time I dry-humped in a car, but this is a whole other level of excitement. We're in the middle of Africa, under an infinite starlit sky, getting it on like animals. I've waited for this for a long time, and I plan on enjoying him before he changes his mind.

I hear him, but my eyes are screwed shut. "Do it. Come for me." The bass in his voice is demanding but delicious. If I could listen to it for the rest of my life, I would do anything he asked.

Colored stars explode behind my eyes, and I scream at top volume, mumbling his name over and over. Heat flushes through my entire body as my head falls on his shoulder.

"That's my Red Hurricane." His chest moves up and down from laughter.

"Red Hurricane?" I giggle.

"Your red hair has been like a magnet from day one, and you are a force to be reckoned with. You came in like a hurricane." He doesn't sing the words.

"You were listening to my music. Luke Combs. Good point. Touché." I climb off his lap. "Now, it's your turn."

"Nope. When we're together, it will be with nothing between us. We need to get home." He pulls back onto the road as we sit in silence. "Thank you for not listening to me and being here, despite my stubborn ass."

"If that's how you're going to thank me, don't let me stop you."

"I owe you one more apology." He sighs. "Wafiq has made the suspect list. Things between us changed after the shooting. Today, he was quite defensive. I can't believe he killed his parents."

"I don't think he did." Beck turns and frowns at me. "Those tears were real, but I think he may know who altered the plane so it would crash. We have so much more work to do."

"Tomorrow, we need to get into the warehouse and find out what's happening. These incidents seem isolated, but they somehow link together," he says with a confidence I haven't seen in him in a while.

The rocking of the car lulls me to sleep again. I wake up in Beck's arms as he carries me into the house and up the stairs. We enter his room, and he lays me on the bed.

"I want you to sleep with me tonight and every night we're here. Today was a close call. You've sparked something in me I need to explore." He bends down and kisses my forehead.

I shuck off my clothes and put on one of his T-shirts, which is three sizes too big for me. My body is still tired, and I need to shut off my mind. The bed moves as he slides in behind me. He snuggles into my back, just like we did when he was sick.

His breath evens out, and he's asleep. The hot air from his nose blows across my ear. His warm, firm arm hugs me in, and for the first time in my life, I truly feel safe. We've saved each other in more ways than one, and I have a premonition there is more to come.

TWENTY-FIVE

Pippa
———————

I'M FLOATING between sleep and awake when I feel his hardness between my butt cheeks. His hands match his hardware. He's my kind of guy in every way. To think I had given up on him, and he turned the corner to apologize in the humblest way.

The title of king hasn't gone to his head, and I need to keep it that way. My connection to him is not like anything I've ever experienced. He understands what it's like to stand on the outside and observe what's going on around you and to how people look at you through different eyes. Some are judging, and others are envious.

"Pip," his gravelly voice vibrates through his chest and into my back.

"Yes, do you need something?" I put my hand over my mouth to hide my giggle. He rips my T-shirt over my head, and we're skin to skin. There is instant heat between us.

"Ha-ha, very funny. I can hear you giggling," he mumbles.

"You realize you're calling me Pip like the character from—"

"Great Expectations."

"I didn't know you were such a literature buff." I lace his fingers with mine.

"You can't attend Oxford and not read Dickens. My real love is poetry." He hesitates. "My favorite is Langston Hughes. He wrote 'Dreams,' 'The Weary Blues,' and 'Brotherly Love.' 'Dreams' is where Martin Luther King Jr. derived his famous speech. I dabble with my poetry. I've never shared that with anyone."

I nod. He's opening up to me more each day. I don't want to blow it by prying. "I have a lot in common with Pip. He's an orphan who is immature, kind, and ambitious. He never feels comfortable with himself. When he lives among the wealthy, he decides that a life of luxury would be more beneficial to him. I've worked hard for everything I have. I don't want anything from you except you," I whisper.

He flips me toward him so we are nose to nose. His fingers push the stray hairs from my face.

"I didn't think you wanted anything from me, and being king is just a title. The amount of money I have lets me live comfortably for the rest of my life. Doing this work allows me to live life instead of watching it pass me by. I'm drawn to your joy of life, kindness, and enthusiasm. We need to jump in and see where this goes. We make a great team. Balance is what it's all about. Your impulsiveness to my calculations." His eyes are soft and sincere.

A shift happens between us, making me believe every word he says. We may only be together for this mission, but I don't care. I'll take anything I can get from him, knowing we'll go our separate ways in the end. I revel in the feeling of him, his skin, hands, smile, eyes, and that baritone voice.

"So, now I'm impulsive." I push him onto his back,

pinning his hands above his head. He could flip me in an instant, but he plays along to appease me.

His broad smile spotlights his white teeth as his chest vibrates from laughter. "I think you've forgotten how long my arms are."

As I pin his wrists, my breasts line up with his lips as he pulls a nipple into his mouth and sucks on it. His lips are heaven as he sucks with the right amount of pressure, and his tongue swirls around my tightening buds.

My wet core slides up and down his hardness, dying to take the plunge.

He stops sucking enough to say, "I don't have any condoms. I didn't plan on meeting someone who drives me this crazy." His eyes sparkle with mischief.

"I do." I wiggle my brows. "It pays to come prepared. Did you see what I did there with my play on words?"

"Yeah, yeah. Off with you. You're wasting the time I could be inside you."

I hop off him, run to my room, and grab a box of condoms.

His cock stands straight up, demanding attention as I place the box on the nightstand.

"Do you always carry XL condoms with you?" He smiles.

"No. Only when I know I'm going to have hot sex with an XL man."

He throws his head back and laughs. "Well, you got that right. Someone was feeling confident."

"Jess thought it would be funny. I'll have to thank her when I get home."

I sheathe him and get back into position.

"Are you ready to ride?" he says in a serious tone.

"Oh, yeah. This might be my sweetest ride yet."

"I'm not as sweet as you think." His lips curl.

I move down slowly to adjust to his size. He's bigger than the average man, but there is pure delight in my heart and body. I love how he fills me. We move slowly at first and sweat slicks our bodies.

"I can't hold back any longer," he says through gritted teeth.

"Go for it."

He grabs my hips and thrusts into me from below. His form is almost brutal, but I can't get enough. I like it rough, the slice between pain and pleasure. I ride the wave with him and float away on our high. "Ready when you are."

A heat wave shoots through my body as I yell out his name. He follows behind me as he arches his back, nailing my sweet spot and prolonging my orgasm. We lie in a heap, trying to catch our breath.

"I promise it'll be longer next time. You've been hard to resist, and I have a lot of pent-up energy." His look is unapologetic.

His smiling face looks free of whatever in his past that holds him down. "Oh, I'm not worried. We have plenty of time to experiment with timing. I have a few tricks up my sleeve."

His dark eyes are stormy. "I'm sure you do. I can't wait to see the kink you bring."

There's a knock at the front door, and I look at the clock to see who would come over at this hour when I realize it's almost noon.

We throw our clothes on and run downstairs to answer the door. Standing in the doorway is Wafiq, holding the back of a man's shirt. He pushes the man into the foyer.

"Here, I found the man who sabotaged the plane. I thought you would want to talk to him." Wafiq crosses his arms in front of his chest, and his mouth is turned down.

The man stands in a white T-shirt and khaki pants with wide eyes. His elbows are tucked into his body with his hands up, ready to defend himself.

Beck says, "Hi, what's your name?"

"Taavi." He glances over his shoulder at Wafiq. "I'm a mechanic at the airport."

Beck's eyes narrow. "What did you do to make the plane crash?"

His hands drop, but they're shaking. "I disabled the air mixing valve."

"Do you know who I am?" Beck stands up taller, taking on the role of king.

Taavi nods. "You're soon to be our new king. I was there the night of the shooting."

Beck puts his hand on the man's shoulder and pushes him toward the door. "Let's talk outside. Wafiq, you can stay here." His voice has more command than I've ever heard from him.

I turn to Wafiq, who is miffed at being left out of Beck's conversation.

This gives me time to go fishing. "Sabeen took us on a tour of the city and her lab. She pointed out your warehouses. Is there any chance you'd give me a tour? We can leave the big guy at home." I point my thumb to the door.

"I don't think so. Those warehouses are off-limits and heavily secured." He smiles like he's got me by the short hairs.

Beck comes back in without Taavi. "Wafiq, that was not the man who sabotaged the plane. He is simply a mechanic at the airport."

Wafiq bristles. "Well, we had to start somewhere. He seemed like a logical choice."

"Have you talked to the police about what we found at the crash site?" I ask.

"No. There's no need to bring the police into this. Besides, we don't have enough evidence or bodies to investigate. We may have hit a dead end." He stuffs his hands in his pockets and looks at Beck through narrow eyes.

"I don't think you're going to find evidence out in the open. Someone has been very clever and has even taken care of the bodies. Let us take it from here," Beck says calmly.

Wafiq's hackles are up. "What do you know about it? You know nothing about what goes on here or the people who live here. How are you going to find out who killed them?"

Beck, a head taller than Wafiq, steps closer and looks down at him. "Because it's what I do, no matter where I am in the world, and I'm about to become king of your tribe. I think I have some pull. You may be too close to everything to see what's happening right under your nose."

Wafiq huffs, walks out, and slams the door behind him.

"Well, that went well. I questioned him about the warehouse, and he doesn't want us anywhere near it."

Beck stands with his hands on his hips and exhales. "Good. Then we're going to hit it tonight and see exactly what he's hiding. I'm done being Mr. Nice Guy. My blinders are off."

TWENTY-SIX

Beck

My blood is boiling. Wafiq thinks he can pull one over on me because I'm new to the city and culture. What he doesn't know is my extensive international training as an operative. I can sniff out a criminal from five klicks out. Taavi is no criminal. He's an innocent man Wafiq has cornered into taking the fall.

Pippa and I make our way to the living room. I plop down on the couch, and she sits next to me. She's a snuggle bunny, and I like it.

Even amidst the turmoil swirling around us, I'm painfully aware of what I've been missing. My relationship with Taylor was on automatic pilot. We never put ourselves in situations where we needed to test our relationship or rely on one another. I pull Pippa into me and kiss the top of her head. There's more give to my rigid ways.

"When I questioned him about the mixing control knob being stuck, he didn't know what I was talking about. The mechanic confessed that Wafiq had told him about the valve. He's not our guy, but Wafiq wants us to think he rigged the plane. Do you still think Wafiq didn't do it?"

She lays her head on my chest. "He might know who did it and is trying to cover for them. I wish all roads didn't lead back to him, but they do."

She looks up at me with her big green eyes filled with worry.

"Blood is thicker than water," I say as I run my fingers through her silky red hair.

She looks confused. "What does that saying mean, anyway?" I appreciate her inquisitiveness. She always has questions that need answers.

"'The blood of the covenant is thicker than the water of the womb' is the full saying, but it's from medieval times. Back then, it meant that bloodshed on the battlefield created stronger ties than the water of the womb does, or family ties. When you stand shoulder to shoulder with a brother in arms, see the fear in the eyes of the enemy, and lose a fellow soldier, you understand the oath you take is an allegiance to your country that can never be broken."

My memories travel back to my time in the military, turbulent for any young soul and a matter of surviving the undertow. "If I am going to be king of this tribe, I need to do what's best for them."

"I'll probably never fully understand how it feels to be in the military, and I'm sure you've seen your share of tragedy and suffering over the years." She draws circles on my chest, her favorite thing to do when we're talking.

"Those were some of my first memories that came back. They were more like nightmares. I had to get out before it destroyed me. There's only so much a soul can take. You pack away your memories, but they always knock on the door, waiting to come back in." I hold her close like I'm holding onto a life raft.

Peace comes over me lying on the couch with her. I put my head back and take in the quiet.

"We need to come up with a plan for tonight. Any thoughts?" she says.

"Does your brain ever take a holiday?"

"Yeah, when I have sex." She laughs. "I say we go with our previous plan and have dinner with Wafiq and Zahara. We need to keep up appearances, and you need to play nice, then we hit the warehouse. We need to go in fully equipped. I don't know how hard it's going to be to get in there or even if we can get in."

The rest of the day is spent doing recon by driving around the city. Keeping the Range Rover gives us mobility. The warehouse is solid, with one way in and one way out. We can't get out of the vehicle to look around. There are security cameras, and even without them, we would look suspicious.

I call Wafiq and ask him if Pippa and I could come to dinner. When I suggest Katoo join us, I'm left with silence.

"I don't know what happened between you and Katoo, but it would be in everyone's best interest if you two patch things up. We're all going to be working together in the future. We can decide about what's best for the city and tribe, but not without mending its past. What do you say?" I hold my breath, hoping he accepts the peace offering.

"Fine. I'll do my best to meet him halfway. We'll see you later." Wafiq sounds tired, as if his battle wears on him.

Clouds obscure the sunset, which will benefit us later when we breach the warehouse. The more cover we can get, the better. My gut tells me we're going to find something I don't want us to find.

Pippa has been on the phone and computer most of the day, trying to hack Wafiq's server without much luck. Peter and his team haven't been able to crack the code, and without getting into Wafiq's system, we don't know what he's up to.

She comes down the stairs in a black fitted halter dress. Her shoes are not Chucks but small heels to accent the dress.

The stories in her ink are on full display, covering her ripped arms, back, and legs. There are words like *be kind, fierce, forgive,* and *lies are like knives* alongside a butterfly, serpent, and the moon with stars. My favorite ink is the one down her side that reads, "You'll never know how strong you are until being strong is the only choice you have." She's a warrior who doesn't need armor. I admire her fortitude.

I grab her by the waist and cover her mouth with mine, grabbing her by the ass, which fits nicely into my large hands. Powerful things come in small packages as our tongues duel for dominance.

She breaks away. "If you keep this up, we'll never get out of here. You need to stay focused and stop thinking about sex all the time."

I hear her giggle, which only makes me harder. "Says the woman with the XL condom box."

Following behind her gorgeous ass is doing nothing to hold down my libido, which has been on full alert since we succumbed to our desires in the most sensuous way.

She jumps in the driver's seat as I reluctantly ride shotgun and throws it into drive, peeling out of the driveway. I reach for the *oh shit* bar above my head and pray we get there in one piece. She weaves in and out of traffic like she's riding her Harley.

We pull up, and she gets out of the car without a care in the world. Sweat beads on my forehead, but we made it from point A to point B.

"What the hell was that, driving ninja?" I climb out of the car and want to kiss the ground.

She smoothes her hands down the front of her dress. "I wanted to see how it handled, and now you're awake for dinner tonight. I've got to have you on your toes. You never know when someone is going to slip up."

"Who's running this op, anyway?"

She peeks over her shoulder at me and winks. Then she slips her hand in mine and whispers, "If you're a good boy, I have a surprise for you later. It includes my mouth and a kielbasa."

Here I go again. I can't get enough of this woman. The evening will be spent trying to get that image out of my head and keep from getting a hard-on. I haven't been this horny since I was eighteen.

We enter the foyer, and Katoo and Wafiq are waiting for us. Wafiq stands tall, with his hands in front of him. His body is stiff, and his face is grim.

I try to break the ice. "How are you two doing this evening? Making friends, I see."

Katoo shrugs. "The best that it can be."

Wafiq nods without a word. Bad blood runs deep and long with these two, but they need to figure it out.

We follow them into the dining room set for a palace. The long table has red candles down the middle, making the silverware and crystal sparkle. Everything else is in ivory. I notice we aren't alone. Several elders stand around with drinks in their hands. They nod in my direction with tight lips.

"I wasn't aware we were having a business dinner." I turn to Wafiq.

"I thought if Katoo was here, we should have other council members here as well, in case anything comes up," Wafiq says smugly.

I take a drink from the tray and slug half of it back. The

champagne is way too sweet for the event. My eyes roam the crowd to find Pippa and Sabeen standing in the corner, laughing and talking. They are easy with one another like long-lost friends.

Zahara is on the other side of the room and makes eye contact with me. She strides over in a royal blue designer gown, wearing a diamond and sapphire necklace and earrings. Her attire from head to toe is well over a hundred thousand dollars. She spares no expense on her wardrobe.

"How are you?" She leans in, giving me her cheek for a kiss. "I heard you found some problems with the plane crash. Do we know who sabotaged it?" She's smiling, which makes me suspicious right away.

"No. We are at a dead end for now." I watch her as I say the next sentence. "We have to do some deep digging to find more clues. Everyone is a suspect until then."

She lifts her glass to take a drink as it covers half her face. "Well, it sounds interesting. I hope you can wrap it up quickly. I'm just glad you're feeling better without other symptoms. That must have been difficult."

She keeps asking about other symptoms, which raises my antennae.

"What other symptoms did you think I should have?"

"Oh, I don't know. When you're dehydrated, you can have memory issues and hallucinations." She tilts her head.

Pippa stands to the side of Zahara and shakes her head minutely. Zahara is a prime suspect in this charade.

TWENTY-SEVEN

Beck

THE REST of the evening involves small talk about many things concerning the state of the city and the mines. They have kept most of the mine information from me, but one of the council members speaks to Wafiq.

"We still have a problem at Mine 3 with some workers. They are demanding more money and better working conditions." He speaks in a low tone into his drink.

Wafiq's eyes shift to me. "Since you're going to be our leader, maybe you'd like to go to the mine with us tomorrow and address their concerns directly."

"Absolutely, I'm well versed in problem-solving with employees."

His face is deadpan, and he turns to the council member. "How is your daughter doing with her soccer game?"

I tune out, looking around the room for Pippa. She's having an animated discussion with Sabeen, and they are laughing again. I want to capture her laugh in a glass jar and bring it out when I miss her. I've never had a thought like that about anyone. She's a woman of many mysteries, and I want to solve all of them.

Katoo catches my eye and gives me a nod to meet him in the kitchen. I excuse myself and wander out of the room. The back of Katoo's head weaves in and out of servers as he makes his way through the exit door to the back garden.

He whips around. "He did this to make you look like a fool." This is the first time I've seen this much emotion from Katoo.

"Relax. I know what he's up to. I run a successful multi-million-dollar company with a board of directors. Running this city with the council can't be that much different. My bigger concern is Zahara's constant questions about my symptoms when I was ill."

"She is not to be trusted. She came out of nowhere two years ago and latched on to Wafiq. She's always pleasant enough, but there is something about her I can't put my finger on. With her background in microbiology, she could have created the poison."

Katoo makes a good point. "We're going out to the warehouse tonight. I need you and Jobi to be our eyes and ears."

I pull two ear comms from my pocket. "Here, you're going to need these so we can communicate. They go both ways. You can talk into them, and you'll be able to hear everyone."

"You certainly came equipped." His lips curl at the ends.

"We'll be in different— "

Wafiq bursts through the door. "There you are. I've been looking for you. What are you two discussing?" His eyes narrow.

I take a long sip of my drink. "Nothing. I had one of my dizzy spells, and Katoo was kind enough to show me to the garden for some air. Do you need something?"

"We're getting ready to serve dinner, and I thought you would like to address the council members before you become our new leader. They will want to hear from you." At every turn, he puts me on the spot, trying to catch me off-balance.

"I would like to address the council and introduce myself as the owner of a multi-national security company. We'll have dinner, and I can open the floor for questions regarding the management and fiscal profile of the city. Sound good to you?" My *I-got-you-by-the-balls* smile comes shining through as he grimaces and nods.

We make our way to the dining room, and the event goes as planned. I stand at a small podium, answer questions, ask questions, and make a few jokes to keep the mood light. All the while, my eyes keep coming back to Pippa. She stares at me with a smile and admiration in her eyes.

Now and then, her eyes get big when I catch her off-guard with one of my responses. Her nod of approval keeps me going. I shouldn't need her approval, but I do. I want her to see me as an accomplished business owner instead of the sick man who lost his partner and can't get over it.

She and I skip dessert and say our goodbyes. Limited alcohol and sugar will keep us sharp for the night ahead.

I decide I should drive home, and she laughs at my suggestion without being offended, throwing me the keys.

The car is quiet as I wait for her to say something about the evening. She rakes her nails up and down her thighs, which is a signal she's anxious about something.

"What's got you balled up over there? Are you nervous about tonight?"

"Balled up?" She laughs.

"It's a saying. Don't deflect."

"You've got me balled up. There are so many layers to you. Physically, you're as strong as they come until you get sick. You've opened up to me about things you've never told anyone, and tonight I find out you're a very successful business owner added to your time as an agent. You have a lot to be proud of." She tells me this while looking at her hands and out the front window.

"Do you think I'm all sunshine and unicorns?"

"Unicorns were real at one point," she says over one shrugged shoulder.

This time, I'm the one who's laughing. She's the only woman in the world who has ever made me laugh about unicorns.

"My life has been full of never being accepted and the ugliness that goes along with being an MI6 agent. James Bond makes it look glamorous, but it's not. Your existence as an agent is lonely, where no one can know your name, face, or voice. You work as a shadow, and it takes a toll on you. Some agents can spend their entire lives living in the dark. I wasn't one of those agents. I met Peter and Sean on a mission in Kuwait and broke protocol to get to know them. Not long after I left MI-6, we started our company."

"Then maybe I will make it as an agent. I'm used to working in the shadows." Her response is somber, and I can't help but feel she thinks she's less than.

Her kind of fire will never last in the shadows. She burns brightly, and what she doesn't know is that I want to hire her away from Neil. We need fiery female agents at the firm. She would be a perfect fit, in and out of the field.

Back at the house, we go our separate ways. She claims she needs to get in touch with Peter about the encryption, but after our conversation, I feel her distancing herself from me. I'm not sure why. I'll have to wait it out and give her the space she needs.

I stand in the room on the top floor with the triangular window and watch as most of the lights go off around the city. As I trudge the stairs, she's dressed in black from head to toe with her red hair tucked under a black beanie. She loaded her backpack with gear, but I'm not sure what is in there.

"You all set?"

"Ready when you are." Her eyes light up with an adrenaline rush I've experienced on many ops.

Katoo and Jobi each have a vehicle and drive us to another part of town to pick up a black Jeep Wrangler. It's outfitted with a winch mechanism and has the top on for cover.

Pippa is still quiet and in her head. Her eyes dart around, scoping out the city scenes.

"Are you thinking about us or our recon?"

"A bit of both. I thought a lot about what you said about being an agent." She stares out the window.

"And?"

"I think I'm cut out for it, but I don't know to what extent." She still doesn't look at me and says nothing about us.

"You'll know after our mission is over." I fail to mention my feelings about us or what I want to come of them. I'll let it sit on the back burner.

The city is asleep at 1:00 a.m. We've got Katoo and Jobi at two crucial locations. They'll be our eyes and ears. I park the Jeep down the street as we make our way on foot. We are loaded with weapons from head to toe.

The building is solid concrete with a steel veneer. Cameras monitor each corner. Pippa crouches down and pulls her laptop from her backpack.

"There's a chance this is a closed-circuit system. It may not be on the encrypted mainframe." She taps away on the keys. "Bingo! We're in. I can run the cameras on a loop for about three minutes before anyone figures out what's going on, if anyone is even watching live."

There's one way in through a steel door with no handle. Next to the door is a keypad and a fingerprint scanner. We stand there, trying to figure out our next move.

"You didn't think it would be that easy, did you?" Before I finish my sentence, she pulls a tube from her backpack, and a feather brush pops out.

She thinks on her feet. "Fingertips leave behind water and oils. The higher humidity will allow the prints to rise," she explains.

I finish her thought. "If you dust it with a powder, we can at least figure out the numbers and run those numbers into a program to get the sequence." We're in rhythm.

She smiles up at me. "You're smarter than the average bear."

I frown at her. "So now I'm a bear?"

"It's a saying. I'll explain later."

She dusts the keypad. There are fingerprints on five numbers on the keypad. I wipe the pad down with alcohol to get rid of any residue.

"I'll put the numbers in later." She stands up. "Our next move is to lift Wafiq's fingerprint and remake it for the scanner."

She looks up at the roof.

"What are you thinking?" The way her brain operates excites me in a way I haven't experienced since...I try not to think about Emilia. Emilia was the overplanner who lacked suspicion, which, in the end, might have been the thing that got her killed. Pippa thinks on her feet and looks for opportunities. Everyone is a suspect.

"I want to get on the roof and see what's going on up

there. Maybe there's a way in." She unloads her mountain climbing equipment from a grappling hook to carabiners.

"I need you to throw the grappling hook up and over the side of the roof. I'll get set up in the harness and ropes."

With two tries, I get the hook to grab the side of the roof. Pippa adjusts her harness and attaches the carabiners. She's left the end of the rope on the ground.

"You should be able to hold me, Big Guy." She winks.

Finally, I get a smart comment from her, and I breathe a sigh of relief. I grab hold of the end and pull. She's heavier than she looks, which accounts for her muscle mass. One hand over the other, she scales the side of the building with ease. She gives me a thumbs-up, and then all hell breaks loose.

"You've got incoming on your six." Katoo's voice comes through the comm with the calm of a veteran.

Pippa whips the rope up the side of the building and is out of sight. I run to the end of the building and flatten myself on the wall when I see a pair of headlights shine on the door.

Wafiq jumps out of the SUV, punches in the code, and puts his thumb on the scanner. The door clicks open and shuts before I have a chance to sneak in behind him.

Pippa breaks in. "I'm going to take a walk on the roof. I'll report back."

The sweat pours down my back. Despite the sun setting hours ago, the night is stifling with heat and humidity. In the distance, the howl of an animal breaks the silence, a reminder we're in the wilds of Africa.

"Nothing up here. High-end solar panels cover the roof, and there is no entry point. There is some serious juice being pumped into this place. Give me the go when it's safe to come down," she says with confidence.

Wafiq comes out in less time than I thought he would,

carrying a briefcase. He rushes to his truck and peels out as the tires throw gravel.

I wait to hear the truck drive off in the distance. "You are clear."

She throws the rope over the side so I can ease her down. We get her out of her harness and hurry to the Jeep.

"Katoo and Jobi, thanks for your help. We'll touch base tomorrow." My comm cuts out as I remove it from my ear.

I turn to Pippa. "You're awfully quiet. What's going on?"

"I get the feeling something big is going on, and we aren't even close to figuring out what it is."

TWENTY-EIGHT

Pippa

My SOLE FOCUS is on this mission, but Beck is a distraction. What I thought would be a fun romp in the sack changed when he bared his soul to me.

There is a lot to him, and he's accomplished in many areas of his life. My only claim to fame is I'm an expert hacker, and because of that talent, I got hired by MI-6, off-book. I don't measure up, and it's daunting. We work well together, and I try to hold my own, letting him take the lead, but I need to keep proving myself. I want him to see me as an equal partner.

Putting space between us will be a good thing and give me time to prove myself to Beck and Neil. There is so much more to this series of events than meets the eye. We're missing crucial information that's hidden in the warehouse. I don't know if we'll find out who shot at Beck or who killed his parents, but Wafiq is up to something.

After sleeping most of the morning away, I meander downstairs to see Beck sitting at the table, focused on his laptop. I stop and watch him from the doorway. He has a regal air about him. The way he sits, shoulders squared as his hand cradles his chin. He's wrapped in a confidence that can't be learned but must be genetic. He senses me in the doorway.

"Come here." He pushes back from the table and waves his hand to sit with him.

I walk over and stop at the end of the table on the other side from where he sits. A frown crosses his face.

"You've been distancing yourself from me. Do you want to tell me why?" His voice is gentle, like he's coaxing a timid animal to come closer.

He's nothing if not direct. I shake my head. "I have a lot to prove, and we have a job to do. That needs to be our focus. I need to stop distracting myself."

He stares at me for a beat. "If you say so."

"I have a plan for tonight to get the thumbprint from Wafiq."

He steeples his fingers in front of his mouth. "Go on."

"We need to have him and Zahara over for drinks and appetizers this evening, by themselves." I pull out a chair and sit down. "Ply them with alcohol, get the print, and try to get some information out of them."

"I like it, but I don't think it's going to be that easy. They're very cagey, even on their turf. But it is time they came here to our turf. I want to see Wafiq's reaction when I ask him questions about the house and my family. We can't determine how much they might drink, but it's a start."

His eyes penetrate me. He doesn't like my proposal regarding the two of us.

"Anything else?" he asks.

"I don't know how to cook, let alone any traditional foods. Breakfast I can do, but I'm lost with anything else." For this, I get a smile out of him.

"Call Katoo or Jobi. See if they can help. I'll reach out to

Wafiq." He dismisses me by focusing back on the screen of his laptop.

I push back the chair. His low voice cuts through the tension. "You and I are not done, if that's what you're thinking." He doesn't look at me.

"Maybe not, but we're on pause for now," I call the final shot as I turn and leave to bring in reinforcements for the cooking detail.

Katoo comes to help me prepare traditional Zambian foods. We stand side by side as we prepare *nshima*—a corn maize dish—relishes, and fruits such as loquat, a plum-like fruit. I add some American twists to the recipes.

"You know, he is very much like his father. Since he arrived, I feel like I'm being visited by a ghost. The resemblance is striking. The way he speaks and gestures reminds me of my dear friend when he was younger. Genes are a powerful force. There is no doubt he is Tadashi's son."

"Would there ever be a doubt?" I'm curious to know where his comment comes from.

"No," Katoo responds quickly.

I tuck it away in the back of my mind. What's more interesting is that Wafiq has never required a DNA test from Beck.

"I wish you could stay tonight. I've enjoyed our time together." My hand rests on his arm.

"It's best that I go. You will get more out of Wafiq if I'm not here." His smile is weak, and his eyes are tired as if he's seen too much.

For the evening, I dress in a simple patterned skirt and lime green short-sleeved shirt. I don't wear shoes. I like the feel of the hardwood floors on my feet. Besides, shoes aren't required in Mubala.

Beck dresses in black pants and a white shirt with two buttons open at the top. He looks irresistible. I want to jump on him and rip everything off. How dare the clothes cover such a beautiful man? But I need to keep my wits about me tonight and pick up on any missteps from Wafiq or Zahara. I can't get sucked into his puff of pheromones.

There's a sharp knock at the door, and Beck answers, welcoming our guests. Zahara wears a sporty ivory pantsuit, and Wafiq is dressed in khakis and a polo shirt. This is the least formal attire I've seen them wear.

We move to the living room and sit down while I offer them something to drink. I put together special drinking glasses for both of them so we can lift the prints. The outside of the glass has a somewhat spongy surface, allowing us to pick up the prints and remake them. They both ask for white wine, and Beck and I decide to have the same.

Wafiq is more relaxed than I've seen him in the time I've been here in Mubala. He sits as if he has the world by the ass.

"Tell me, did you get the problems solved at Mine 3? Sorry, I couldn't make it. Work at home called me away," Beck says.

Wafiq waves his hands to dismiss the comment. "It was nothing. They like to complain every once in a while. How are things with your business at home? Do they need you back there?"

Beck takes a long swig of his drink. "No, my partners will manage everything. They know my total focus is on what's going on here. Do we have any more leads on who killed our parents?"

Zahara stares at her drink, and Wafiq moves in his chair. "No, with no bodies, it doesn't look like we're going to get any answers." There's a sadness in his voice that hadn't been there before. I'm sure he misses his parents, but until now, he's shown very little grief.

I reach over and cover his hand with mine. "Be thankful

you got that time with them. They sound like they were wonderful people. Not everyone gets to know their parents like you did." I squeeze his hand, and he squeezes mine back.

Zahara shoots me a frosty glare as she finishes her wine. "Can I have a refill, please? I'm parched tonight."

"Sure. Maybe you'd like to help me get the appetizers in the kitchen?"

She forces a smile and follows me to the kitchen.

I bend down to pull the food from the oven.

"You and Dacari need to pack up and go. The message has been clear that he's not welcome here. The people don't know him and are unsure of what kind of leader he will be. The situation has made things very tense. If he wants to do what's best for everyone, he will go back to his life in the US."

My back is to her while I form a response without slapping her. I turn around slowly. "We'll stay until we know what is going on here."

She straightens her back. "What do you mean?"

"First, someone kills his biological parents in a plane crash. Then Dacari is shot at, but they miss him and hit his sister instead. Finally, he's poisoned."

"What do you mean, poisoned? I thought it was food poisoning?" I watch as she becomes a little unraveled, her composure slipping.

"We thought it was food poisoning at first, but the more we looked at his symptoms, they didn't add up as just food poisoning."

"What were his other symptoms? I might be able to help. I am a doctor, after all." Her eyes watch me intently.

I come face-to-face with her and tilt my head. "Wouldn't you like to know? I think I'll keep that to myself. But in case you're wondering, you've made the suspect list. Now, let's go to the living room and put on a pretty smile for the boys."

TWENTY-NINE

Beck

PIPPA AND ZAHARA come back into the room wearing fake smiles and tense bodies. Knowing Pippa, she said something to rattle Zahara to see what she could shake out.

I offer to refill Wafiq's glass and take it into the kitchen, replacing it with a fresh glass. The print needs to be clean to remake his thumbprint for the scanner. His glass gets placed in the freezer for later.

I hand his wine to him. "Tell me what it was like to grow up in this house with our parents."

Wafiq looks in his glass and gets quiet. "It was a wonderful place to grow up in. Our father was a special man loved by everyone." There's a faraway look in his eyes as he takes a sip. "As a child, there are so many things you don't know about your life, hidden from you."

His words catch me by surprise. "What do you mean?"

He snaps out of it. "I guess I was thinking about how our lives have intersected. I didn't know how to run a tribe or a city when I was younger. Father kept me from most of it, even when I got older." His lips are tight.

He looks at me with resentment in his eyes. "You'll be

crowned as our leader soon. The position is honorable and not to be taken lightly."

"I'm aware of the significance of the tradition and position. No one will take it lightly, especially me. We'll go through the ceremony, and then I will have the power to hand it over to you."

He nods, not convinced that's what is going to happen. Something pokes at me, telling me he may be right. The road ahead has more curves than a dragon's tail. If we find out he has anything to do with the deaths and the shooting, it's game over.

"As I look around the house, there are no pictures of me. I guess they wanted to forget about me forever." I've accepted my place in this pecking order.

"Trust me, they didn't forget about you. They talked about you often with me and Sabeen. In our culture, you never forget your firstborn." He finishes his drink and places it on the table with more force than is needed.

The evening continues for another hour as Zahara tells us about her research at the biotech company where she used to work. Pippa plies her with questions. Zahara gives vague answers and seems distracted.

They get up to leave, and I feel exhausted from trying to navigate their answers and what they mean.

Pippa closes the door and leans up against it. "That was interesting. I feel like I've gone a couple of rounds in a boxing ring."

"My thoughts exactly. What happened between you and Zahara? The ice storm came in with you from the kitchen."

Pippa explains how she told Zahara about the chemical poisoning to see her reaction and how she's made the suspect list. Now, we wait to see what she does.

"Good move. She was quiet tonight, not her usual personable self."

"I think I caught her off guard, and she's not used to that. She didn't ask any more questions about you, though."

Pippa rubs her arms as if she's cold.

"You seem chilly. Do you want me to get you a blanket? I think I saw one up in my closet."

"I'm tired. When I get tired, I get cold. Thank you." She shuffles to the couch as I turn to go upstairs to find a blanket.

I head toward the closet, where I saw the blanket, and open the door. On the top shelf is a red blanket. I reach for it easily, but when I grab it, a binder falls out with it. I catch it before it hits the floor and take it with me. Excitement pumps through me. This may give me more answers to my past.

Pippa is curled up on the couch, and I cover her with the blanket.

"What do you have there?" Her eyelids are half open.

"It fell out with the blanket. I think it's a photo album."

I lay it on the coffee table and open it from the beginning. The album contains photos of my birth parents' life before they had children. They were young and in love. Page after page shows the happy couple on safari in Kenya.

I touch the photos, noticing how much I look like Tadashi. He was younger than me when the photos were taken, but I can't deny how much we look alike. I notice the scars in the shape of stars on the side of his face. Warmth fills my chest as Pippa puts her hand on my arm.

Farther into the album, they are with a group of people sitting around a campfire. Everyone is having a good time: laughing, drinking, and eating. The photographer zooms in on each couple to capture the moment.

What I see when I scan the snapshots leaves me speechless. My excitement leaves me, replaced with dread.

I take the photo out of the plastic pocket and stare at it. I would know these faces anywhere, young or old.

"Beck, what's wrong?" I hear Pippa's voice, but it's far away.

I flip through the pages, looking for the photo that will answer my question. There it is. The photo is of the four of them together, smiling at the camera with their arms around each other as if they are old friends. My hands shake as I take it out of the plastic protection.

"Beck?" Pippa looks over my shoulder. "Who are they?"

"Those are my parents." My voice cracks.

"I can see that, but who are the other couple?" she says softly.

"Those are all my parents, together on safari in Kenya many years ago before I was born." My mouth is dry.

She gently takes the photo from me to examine it. I've never experienced the pain of this betrayal. I'm angry and hurt, with more questions without answers. I've spent a good deal of my time worrying about telling my parents, and they knew from the beginning.

My cell rings, telling me my parents are on the other line. I send it to voicemail. I'm not ready to deal with their lies. My anger will be at the forefront and only make things worse.

My hands turn into fists, and the tears burn my eyes, but I will them not to fall. Pippa has already seen me sick. Now, she'll see me at my weakest point. A flood of emotions comes to the surface out of my control, and I can't stop. I take the album and throw it onto the floor, watching as the photos scatter everywhere. They rip out of their protective plastic, exposing themselves. My breath is shallow, and anger takes over. I'm embarrassed by my reaction, losing my composure, but to hell with it. I've had enough of this place and its secrets and betrayals.

Pippa sits with the photo in her hand in silence. She watches me come undone by my past. There's no fear on her face, just compassion. She looks as if she knows something about betrayal and how it cuts deeper than any other lie because someone else holds the key to your vision of life.

I leave her sitting there and go to my room, slamming the door behind me. I want to throw things, destroy this house, burn it to the ground, and pack my shit up and leave. Only, I won't be going back to the UK, ever. They knew and never told me. What was the purpose of that?

I throw my clothes in a pile on the floor as I lie naked in bed, and darkness surrounds me. I know sleep will never find me tonight. The tears have dried, and fury is my companion.

The door creaks open and then closes. Pippa lifts the sheets and curls in beside me. She moves toward my pain, not away from it. She's come to comfort me once again.

"You shouldn't be alone. I can take your pain and help you through it. We'll get answers tomorrow."

She puts her head on my shoulder and strokes my chest. It's the comfort a mother would give a child. I have two of them, but neither cared enough to tell me the truth.

THIRTY

Beck

I KEEP TELLING myself there are worse things in the world than biological parents who gave me up to people they knew and probably trusted. I was the black sheep of the family, literally. When I look back on my childhood through a new lens, they always made sure I took the correct steps. Could they have been preparing me for what was to come?

My boarding school training, which led to Oxford and then into the military, might have been the steps I would have taken had I grown up here in Mubala. Each step prepared me for navigating the city both financially and from a defense standpoint for the tribe's mining territory. My head spins as I tried to peel back the layers of my life.

Dawn peeks around the corners of the shades to greet me. I haven't slept a wink. Pippa is curled up next to me, slumbering without a sound. Having her here with me calms me down once again. This is miles from where we started. She's turned out to be one of the strongest women I know. I fold back the covers and sit on the edge of the bed.

"Where are you going?" a groggy voice says from behind me.

I look over my shoulder at my angel warrior. Although, she's not mine yet. She's been resistant to continue what we started, and I don't have the strength to pursue her reasons.

She props herself up on her elbow. "Your eyes are blood-shot. No sleep last night, I take it."

She comes up behind me and rubs my neck and shoulders. Her hands send tingles through my body. I want to turn around, throw her on the bed, and bury myself in her for the rest of the day to escape the scenarios running in my head.

"You realize in the time we've been here, you've spent most of your time taking care of me. I've been in deadly situations in some of the most dangerous parts of the world and survived, but I came to Africa to see my long-lost family, and I'm a mess and helpless."

"You're still one tough guy. Families have a way of turning even the toughest person into an emotional blob."

"I think blob is a strong word. I'm still in good shape."

She laughs in my ear. "You need to call them and hear their side of the story. There has to be a reason they didn't tell you."

My shoulders hunch over, and I can't think straight due to the pain in the middle of my chest. "How about you make me one of your world-famous breakfasts, and we'll see where we go from there." I reach behind me and stroke her leg. She gasps.

"Sounds like a plan." She kisses me on the cheek with a tenderness that warms me.

The softness brings back a memory of when my mother kissed me goodnight. She gave me the seal of security before I closed my eyes. As a young boy, she made me feel like everything would be okay, but time alters our perceptions.

We eat breakfast in silence. Pippa cleans up and then puts her hands on my shoulders as she stretches upward.

"You need to call your parents and talk to them. Hear their words and be open to what they have to say. While you're doing that, I'm going to run the numbers from the keypad through my program and see what pops up."

"Yeah," is all I can muster. In no reality, am I looking forward to this conversation.

"To take your mind off things, I say we hit the warehouse again tonight and look around. Now, bend down." She gives me a quick kiss on the nose and turns away.

Her kiss sends me reeling to when my mum used to plant a soft kiss on my nose before I went to school each morning until I grew out of it. Truth is, I never grew out of it. I loved the special touches that only a mum can give a child.

I hold my cell phone in my hand, dreading the call I need to make to set things straight. There's only an hour difference, so they are getting ready for work.

My mum picks up on the first ring, and we're on a video call. "Good morning, Beck." She takes one look at my face and knows something is not right.

"Good morning, Mum."

She turns her head away and calls for my father. His face enters the frame, and he gives her a silent nod.

"Beck, how are you?" Concern covers his face.

"I'm in Mubala, Zambia. Ever hear of it?" I immediately regret my snarky tone.

Tears form in my mum's eyes. "Oh, Beck," she whispers. My father puts his arm around her shoulder and kisses her head.

"Why didn't you tell me? Why did I have to find out this way?" My voice is the hurt child and not the man who should be able to handle this.

"We couldn't tell you, ever. We signed an agreement with… your parents."

I cut him off. "They're not my parents. You are my parents. You're the ones who raised me to be the man I am today, and I'm proud of who I am because of you."

My mum covers her mouth with her hand while tears stream down her face. "We wanted to tell you so many times. Your heritage is something to be proud of."

I'm quiet, waiting for a more detailed explanation.

My father continues the story. "We met your... Tadashi and Aafia on safari in Kenya. We clicked with them instantly. They were warm and fun, and we had a lot in common. We kept in touch with them over the years. Then we got the call." He looks over at my mum. "Their tribe was going to war, and the enemy threatened to kill their eldest son. They covet the eldest son to carry on the family line and become king one day. We were having trouble getting pregnant, and then Aafia called your mum. We accepted under the condition that we never tell you where you came from. They wanted to make sure they always protected you from their enemies. As you got older, we didn't feel the need to tell you and upset you. You had a life you had built. We weren't sure you wanted to know, and you never asked."

From miles away, we face each other in silence and heavy contemplation. My mum grabs the phone and holds it close to her face, wiping at her tears.

"This was the hardest decision they ever made. Tadashi and Aafia loved you so much. Every day they were away from you, it killed them on the inside a bit more. I sent photos of you over the years. I wanted them to know what a fine individual you had grown up to be. Please don't be angry with them. They had to protect you, and we were their first and only choice."

"Mum, stop crying and catch your breath. I take it you

know they perished in a plane crash in the jungle. Is that why you've been calling me?"

The phone zooms out again to include my father's face. "Yes. Katoo called us to let us know. We were going to share your story with you. We are devastated."

"So Katoo knew you were the couple that adopted me?" My voice raises in pitch.

"No, not at first, and then he too was sworn to secrecy. The fewer people knew, the better," my father begs.

I pinch the bridge of my nose. "We discovered someone sabotaged the plane. Tadashi was an excellent pilot, so this was not his mistake. We have evidence to prove it."

Their brows furrow. "Are you investigating it? Is that why you're there?"

"Katoo contacted me. I came to discover my roots and become king of this tribe." I leave out the part where I've been shot at. "The plan is to become king long enough to hand it over to Wafiq, my younger brother. Then I'm going back to New York. I might stop by on my way over. I need time to process this. This is a lot to handle."

"Beck, we love you, no matter what. You will make a fine king. You should think about staying for a while." My father speaks from his heart.

"Things are not what they appear here. I'll leave it at that."

Terror shows up in my mum's eyes. "You're not in danger, are you?"

They know about my security company, and I briefed them on my career at MI-6 after I left. "When am I not in danger? It's part of the job." I force a smile. "I'm a trained professional."

"Please be careful." Spoken like a true mum.

"I will. We'll talk later when I've had time to digest all the information." On instinct, I touch my nose and then the screen as I sign off. We've been saying goodbye like this for years.

I solved one mystery while the other mysteries about Mubala floated in the wind.

THIRTY-ONE

Pippa
_____

THE FIVE NUMBERS from the warehouse run through my computer program, generating over one hundred thousand combinations. Once I have the combinations stored, it will be faster to hack into the system and find the correct code. Thank God this is child's play because I can't stop thinking about Beck.

The news of his parents' betrayal cut deep. They better have a damn good explanation for why they never told him about his family lineage.

I wasn't so lucky. I know exactly where I come from. I've never dwelled on the misfortune of being a product of my parents because what good does it do? The scars show up in my lack of trust in people as I stand away from them to avoid getting burned.

There's a knock before Beck opens and peeks around the door. His face is drawn, and his sad eyes are laced with confusion. I recognize the look on his face from looking in the mirror.

"How did it go with your parents?" I turn in my chair as he sits on the bed.

His shoulders slump over. "They admitted to knowing everything but were sworn to secrecy to protect me. The situation is messed up. They were very close to Tadashi and Aafia. This doesn't change how I feel about them. They are wonderful parents. I wish I would have had the chance to know my biological parents."

I want to reach out and hold him to me, taking the sorrow I'm familiar with as my next breath. He and I are alike in many ways, from being loners and traveling outside the circle to our workout regimens. The place where we are worlds apart is how we grew up. He has an incredible family who supports and loves him. I have nothing but foster parents who used me to make money.

"It sounds like you have wonderful parents who care deeply for you. You should feel very fortunate." I bite my lower lip.

His face is etched with pain. "What about you? What about your parents?" he chokes out.

"I was left behind by parents who thought a con was more important than their child. They did time and then disappeared. Yeah, they're real gems. My battles have scars that no one sees, but I won't let it keep me down." I swallow my tears.

"I'm sorry," he whispers.

I need to get out of this loop. "We should work on the fingerprint. I've run the number combinations. If we have both, we can get into the warehouse without any trouble."

His eyes give off a faint glow. "How about I show you how it's done?"

Teaching me to make a print would keep his mind off family drama. We walk down to the kitchen and pull the thumbprints we got from Wafiq.

He puts hot glue on a glass plate, quickly coats the finger-print with Vaseline, and presses it into the glue.

"Pray this works. We need enough of a print to press into the glue," he says, focused on the hardening hot glue.

"I'll lift the print and cover it in favicol, a rubbery material that will give us the print. We have to wait twenty-four hours to peel it out, so we'll have to hit the warehouse tomorrow night." He smiles.

"You're amazing," I mumble.

Too amazing for the likes of me.

His face hardens. "I need to meet with Katoo. There are questions I have that only he can answer. You need to be there when I talk to him to read his reaction."

He scrubs his hand over his face, turns to me, and places his finger under my chin. The heat rolls off his body as my legs squeeze together. The attraction to him is at a whole other level where I submit with a single touch.

My hormones and head are warring with one another. He reaches a space in me I've kept out of reach from anyone else, even Jess. His raw emotions and honesty grab my attention and won't let go.

"I've spent my life living out of sight, a ghost operating in hostile lands, until you brought me your light. From what you've told me, you come from a much harder life than me, yet you refuse to let it dictate how you live. You've given me the courage to step out and let people see me. Although I am kind of hard to miss." He shrugs and smiles. "I waited too long to let Emilia know how I felt." His throat moves as he swallows. "I'm not making that mistake again."

His thumb caresses my cheek, and it's all I can do to not hump him like a dog in heat. He's so much more than me that I shrink in his shadow.

I pull his finger from under my chin and focus on his Adam's Apple. "You're a lot of man to handle."

He laughs. "Says the woman built like a warrior and will go to the ends of the earth to find answers." He tilts his head and frowns. "Is this what your distance is about? You think you're not good enough?"

My throat tightens with the words I want to say. *I won't apologize for who I am or where I come from.* Usually, I'm not easily intimidated, but he has me tied up in knots.

He hugs me to him as I melt into his body. "You're more than good enough for me. You are my queen if you'll let me be your king."

His words rocket through me, spearing the place no one dares to visit. My fingers skim the marks on the side of his face.

"You might call those birthmarks, but I was branded as a child." He waits for my reaction.

"They're sexy as hell." I trace his lips, remembering their taste.

I try to push away from him as his full lips capture mine in a gentle kiss that teases my heart with things to come. His hands encompass my face as my knees buckle, and I grab his arms.

His face is soft and bright. "I have a phone call to make. We'll pick this up later." He walks away, shoulders back and head held high.

What in the fresh hell just happened?

Tears swim in my eyes, but I refuse to let them fall. He called me his queen. In chess, the queen has the most power, even more than the king. Maybe he's right. It's time to come out of the shadows and into the light. Being in the spotlight will be uncomfortable, but everything is in baby steps.

I wipe away the saltwater gathered in my eyes and shake out my hands. I'm drowning in questions I have for myself. Can I live out of the shadows? Can I be the woman he needs me to be? I'm lost in my thoughts when he returns to the kitchen.

"Katoo is coming over, and he doesn't sound too happy about it. I demanded he see us to discuss everything we should know about what's going on. Are you okay?" He stops in front of me and rubs my arms as I hold onto his.

"Yeah, you seem to know how my brain works. I'm constantly thinking about everything at once. Bad habit." I let go of his arms and step back, missing my anchor.

We wait in the living room for Katoo. I sit on the couch as a spectator for this match. Beck won't go easy on him. His emotions are fresh from his conversation with his parents. He folds and unfolds his hands several times before the knock comes on the door.

I open the door, and Katoo stands there with a scowl.

"Good luck. You're going to need it. He wants answers." I pat him on the shoulder and close the door.

Katoo cocks his chin up and moves past me to the living room.

Becks stands up out of respect for his elder. "Please, have a seat."

They're civil toward one another, but that may not last long.

"Thank you." Katoo adjusts his jacket and sits with his hands on his knees.

Beck sits across from him and rests his ankle across his leg. His casual look is deceiving. I take the spectator's seat on the couch.

"I've spoken to my parents. You've known about my past the entire time but lied and kept it to yourself." He leans forward, resting his elbows on his knees. "I want to know why, and I deserve an answer."

Katoo sighs. "Your father and I were close enough to be brothers. We met in primary school when he pushed me in the mud, and I pulled him down with me. Your parents were young when they had you, and he had been crowned. Like they say, life is a bed of roses until you lie on a thorn."

His lips tighten. "His thorn was the leader of the Yagi tribe. They were going after the rights of the diamond and emerald mines and promised that his family's blood would pour. He got you and Aafia a safe passage out of the country. But then they threatened to find you and kill you, just like they did to your uncle. Your father was crowned, lost his older brother, and had a baby boy inside of a month. We had to get you to safety, and Ellen and Albert agreed to take you. Our tribe joined forces with another tribe and defeated the Yagis, but it was a battle that took many years and many lives."

"Why not bring me back when it was safe again?" Beck's words cut through the air.

Katoo holds his head in his hands. "You were older, in school, and doing very well. Tadashi and Aafia thought you might be better off staying in the UK. You would have more opportunities than you would here in Mubala."

Beck shoots up out of his chair. "Everyone made decisions about my life, and no one asked me." He slaps his hands against his chest. "You didn't even tell me where I came from. I never had the chance to get to know them."

He gets closer to Katoo with his hands on his hips and bends down. "And you want me to be your king? What if I refuse?"

He looks up at Beck. "You cannot. This is your destiny.

Your father and mum wanted this for you, and they groomed you for it. Albert and Ellen want this, too."

Katoo gives the final blow as Beck jerks back. Katoo stands up.

Beck looks at me sitting on the couch. "We have everything we need to hit the warehouse tomorrow night. I'll need your help and Jobi's. Thank you for coming by," he says tersely.

The door shuts with a soft click after Katoo leaves.

I don't say a word as I let Beck get his bearings.

"I love when people play God with innocent lives." He looks at me with eyes wide open. His words are heavy, and there's a change in the air. "Now, everyone will play by my rules since I'm the king."

THIRTY-TWO

Beck
_____

"Katoo is not the enemy. He's on your side," Pippa says in a low voice.

"I'm surrounded by liars and secrets." I bite out my words. I close my eyes and rub my forehead. "I'm sorry. I've had a rough day."

She smiles. "Rough might be an understatement. Why don't you take your mind off things for a while? I have some hacking to do." She rubs her hands together. "I also need to get in touch with Peter and see if he's come up with anything to break the encryption."

I pull her to me and rub her arms. Goosebumps form under my fingertips. The energy between us is stronger than ever, and her body gives her away.

"No, you can't use me as a distraction. We need to keep our heads screwed on straight. Okay, that might not be the best choice of words." She laughs.

I wiggle my brows. "I always keep my head on straight." I kiss her nose. "I'm going to drive to the mine and see what's happening there without Wafiq. The workers may talk to me without him around."

My day has already gone to shit, what's one more thing to add to it. Grabbing the keys to the car, I head for the door. The day is overcast, which I've learned means one of two things. The clouds will blow over, or we'll get a deluge of rain. Either way, I'm protected from the elements.

I drive out of town, away from where I think my problems are, but they started long ago. The memories of my childhood make sense. I've been here before, and I remember the feeling of being in the house with my parents.

The house was filled with love, fun, and laughter. I wish I could remember their faces smiling at me. The loss grips me in my chest, which is odd for people I don't know.

I traveled down the road, getting lost in trying to remember everything about my time here as a child. Small drops of rain hit the car, making a pinging sound on the roof.

As the rain gets heavier, coming down in sheets, rivers of water form on either side of the road as the barren earth can't absorb it. The windshield wipers can't keep up, and everything is a blur. Water on the road is swift and rising.

Up ahead, I see the red blinking lights of a truck I can barely make out on the side of the road. I pull in behind it as four men stand next to the truck. The rain has soaked through their clothes, but they seem unfazed, standing up to their ankles in water.

I step out of my car in rushing water up to mid-shin and wade toward them. My clothes cling to me within minutes as the torrential rain covers me. The front of their truck has gone off the road and is stuck in a ditch. With a broken axle, this truck isn't going anywhere.

The men look at me with confusion. Their clothes are holey and frayed. The SIG logo on their shirts is barely visible. They look at each other, turn to me, and begin to kneel.

"Stop!" I shout out over the crashing rain.

They are bent at the knee, frozen, waiting for further instructions.

"You don't need to kneel. I'm going in that direction, and I can give you a ride." I need to do a better job of accepting the role of king, but I don't need everyone kneeling every time they see me.

They shake their heads and walk down the road in the direction their truck is facing. I run to catch up with them as the rain pelts my face like needles.

"I'm going to the mines, anyway. Please, let me give you a ride." I need to get information on what's going on because these are not the workers I saw at the mine I visited with Wafiq. Those men were in clean uniforms and looked well-fed.

They speak to each other in a foreign language, and their bodies are stiff. One of them speaks in broken English. "Yes, we go with you. You are special for helping us."

Sopping from head to toe, we pile into the car. They look at me with wide eyes but don't utter a word. The storm is letting up, giving me more visibility.

"One of you will need to tell me which road I need to take."

The one who spoke sits next to me in the front seat and nods. He guides me through the hills and beyond the mines I've been to with Wafiq. I'm interested in where he's taking me.

We round the corner as the earth gapes open with a raging river at the bottom. Men and children line the banks with sifting trays. The men climb out of the back seat and shuffle down the bank.

The river rolls by, but the workers stand frozen, staring up at me. I grab the arm of the man next to me.

"What's going on here?" I can barely get the words out because I dread the answer.

"We look for diamonds, sometimes emeralds." He frowns like I should know this.

"I've never been here before. Wafiq took me to the mines over there." I point in some random direction.

"That's what he wants you to see." He laughs.

My head whips in his direction. "What do you mean?"

"A lot of the mining happens here. We get two kwachas for each diamond we find, depending on the size. Some families barely have enough for food each week." That's just over one dollar for every diamond they find. No wonder they don't have enough to eat.

"And what about the children? Shouldn't they be in school?" I stutter.

"They need to work to feed their families." He shrugs.

"Where is everyone from?"

"Everywhere. Some of us are from the Congo over the border." His gaze darts toward the workers on the bank.

"Where do you live?"

He blinks several times and shakes out his hands. "On the other side of the ridge, out of sight. But we know who you are. You are going to be our new king." He smiles.

"Yes, and this new king is about to make some changes." I reach out my hand, and he looks down at it before shaking it. "Thank you for answering my questions. You'll be hearing from me again."

I walk back to the Range Rover, which is out of its element in this environment, even covered in mud. Wafiq needs to explain why these workers are in this condition and at wages that can't feed their families. Thank God the ride back is long enough to cool me down. I can add another liar to my endless list.

My blood boils thinking about the living conditions of the workers behind the ridge. There are children without a childhood or education and parents who can't provide food for their families. I feel sick thinking about how big the profit margin is for a gem industry that's so lucrative.

The voice command in the car connects with the person I need to see. "I hope you're home, brother, because I'm coming over. We need to have a chat."

He gives me a one-word answer, and I click off.

I slam the car into park in front of Wafiq's house and storm up the stairs in twos. The door opens before I knock.

"How nice of you to call first," he sneers, looking me up and down. "What did you decide to do, go for a swim?" The niceties are gone for both of us.

"Do you want to tell me about the workers beyond the ridge?" My fingers grip my hips to keep from taking a swing at him.

He looks down and crosses his arms. "What workers beyond the ridge?" I stalk over to him and get in his face. His arms fall at his sides.

My teeth grit together. "The workers who stand in water up to their knees, sifting for a diamond that may get them two kwachas for their trouble. Most can't feed their families. What kind of monster are you?" The words leave my mouth before I think about it, but I don't regret saying them.

He doesn't back down. "So now I'm the monster. What would you know about it? You come waltzing in to do what? Save us all? You're going to make everything better?" He backs away from me, waving his arms in the air.

"You weren't here all these years to understand how this city works. We have an image to maintain and still get the work done. Those workers are our meal ticket. It's always been this way, but you wouldn't know that. The circumstances will not change, no matter what you do. This is engrained from generation to generation." His neck strains.

"They are our people. How can you treat them like this?" I bellow enough to get Zahara to come out of hiding.

"They are not our people. They come here from all over, looking for work, and we give it to them, offering them a place to live on the outskirts of town."

Zahara floats in to stand by her man with her chin held high. I ignore her and focus on Wafiq.

My head shakes. "No. This is not the way it needs to be. You're keeping them as slaves."

"They can leave anytime they want. No one keeps them here against their will," he shouts.

"Those people can't leave because they don't have money to go anywhere," I yell.

Wafiq smiles as it takes everything I have not to punch him square in the face.

My fight-or-flight instincts kick in, and I decide to take flight. I shove him out of the way.

"This isn't over," I say over my shoulder.

He takes rapid breaths. "It's more over than you think, my brother."

Those are the last words I hear as I storm out of his obnoxious house. If I am to be king, then things are going to change, come hell or high water, if he doesn't try to kill me again.

THIRTY-THREE

Beck

My feet can't carry me out the door fast enough. The tires squeal, peeling out of the driveway and into the street, missing a bus by millimeters.

Blind fury takes over, and I can't wait to get home. *Home?* I've found security and peace in my parents' house, even if it's empty of their spirit. How did they spawn someone like Wafiq, who is heartless with his people?

I've reached my limit with this situation, but it makes me want to dig deeper to find the truth. It's not bad enough that these people work hard for a living, but they do it under less than adequate circumstances. I grew up wanting for nothing, but seeing the workers today up to their knees in water and mud was like a punch in my gut. My reign as king has a new top priority.

I pull into the driveway and sit with the motor running, trying to calm myself down. My head rests back on the seat, and I close my eyes. I don't know how long I sat here until Pippa opened the door.

"When I said take your mind off things, I didn't mean do

a mud race in your car." She looks at the car with a smirk and reaches in to turn off the ignition.

I keep my eyes closed and listen to the slight twang in her voice. A smile forms on my lips without thought. She can do that to me, bringing me back to center, along with a host of other things my body and soul crave.

"You know, I'm going to have to take this car back to the States with me." I look over at her.

She hangs on the window with her hip cocked to the side. "Why is that?"

"It smells like you and holds my most important memory." I smile.

"You know what else it holds? The stink of wet leather and mud." She pinches her nose.

She deflects from what I want her to see, that she's important to me. I wasn't kidding about taking the car with us. *Is there an us?*

"Why don't you come inside, and we can peel you out of those wet clothes?" She wiggles her brows.

"Promise? I might need you to dry me off, too. Maybe a body massage with some coconut oil."

She shakes her head and laughs. This is what I need. I need the banter with her and her cute smile with the one crooked tooth. "You're pushing it today. I see someone is confident."

I get out of the car and pull her to me as we touch from chest to hip. I whisper, "I didn't get this far without being confident and knowing what I want. The king has arrived."

She shivers. I hold her hand as we walk into the house. I need to touch her and make our connection.

The door closes behind us, and I pull her into me, tucking her in my arms. Home is not in this house. Home is wherever she is. I keep circling back to her, seeking her out like a beacon in a fog. Each time I reach for her, she is there without question. The time has come to let go and hold on at the same time.

"I think Sabeen should live here. She seemed to have a happy childhood here, and it brings her back to the old neighborhood. The people love her. She will make an excellent queen. Maybe the first for this city and tribe."

Pippa's body stiffens. "I thought I was the queen. What about Wafiq being king?"

"Wafiq and I have a huge difference of opinion on the things that matter. He's no longer my choice for such an important position." I bend down to kiss up her neck and gently bite her earlobe. "You're a different kind of queen. A queen who needs to be worshipped from head to toe. This king is about to show his gratitude."

She hums as her body loosens. "Are you sure you're ready for every part of me?" She doesn't push for more answers than I'm willing to give.

My fingers trace her face, knowing what she means. "Emilia was a free spirit and a lot like you, but she was always on the job. I admired that quality at the time. You remind me there is more to life that needs to be lived, nurtured, and enjoyed. You're fierce, compassionate, and loyal. And Taylor was my 'in the meantime.' We weren't destined to be together forever."

Her face softens. "What you're trying to say is you want to give the craziness of us a serious try?"

"Yes, I would like to try, preferably naked."

Our laughter echoes off the walls in the foyer. There is a flash of memory of laughter, where hide-and-seek wasn't at my expense. The warmth feels familiar.

My mouth devours hers as our hands grab each other's clothes. She strips off the wet clothes clinging to my skin, unleashing the beast who points in the direction he wants to go in.

She backs away as I stalk her like a panther, and her breath grows rapid. Without a word, I lead us to the living room. Her knees hit the carpet as she peers up at me with wonder. Questions swim in her eyes about whether she's ready for this kind of leap. I won't be another man who uses her for his own gain. I want us to be equal in our journey together.

I slip into the warmth of her mouth, holding back from taking what I want. I let her give me what she offers. My eyes close as I focus on the place where we meet. She's an expert and knows exactly what I like based on instinct. There's roughness in her approach, just the way I like it.

Before I hit my maximum restraint, I pull her up, with her red swollen lips and a blush to her cheeks. "That's not where I want this to end. Get on the couch and show yourself to me." I slap her ass as she walks away. She doesn't flinch, giving me ideas for later.

Her red hair fans out around her head, and her legs are spread with no hint of embarrassment. I look down and start laughing. She has shaved her hair between her legs in the shape of a red arrow.

"Oh, love, I know exactly where to go. There's no need for arrows, my little vanilla Pip."

"Vanilla? Who said anything about vanilla, Chocolate Thunder? I had to make sure. I understand men are visual creatures." She wiggles her hips on the couch.

I bite my lower lip before licking her sex, the sweetest tasting fruit I've ever had, eating to my heart's content. She writhes as my hands grip her hips to keep her in place. She comes for me several times, like a rock star for a man's ego. I crawl up her body and poke her entrance with my joystick. I smile.

"Why are you smiling?"

"In my head, I just called my…" I look down between us, "a joystick." We laugh as I glimpse the most minute shift in her eyes as her brow wrinkles.

"Is there any chance you have condoms nearby?" I say.

"It's okay. I'm clean and on the pill."

I shake my head. "I won't ever take a chance like that with you. We need to be fully on board with each other before we take the next steps. We need baby steps and not the humankind… just yet."

Her breath hitches. "My purse is in the foyer, center pocket."

As I come around the end of the couch, her legs close, and she stares at the ceiling. I hesitate, questioning if we should continue. She looks down and sees me, smiles, and opens her legs.

"Would you hurry up? That anaconda needs some lovin'." She giggles.

A snap of energy pulls us together as my hands caress her body. The pads of my fingers light up her skin as she gets goose bumps. She's wetter with every touch. I play with her nipples, taunting her. I want to savor every moment. Rolling on the condom, I slide into her tightness, stopping to gaze at her, watching her eyes close as I stretch her, and she takes me, all of me, just the way I am.

We make love for the rest of the evening, feeding each other grapes, chicken, and other finger foods to keep up our strength. None of my relationships have ever been like this, so easy, freeing, and fun, yet intense.

She's like a precious bird you want to put in a cage but

won't because you can't wait to see her fly. I can't take my eyes away from her when she's in flight.

Every part of her body fits with mine. She loves it a little rough and a bit naughty. I don't have to hold back, and I have been holding back for years. My inner dominant unleashes and seems at one with her zest for life as she holds on to me and asks for more.

I live for her every sigh, moan, and scream. She doesn't let me keep anything from her, embracing my raw energy. We're in sync, which is a good thing because tomorrow night may change everything.

THIRTY-FOUR

Pippa

HE IS the most spectacular lover I've ever had in my life. If sex were an Olympic event, he would score a ten and win gold for form, stamina, and most big Os. My lady parts are sore, which is a first for me. He can be wickedly rough or smooth like butter, and butter is my new addiction. He makes love to me in all the right places, as if he knows my body's secrets.

A piece of me worries he won't need me after we complete this mission. He will have gotten what he wanted and move on even though he talks about more.

Old abuses with people who used me to get what they wanted and disposed of me run deep. But I've got to keep my eye on the prize, getting my next assignment with Neil. My appetite for adventure has increased since being on this mission with Beck. I want more excitement, intrigue, and challenges.

However, being with Beck is challenging in itself. If I keep my mind focused on the moving pieces of this case, I won't have time to think about the fallout with Beck.

I still have no word from Peter on a break with decoding

the encryption. Once I have that, I can get into Wafiq's mainframe and snoop around, my second favorite thing to do on this trip. We could break this mission wide open depending on what we find tonight, paired with getting into the mainframe.

Beck opens the door. "What are you doing up here?"

I'm perched on the bench by the triangle window overlooking the city, watching the sun go down. "Do you think there's anything odd about this city? It seems too perfect, too clean, too everything."

He picks me up with little effort, spins me around, and plops me on his lap. I have a fit of giggles as he nuzzles his nose into my hair.

"The scent of vanilla, you're anything but." The low rumble of his laugh reminds me of my V-rod Harley Davidson. My ride is satisfyingly fast, handles like a champ, and the vibration from the tailpipes speaks to my need for adventure.

"You should talk. Kink Master." He has mastered my body like a finely tuned violin.

"I only want to get kinky with you. By the way, that's Master Kink, my queen."

He holds me to him and rocks me. We don't say a word. These are the moments that center me and calm down my internal engine, which is constantly going. I have a hard time shutting it down, and my adrenaline is full steam ahead in anticipation of tonight.

"I think there are many odd things about this city, and we're going to uncover some of them. You ready to hit the warehouse?" he asks.

"I keep going over all the possibilities of what we might find. What is he hiding in there?"

"We're about to find out. Let's get dinner and head out."
He stands me up and takes my hand.

I was never much of a hand-holder until he came along,
grabbing his hand at every opportunity. The connection is an
intimacy I never thought about until I found someone who
wanted to hold my hand.

Katoo and Jobi are back on the job, watching our six. I've
picked up some lingo along the way, and I use it every chance
I get.

We dress to blend in with the night, this time armed with
night-vision goggles. Beck peels the favicol off the fingerprint, hoping we can use it to gain access to the warehouse.
When we get closer to the keypad, my computer will generate
the code.

Everyone gets into their vehicles, driving down empty
streets at two in the morning. The air is heavy and thick,
almost foreboding, giving the early morning an eerie vibe.

Beck hasn't said a word. His head swivels, identifying
anything out of place in the surrounding areas. His fingers
grip and release the steering wheel intermittently.

We pull up behind the warehouse, and he cuts the engine
and lights. We need a way to get out fast. Katoo and Jobi
report that they are all clear in their areas.

He turns his body toward me. "I get the sense we don't
have a lot of time in there. Take as many photos as you can of
everything, and then we'll analyze them later. Ready?"

"Let's do this." Excitement runs through my veins like a
roller coaster on the downslope.

I lay my laptop on the ground and start the program using
the numbers we discovered from our last recon. Five numbers
pop up: one, zero, zero, three, eight. I show the screen to
Beck, and he stares at it a beat too long as I watch him
swallow.

"What's wrong?" We don't have time to waste.

"Do you find it strange that the combination is the zip code for my security company?" The screen makes his face glow.

"Honestly, so far, everything's been strange. Let's get in there and see what's up." I close the laptop and shove it in my backpack. "I find it odd that he didn't use a hand scanner. It's more secure."

"I don't think he expected anyone to break into his warehouse in the middle of Zambia."

Beck places the rubber fingerprint on his thumb and takes a deep breath. He presses his thumb on the scanner, and there's a beep that it's been accepted. He punches the code into the keypad, and the door clicks open.

The warehouse is so dark you can't see your hand in front of your face. Our night-vision goggles are useless. They need some ambient light to work. The air is chilly enough to refrigerate meat.

We use the flashlights on our cellphones to light up the area and split up to search. The room is massive, with rows of enormous machines humming away. In my research, I came across these machines. They create diamonds under extreme pressure. Wafiq coded each machine with a number and a country listed with several cities. I take photos of each one.

"Pippa, look at this."

Beck calls out from the other end of the warehouse. His light shines down on something.

"What is it?"

On the floor, stacked two high, are armored boxes with the names of countries. They are sealed at the edges and locked with a highly secure padlock. I take photos of each box and the padlock.

"I'm guessing they filled these with lab-created

diamonds, but why? They make and house these types of diamonds in another location in the city."

Beck turns to me and frowns.

I point my thumb behind me. "These machines create diamonds. Why are they separate from the other warehouse, and where are these crates going?"

We probably have minutes left as we shine our flashlights around the warehouse, trying to get a sense of what's going on. Out of the corner of my eye, my beam of light picks up something glittering on the floor. I pick them up and stuff them in my pocket.

Katoo breaks in on the comm. "You have incoming. Several unmarked cars headed this way in a hurry. Not sure you have time to get out."

Beck replies, "You and Jobi need to get out now. Stay on the line in case we need you."

"Roger that, Pippa."

Smart-ass.

"We need to get to the breaker box so they can't get to the lights. We'll have more cover in the dark." Beck is the calm at the center of the impending storm.

"Based on what I saw on the roof, the cables come through at the other end. The breaker should be there."

Beck rips open the box and trips the breakers. He doesn't want to leave any evidence of criminal intent. His flashlight follows the wires out of the box and up the wall to a catwalk along the ceiling of the warehouse.

"We need to get you up there. Did you bring your climbing equipment?"

I argue with him. "Of course, but I can hold my own down here."

He grabs me by the shoulders. "I'm not worried about you

holding your own. I'll cover the bottom. You are on lookout from above. Got it?"

"Yes, sir."

"Don't say that. It does things to me."

My heart skips a beat as I shine the light on the catwalk so he can throw the grappling hook. He catches the railing in one throw. I grab the rope and scale the wall with his help. Another rope hangs over the side, and I tie it to the railing.

I angle my flashlight at the beams in the ceiling and heave the grappling hook toward the middle one, hooking it. A tug on the rope tells me it's secure.

Beck stands over by the breaker box, flashing his phone so I know where he is, and then he goes dark. The minute they figure out there's no light, they'll head for it, which is exactly what we want.

The door clicks open, and they flip the switch for the lights. Four flashlights switch on as they fan out to search for the breaker box. The guard coming toward the box goes a couple of rounds with Beck before he gets knocked out. I watch as the light from the guard's cell phone disappears.

From up here, it looks like some sort of video game with bouncing lights. Beck can see the lights, too. In the middle of the warehouse, a thud comes from Beck as he knocks out another guard, but the two that are left also hear it.

Their lights split up and go around the outside of the machines to get to Beck from both sides. I untie my rope from the catwalk, getting ready for action. One flashlight goes off as the guard tries a sneak attack. This is Beck they're dealing with. They have no clue he's a highly trained agent.

The last guard is behind him with his flashlight on as I swing down. My flashlight shines in his eyes. Move over, P!nk, there's a new highflyer in town. Her flying is just a lot prettier than mine.

"Hit the deck!" I yell to Beck as I raise my legs over him. He lies flat as I hit the last guard in the chest, and he flies into the wall, knocking him out.

"Shine your light on him. I want to see who we're dealing with." Beck breathes heavily.

The guard is wearing a black ski mask. Beck grips the bottom and pulls it off. The guard is of Asian descent, indicating the Chinese are in this game.

"Just as I thought." He grabs my hand, and we make a run for the door.

He stops at the door and scans the area. I peek around him and see Wafiq sitting in his Range Rover with the window down. He keeps looking at his watch, waiting for the guards to come out. He speaks into his watch and waits for a response. When he hears nothing back, he starts the car and peels out of the gravel driveway.

We round the corner to find four flat tires on the Jeep Wrangler. Beck presses his comm.

"Katoo, you still there?"

"Yes."

"I need you to get rid of our ride. Four flats. Strip it with nothing left and burn it. We're headed south, following the streets with no lights or cameras. Jobi, we need a ride."

"Got it," Katoo says.

"I'll find you," Jobi responds.

We make our way through the dark streets. Without light, the cameras can't detect us. Headlights come up from behind us as we duck into a stairwell.

"It's me. I'm behind you. Jump in."

Jobi stops long enough for us to hop in and races toward the house. Beck is quiet, staring out the window.

"What's going on?" I ask.

"We'll talk when we get home." He shifts his eyes in Jobi's direction.

He can't possibly think that Jobi tipped off the guards. I refuse to believe he had anything to do with tonight's siege, but the proof will be in the evidence.

Jobi drops us off, and Beck nods. We get inside, and I strip off my clothes, damp with sweat from a night on full throttle. As I empty my pockets, I come across what I picked up in the warehouse. I open my hand to show Beck the two large lab-created diamonds. They must be at least two carats each.

"Where did you get those?"

"They were lying on the ground. Someone must have dropped them. They didn't make it into the armored boxes. Luck is on our side for once."

He picks one up and holds it to the light. "What makes these different?"

"I don't know, but we're going to have to come clean with Sabeen. We need her help."

Beck nods. "She's not the only one we will need help from."

THIRTY-FIVE

Beck

THOSE GUARDS WERE HIGHLY TRAINED. My knowledge of karate and Krav Maga allowed me to hold my own against them. They were expecting an easy takedown. Surprise. I've never been easy.

The guards were more than likely Chinese. Wafiq is up to his neck in nasty shit if he's in with the Chinese. There still may be a way to get him out, but first, we need to find out about the diamonds and Jobi.

We sleep in after a long night, and my midday wake-up call for Pippa makes me feel better already. She's always willing and able to accept my foreplay. I play with her nipples and caress her body, warming her up. She bumps her butt into me, and I have my cue. I sheathe myself and push into her from behind, gripping her hips for leverage. Her moans strengthen my libido as she moves with me. Heat radiates off her in waves. Those waves can take me under without a fight.

"In case I haven't told you, you were frigging amazing last night. You came in like a wrecking ball." I'm holding on, waiting for her to come.

"No, not Miley, P!nk. I just needed a sequined bodysuit. If the lights were on, I would have looked spectacular," she says through sighs of satisfaction.

"You have enough ink; you don't need a bodysuit. The visual of you swinging naked across anything makes me crazy."

I pumped harder into her. The friction and the slice of pleasure make her detonate. The stars have never been brighter. I roar with ecstasy as we come together, sticky with sweet sweat.

Best sex ever. Everything with her feels different and fresh, but I can't pinpoint why. But this time, I don't want to question it; I want to enjoy it. She lies with her head on my shoulder.

"Jobi didn't tip anyone off," she mumbles.

Her mind doesn't stop even during sex. I don't know if I should be offended or not. "Do you think this is the time to bring up another man's name?"

She sits up. "Yes, I do because I know you think he tipped them off, and it's been on my mind. I'm going to run a systems check. I think when we went in there, it tripped an alarm somewhere. Probably in Wafiq's bedroom." She rolls her eyes.

Someone pounds on the front door, and Pippa jumps up.

"I'll get it."

She slips out of bed, taking her heat with her, and pulls on my T-shirt that hangs to her knees.

"You look like a rock star in my T-shirt. Let me get dressed, and I'll follow you down. I don't want anyone to get any ideas." I haven't been this possessive of a woman since... ever. Selfishly, I want to capture her strength and zest for life, infusing it into my soul.

"I won't seem like a rock star to whoever is on the other side of the door after I slam them over the head with a guitar for coming here so early."

Wafiq yells. "Open this door!"

Pippa opens the door to a puffed-up Wafiq and the commissioner of police, who stands behind him with a pained expression.

"Wafiq, please come in. We were getting ready to have brunch." I wave my arm toward the kitchen.

"I'm not here to eat. Where were you last night?" he bellows.

I look at Pippa, and she looks at me. Acting is part of the job. You're only as good as your last undercover lie.

"We were here at home. Why? Where were you?" Pippa crosses her arms and frowns.

He's startled by her response. "I'm asking the questions here."

I'm annoyed. "What's your concern? Did something happen?"

"You know exactly what happened. You broke into my warehouse, snooping around. My men saw you and her." He points his finger at Pippa with a scowl on his face.

"What you're saying is they could pick me out in a lineup and can describe exactly what I was wearing last night." With each word, I step closer to Wafiq. The commissioner shrinks and hasn't said a word. "Did you dust for fingerprints? You and the commissioner should probably start there."

He turns to the commissioner. "Show them what we found."

The commissioner moves his hands from behind his back and reveals the grappling hook and rope we left at the warehouse.

Pippa shrugs. "And?"

Wafiq turns to her. "I'm sure if we searched this house right now, we would find the other equipment that goes with this hook and rope." He smiles smugly.

Pippa pushes me out of the way. "I'm sure that you can't do that. According to your bylaws, the king's house is sacred ground. Therefore, you would have to have not only his consent but the consent of the commissioner." She looks over at the commissioner as beads of sweat form on his forehead. "But he hasn't said a word."

Wafiq shows his teeth with fists at his sides. "He's not king yet. You white bitches are all the same—" Before he gets out another word, I coldcock him. Pippa doesn't move as Wafiq falls to the floor, holding his jaw. The commissioner jumps back.

I grab Wafiq by the lapels of his jacket and bring us nose to nose. "Don't you ever speak to her like that again because I can't guarantee I won't beat the shit out of you, even if you are my brother. You're going to apologize and get your sorry ass out of my sight."

Wafiq gets up, stumbles while mumbling his apology, and leaves with the commissioner in tow.

Pippa closes the door behind them. "That went well. Nice cross hook, but I had it under control. I've been dealing with guys like him my entire life."

I pull her into a hug. "Not on my watch. I won't allow anyone to disrespect you. By the way, how do you know about the bylaws?"

"I did a lot of reading while you were sick. Thought I could make good use of the time." She smiles.

Every time I turn around, this woman amazes me. I hold her face as she puts her hands over mine. No one has ever looked out for me the way she has in the last couple of weeks.

"We need to get in touch with Sabeen before Wafiq tries

to turn her against us. I don't think she knows what's going on. I also think we should take a bubble bath."

I smile. "Why is that?"

"You have some spots that need massaging." She curls into my chest.

Her green eyes pull me in. "I have an important phone call to make. Enjoy your bubble bath, and then we'll talk to Sabeen." I kiss her on the nose, our new thing.

We part ways as she goes to the master bathroom, and I go to the triangle room on the top floor of the house. There's privacy, and it has the best reception. I didn't want to have to do this, but I have no choice, given what we've learned about Wafiq and the Chinese.

If I know my team, they're in early this morning, and this call won't make their day. I call Sean's private line through Vibe.

"Hey, King, what's up?" Sean is way too perky.

"You've already changed my code name? You're chipper this morning." I dread his response because I know what's coming.

"That's what happens when you fall in love with the woman of your dreams twice." He laughs.

"We need a conference call with the alpha team." The three partners, me, Sean, and Peter, along with Mac, Dean, and Declan, are referred to as the alpha team, but Mac, Dean, and Declan don't know it.

"We have a new member, Campbell, Mac's other brother. I'll get them on the line."

Mac won't be happy. He has a new baby girl, Dalia. The man is way overprotective and won't leave her side.

Sean cuts back in, "We're all here. Tell us what's going on."

Everyone's face pops up on my screen. Given the six-hour time difference, most of them are at the office, working out, or getting breakfast.

"I need the team down here. We hit the warehouse last night, and the Chinese showed up. Ring any bells? There are armored boxes with the names of countries on them, and I want to see where they go. We need a full tactical team with all the fireworks. Peter, I know you're working on the encryption, but maybe you can work from here. Mac, I apologize, but we need your expertise on the logistics. Campbell, welcome aboard. Nothing like hitting the ground running."

Campbell nods at the greeting.

Mac chimes in, "Thank God. I need a break. I love my daughter to the moon and back, but I'm overdue to kick someone's ass. Mara can get her sisters and Mama to help. When are we wheels up?"

This gets a laugh from everyone. "I need you here ASAP. You're taking the private jet. Load it up with everything you can get your hands on. Not sure what we're up against, but my brother is in with the wrong people. You'll be coming in at night. I don't want anyone to know you're here just yet."

"Family member gone astray? I can relate. Hang in there. He may not be in as deep as you think. We might be able to get him out," Dean says. He has issues with his father, head of the ASIS in Australia.

There's a long pause. Dean moves closer to his camera. "What's it like to be king? Do you have a harem? I know how you like your threesomes." He wiggles his brows.

Out of the corner of the screen, a female hand hits him on his shoulder, and he cowers away from her and laughs. Leigha, his photographer girlfriend, has a long road ahead of her with his smart mouth and dirty mind.

I give him one of my shit-eating grins as I angle my face closer to the camera on my phone. "Well, now, wouldn't you like to know? A king never gives away his secrets. See you tomorrow, boys."

As I click off, I hear Dean protest in the background. He's always good for a laugh, which is what I need right about now. Even with the talent on my team, we'll have our hands full trying to get a handle on the situation.

THIRTY-SIX

Pippa

No one has ever stood up for me the way he has. I've always had to fend for myself. The feeling of security with him is something new and unfamiliar.

I relax in the bubbles up to my neck. The warm water surrounds me, reminding me of Beck, who has had my back since I arrived here despite not wanting me here in the beginning. I can overlook that because he has more than made up for it.

Our roles have changed. We started by me taking care of him, but he takes care of me equally. If I had to guess, I would say he called in the team for backup. I can't blame him, but this puts me on the back burner again. He'll want me out of the way so the team can handle everything. I'll be relegated to a laptop somewhere to oversee the technical logistics.

Beck enters the bathroom without knocking. I slide down with the bubbles up to my chin.

He sits on the edge of the tub. "You look relaxed in there." His sigh is heavy as if he carries the weight of the world on his shoulders. Staring down at his fingers, he rubs them together.

I dip my mouth underwater, hoping to catch some bubbles on my upper lip. "What's wrong?"

He looks up and gives me half a smile, not the reaction I was hoping for. The deep rumble of his laugh goes straight to my sex. He wipes the bubbles from my face.

"I called in the team. We don't know how big this is or if it involves Deep 8. If Deep 8 is here, do they know we're here? They might want revenge of epic proportions after what happened in Afghanistan." He goes back to rubbing his fingers.

In Afghanistan, his team succeeded in getting everyone out alive but failed to take Isaad, the ringleader, in for interrogation. They also blew Deep 8's shit up, leveling it. The mines they coveted so much are under top security. Yeah, they might want revenge.

I sit up and hold his hands in mine. "Is that fear I see, Beck McKenzie? You're one of the bravest men I know."

"'The brave man is not he who does not feel afraid, but he who conquers that fear.' That's a Nelson Mandela quote. This brave man must conquer the fear of losing someone close to him again. I haven't been able to shake the fear since I lost Emilia. Fear sits like a monkey on my back. The older I get, the worse it gets. I'm starting to look at life like I have a future."

His shoulders droop. "The men on my team have other people who rely on them. Mac and Mara just had a baby. What if something happens to him out here?"

I stand up and step out of the tub as he offers me his hand. My skin is red from the heat of the water, which isn't hard to do, considering I'm white as a ghost except for my ink. I pull him to me and cradle his head to my chest. His large hands grab my backside, and there is nothing sexual about it.

"'Inaction breeds doubt and fear. Action breeds confidence and courage. If you want to conquer fear, do not sit at home and think about it. Go out and get busy.' That's a quote from Dale Carnegie. You can't control who lives and who dies. Your men do what they do because it runs in their blood, like gasoline in a car. They have a calling, a need to help others and stamp out evil. Don't get caught up in playing the role of God. It's a big job. The people in your life played God, and look how that turned out."

I push back from him, hold his face in my hands, and run my fingers along his scars. "We need to keep moving forward and get Sabeen to look at those diamonds. Something is not right." I kiss his nose like he kissed mine.

The light in his eyes shines for a blink. "My mum used to kiss my nose when I was a little boy before I left for school."

"Your mom sounds wonderful. You may not have known your biological mother, but I'm willing to bet your mother and father are both here with us now, watching over you. They want you to find out what's going on."

"I hope you're right. I'll take all the help I can get. You get dressed, and I'll call Sabeen." He slaps my butt before he leaves. "Damn, that's a firm ass."

"I hope you didn't hurt your hand," I say over my shoulder.

My outfit, if you want to call it that, includes one of his black T-shirts, tied at the waist, Doc Martens, and a pair of orange cut-off shorts. I pull my hair into a messy bun on top of my head and meet him downstairs.

He stands on the far side of the living room, staring out the window.

"Hey."

He turns around with his hands on his hips. "How do you expect us to get out the door when you look that friggin' sexy?"

My hand drags along the back of the couch. "If you're a good boy, you'll get something special later."

"And if you're a good girl, I'll still spank that fine ass of yours."

I wrap my arms around his neck. "This is going to turn out fine. We have to get to the heart of what's going on, and once we do, your instincts will kick in, and the team will be with you one hundred percent. Feel the fear and do it, anyway."

Our lips meet, and we kiss deeply and honestly with raw energy that strips us bare. For the first time, I feel like we're in this together. He accepts me as part of the team.

"Thank God you're on my side. I like having the strongest warriors on my team. Let's go see what Sabeen can tell us about these rocks."

When he says things like that, it's like a shot of tequila to my soul. It goes down smoothly and finishes with a bite that grabs your attention. Maybe he'll have me as part of his team after all.

Beck drives and holds my hand for the entire ride to Sabeen's lab. He never lets go until we get to our destination. I hope he always hangs on to me.

One of Sabeen's labs connects to the warehouse that creates the diamonds. We're buzzed up as we step into a warehouse almost exactly like Wafiq's on the other side of town. Sabeen waves to us as we climb the stairs to her office.

She drops what she's doing and gives each of us a hug. "What brings you two out to my lab today?" She's smiling and happy to see us.

Beck takes the lead. "Did Wafiq tell you about the break-in at his warehouse last night?"

"No, he said nothing to me about it. He's been distant lately. Something is going on, but he won't talk about it." She twirls a pen on her desk.

Beck looks at me as if to say, "Here goes nothing."

"Can you look at these diamonds for me? I don't know what I'm looking at or what I'm looking for. It's a good thing I'm related to an expert." He gives her his big brother smile.

She takes the diamonds from him and puts them under the magnifier. "Not a problem. Where did you get them?"

I speak up. "We found them." I shrug at Beck while she's looking at them through a high-powered lens.

"First off, these are lab-created diamonds." Her body goes still while her hand turns the diamond in the forceps.

"There appears to be something in these I've never seen before. It appears to be a silk thread, almost transparent. Here, take a look."

She moves to the side so Beck can look. After a few seconds, he says, "I have no idea what I'm looking at. Pippa, what do you think?"

I peer through the lens and can't believe what I'm seeing. Turning the diamond, I follow the threads. The configuration is correct for its purpose, but I didn't know this existed.

"What is it?" Beck asks.

"On the dark web, they discuss this technology, but no one has come up with a way to do it until now. This diamond holds an invisible chip that can be activated to grab digital information. Take another look and watch the pattern of the threads."

Beck and Sabeen each look at the gem again and nod their heads.

"How is this possible?" I ask.

"It depends on what you put on the seed plate of tungsten. We make these diamonds under HPHT conditions, so interrupting the process would be difficult. I'm not familiar with this technology." Sabeen looks at us with suspicion. "Lab-created diamonds are atomically identical to mined diamonds and can be passed off as the real thing if you don't know what to look for."

"You lost me at HPHT." Beck rubs his forehead.

"High pressure- high heat," I mumble, lost in my thoughts. "Lab-created diamonds take about two weeks to make and are cost-effective, depending on the equipment."

As I look across the warehouse, I realize the machines we saw in Wafiq's warehouse are much different. Sabeen's machines are orbs, whereas Wafiq's are cubes.

"What if Wafiq is making diamonds with an invisible chip in it that can scrape finances or other information from a computer? If you think about it, women and men wear their jewelry all the time. It's the perfect way to extract information you can use."

"Sometimes, the way your mind works is frightening. I'm glad you decided to wear the white hat." Beck's lips tug into a smile.

Sabeen crosses her arms. "Does someone want to tell me what's going on?"

"We think Wafiq is in with the wrong people. The Chinese have a foothold in Zambia, and it's not what's best for the people who live here. Pippa found these diamonds at Wafiq's warehouse."

He holds her shoulders. "I think we can get him out of the mess he's in, but we need your help to keep this quiet." He leaves out the part where Wafiq may be up to his neck in Deep 8.

Sabeen hangs her head. "I had a feeling he was in trouble.

He's been in a foul mood and keeping to himself. I've never seen him like this."

Beck lifts her face with his fingers. "Try to stay positive and don't let on that we had this conversation. It could put you in danger."

"Wafiq would never do anything to hurt me," she protests.

Beck's eyes drift my way as he lets go of her chin. "The bullets at the celebration were meant for me, and you got caught in the crossfire. Wafiq may have been behind it."

Sabeen's mouth turns down, and her eyes get big with questions she doesn't ask. "I'll help in any way I can." She hands the diamonds back to Pippa with a loupe magnifier. "You might need this to look at them again."

"I'm going to inspect these and see if I can identify exactly how they work." She grabs Sabeen's hands. "Thank you for trusting us."

"When Wafiq ships out the gems, what time of day does he do it, and how does he transport them?" Beck asks.

"He rotates the schedule because of ambushes. The convoy takes them to our small airfield and flies them out to either Lusaka or Nairobi, depending on where they are going internationally."

"Do you have access to the schedule?"

"No, Wafiq handles the transports."

"Of course he does." Beck brushes his hand over his head.

"I have no access to anything he does, but we do weekly transports." She looks at him through worried eyes. "I've been in the dark for a long time."

I speak up. "I think he's kept everyone in the dark."

"I just hope you're able to bring our brother back from the dark side." Her eyes plead with him.

THIRTY-SEVEN

Beck
————

PIPPA and I prepare the rooms for the team, including a room for Peter downstairs to accommodate his wheelchair. The house is enormous, and with its open floor plan, we have plenty of room. Having them stay here will give us time to strategize our plan of attack.

Pippa has been like a yo-yo. She keeps her distance and then lets loose when we have crazy sex. I've made love to women in the past, but she surpasses that depth of intimacy. If I lose her, my life will become more restrictive than it has been.

I catch her from behind and put my arms around her waist. My nose seeks out the vanilla scent of her hair. "What do you say we room together and give the guys some extra space?"

She turns in my arms, shakes her head, and pauses as she collects her words. "I want to be seen as one of the team members, not your girlfriend. They have to take me seriously. I can't be taken seriously if they listen to us doing the rough and tumble."

"Rough and tumble?" I smile.

"Well, we are rough, and we tumbled onto the floor the other night." Her eyes have yet to meet mine.

I'll give her time to see where this road might lead us. She needs to come to me because I'm already here waiting for her. In the middle of everything going on, this should be the last thing on my mind, but my heart has other plans. My queen needs to be in my life.

She tilts her head so I can see her beautiful green eyes. "There's been no one like you. There's never really been anyone besides hookups who hung around too long until they became clingers, and then I had to end it. You're special and accomplished. You let me be me. We complement each other, and yet we're so different."

"You're talking about our childhoods." My thumb slides down her soft, milky white cheek.

In a voice barely above a whisper, she says, "I have no one to bring you home to. My parents thought running a con game was more important than raising a child. Jess is happy with Sean, and she's moved on with her life. I've been alone so long, it's all I know. You have parents, siblings, and new people in your life. Your world is full and colorful. There's no one waiting for me when I get home." A piece of my heart chips away with each of her words.

The first tear slips from her eye. I don't wipe it away because I don't want to dismiss her pain. The warrior has put down her shield to expose how she views herself, and I must respect her vulnerability.

I grab her by the back of her hair to get her out of her head. Her body understands my physical messages better than anyone I've ever known. Her eyes close gently, giving in to my dominance. She needs to understand surrender to become part of us. Tears crest in her eyes.

"Open your eyes. You can't shut me out." Her eyes flutter

open, and the green glitters with unshed tears. "You are not alone. When you became a part of this team, even if you're technically working for Neil, you became a part of our family. You will always be an equal. You've proven you can take whatever I throw at you. A strong, powerful warrior with compassion for others. They don't come better than that. What do I have to do to prove to you that you are part of my world here and back home? Tell me. I'll do whatever it takes."

She tries to sniff back her tears. "I don't know." She takes the back of her hand to wipe them away. "I don't know how to break out of this mold. I want to be part of the team, but I've been running solo for so long, I'm stuck. I balance between two worlds, the one I know and the one I want."

"Give yourself time to adjust. Change is scary. Most people don't like it, including me. Family comes in many different forms. You're part of our family now." I hold her to me and rub her back as she curls into my chest like a child looking for comfort.

For a moment, I think of myself as a father. What would it be like to have a daughter, someone so fragile and yet so strong?

Pippa calms down, reaches up, and kisses me. Her kiss holds gratitude, honesty, and trust. I'm sure she has spent her life not trusting anyone, and she hides it well, but she'll never doubt that she can trust me. She excuses herself, saying she needs time to think. I spend time coming up with a plan.

The plan includes Katoo and Jobi taking the Range Rovers outside the city walls to the pickup location. The team is bringing a lot of equipment with them. After Pippa did some research and snooping, she cleared Jobi of any wrongdoing. He didn't tip anyone off. Wafiq has an app on his phone that lets him know when someone goes into the warehouse. The question is, who is he keeping track of?

Pippa keeps to herself for the rest of the evening, claiming to be working on cracking the encryption. We try to get some sleep in our rooms before the team arrives with their chaos.

I toss and turn, unable to take my mind off my conversation with Pippa and my concern about the mission. I want her to feel safe and accepted. She's taught me so much about living life to the fullest, but she seems to have retracted into her shell.

I hate seeing her like this, and I need her firing on all cylinders. The success of this mission depends on the moving parts of everyone on the team.

Three in the morning arrives with a bang as the front door opens, and chaos enters the house. Their voices are the most wonderful sound I've heard in weeks. There's nothing like it when the team comes together for a mission. Pippa follows me downstairs to greet them.

"Hey, King, we're here," Dean calls out.

I come down the stairs looking calm and composed, but inside, my engine amps with excitement. Dean is the first in, followed by the rest of the group, each carrying overstuffed duffle bags as if they're going on an all-inclusive resort holiday.

Peter rolls in, spins around, and whistles. "Nice digs, King." I've accepted this as my new handle. "Where is the harem?" He wiggles his brows.

Mac's brothers, Declan and Campbell, come in together as I introduce myself to Campbell. Both are quiet, checking out the house and where they fit into the team dynamic.

Sean enters next with a huge grin and a gleam in his eye. He's always ready for action. He grabs me in for a bro hug. His edges have softened since Jess has come back into his life, but when it comes down to it, he's the same fierce soldier he's always been.

Bringing up the rear is Mac. His phone rings with the Stevie Wonder song, "Isn't She Lovely," which means Mara is on the line.

"What's wrong? It's late for you to be calling, Leannan." His Gaelic term of endearment for her.

He's got her on video, and we can hear the conversation. "Dalia won't stop crying. She misses her papa putting her to bed at night. I don't know what to do," she pleads with him.

He looks up from his phone at us. "Not a bloody word from any of you," he says in a heavy Scottish accent.

"Put the phone up so she can see me. Hi, lovey, it's Papa."

Dalia stops crying long enough to take a breath and register his voice. He sings "Dream Angus," a Scottish lullaby, as we stand there stupefied. The man is tough as nails but will do anything for his daughter. As he nears the end of the song, he shows us his screen. Her eyes are closed as she lies limp in Mara's arms. He does a fist pump that Mara can't see.

"You're the best, Highlander. Have fun in Zambia, but come back to us in one piece, please. Love you." Her voice has a dreamy quality. There's an instant feeling of dread I push away, hoping the outcome is best for everyone.

"I love you more. Talk to you soon." He clicks off the screen and looks at us with a dare for one of us to say anything. Dean's not even brave enough to tackle this one with a joke.

Declan pipes up, "I guess you have the fatherhood thing mastered like everything else." He turns and trudges upstairs.

Mac shrugs. "Families are always a work in progress. He'll be fine."

THIRTY-EIGHT

Pippa

BECK HAS RUINED me for every other man out there. He's not backing down, won't leave me behind, and he's made it clear we're together. My lungs struggle to breathe his air, the air that knows the love of family and friends. I want to suck in the security of knowing someone has my back, no matter what happens.

Folding myself into him feels like home. His powerful arms are only the physicality of his spirit as a rightful king. He's stepped up to the calling and will keep his promises. But first, we need to get through hell to feel the fire of Deep 8 and how close they are to the SIG operation.

I follow the noise downstairs, coming from the kitchen and dining room. Laughter echoes through the house with loud voices and grumbling. As I turn the corner, a long table full of men eat to their hearts' content. I lean on the wall and listen.

"What? No green tea, King?" Dean laughs.

"Yeah, that kicked my ass, literally. Declan, we could have used your help had I known you have a degree in biochemistry."

Declan shrugs. "You would think with a degree in biochemistry, I would have known better than to become an alcoholic." His Scottish accent rolls off his tongue.

The room stills, and all eyes are on Mac.

"I don't think those two things go together. Besides, you've been clean for a year. That's something to be proud of. Not everyone gets that far." Mac is always the cheerleader.

"Aye." A small smile tugs at Declan's lips. This is the first time I've seen him smile since we met on the Afghanistan mission.

All at once, they notice me.

"Red!" they say in unison. They call me by my code name, leaving behind any doubt I'm part of the team.

I belly laugh and double over. Hands wave me over, offering me a seat next to them.

Declan looks at me with trepidation. When we first met in the Afghan forest, he said I reminded him of his sister, Kendall. We made a connection like siblings. He gets out of his chair and hugs me. I feel his body relax. When I move back, his face has a slight glow to it. He's happy to see me because he always considers it a good sign. Let's hope he's right.

"I have to go make myself some coffee. I'll be back."

Beck stands up. "No. You come and sit. I'll make your coffee."

All eyes turn to me like they're watching a tennis match.

Dean smiles. "Don't argue with the king or free coffee."

I raise my chin and walk toward Beck. "Maybe the king shouldn't argue with the queen." I sit in his seat, and he kisses me on the top of my head. The men shovel food into their mouths and smile at me like they know our secret.

"Welcome to the family." Sean grabs my hand and squeezes.

My teeth dig into my lower lip to hold back the tears or excitement, I'm not sure which, and I let out a breath from somewhere deep in my core. Acceptance. They want me here.

"Thank you," is all I manage to eke out.

Beck comes back in with a cup of coffee and blueberry pancakes.

"My king, have you been holding out on me all this time while I've been making breakfast?"

He bends over, leaning his hands on the table. "Did you just call me your king?"

Oh, crap. Did I?

"Yes." I leave it there.

"Good. Don't forget that." He kisses me on the lips with a tenderness that seals the deal between us. I am his.

"Move over. I need to sit next to my queen," he says to Sean.

"God, I think I'm going to puke," Declan mumbles.

"Don't worry, Dark Lord, your time is coming. I can't wait to watch you fall." Mac laughs as Declan scowls.

We spend the rest of the day strategizing on how best to put surveillance on Wafiq and the warehouse. Katoo brought over maps of the area in and around the city. We created several plans, including using the drone Peter brought with him. Each plan fails miserably at keeping our operation undercover and from everyone being discovered.

"Even if we can get info on when the transport is happening, we can't rally fast enough to intercept it," Mac observes.

The room is quiet as everyone is in their head about how to get to the transport trail. Peter's ringtone of "The Imperial March" from *Star Wars* interrupts the silence.

"What? I thought it was appropriate given that Beck's the king, Declan's the Dark Lord, and I'm a Star Wars geek." He answers his call. "Tell me something good."

He wheels away, listening to whoever is on the other line. I can pray that they have cracked the encryption so we can get more information.

"Well, what now? We've gone over every scenario." Beck sits back, slumped in his chair, staring at the table.

From the other room, we hear Peter yell out, "Antonio Bianchi, I love you."

"Is he playing for the other team, and someone forgot to tell me?" Dean frowns.

I've met Antonio. If there is anyone out there who can make a straight guy play for the other team, it would be him. Handsome, smart, brains for miles, and a smile that could melt your panties.

Peter tears back into the dining room. "We got it. The boys figured out the encryption. They've been working day and night. They deserve a raise and time off. Red, come with me. We have work to do. Guys, go clean your weapons or something. It's gonna be a while."

The room comes alive, and everyone buzzes with activity. They disperse in every direction, and I follow Peter to the living room.

He opens his laptop and turns it in my direction. "The boys back home are going through the stuff you downloaded from Isaad. I'm going to let them handle it because it's going to take a lot of digging, but we need to focus on Wafiq's mainframe and cloud."

As he's talking, I'm watching the screen uncover every-thing we ever wanted to know about Wafiq's operation. We have access to his entire system, including emails, transport schedules, and encrypted communications with the Chinese. Then there's the diamond in the rough we've been holding our breath for.

"We need to tell the team about this."

He's wearing half a smile. "And spoil the biggest secret of all? I want you and I to nail down everything, including the transport route and where it's all going, before we spring it on the guys. We need to have the logistics laid out before they can deal with the tactical end. Trust me, the more they know, the better."

At that moment, Peter made me feel like I'm the cog missing in the gear. He and I are in lockstep, and things flow like only things can between techies. He used to pop up on the dark web and send me messages, trying to figure out my angle. Now, we're sitting next to each other, fighting evil together. This gray hacker has turned into a white hacker, and it feels damn good.

We get into the zone, work through dinner, and compile plenty of information to present to the team to move forward. If Wafiq were operating in the States, we have enough information to put him away for life. The implications are incriminating and brilliant. As we drill down deeper, it's obvious he's working for someone or something. There's no way he's this bright because what they've come up with is absolute genius and needs to be shut down immediately.

The team is getting restless. They're eager to move forward and roll up their sleeves. We call the team into the dining room. Everyone looks at us with anticipation.

"Beck, I have some news you're not going to like. We almost have a face to go with our nemesis," Peter says cryptically.

Peter turns the laptop so everyone can see it. The background color is royal blue, and floating in the middle of the screen is a gold capital letter D with an infinity sign running through it.

Beck puts his head in his hands. "This can't be happening."

THIRTY-NINE

Beck

"You're confirming that my brother works for Deep 8. We can make him an asset and get information about the organization from him." I make a definitive statement based on uncertainty and desperation. The one thing I didn't want to confirm about Wafiq stares me in the face.

"Can you turn him?" Campbell speaks up for the first time since he's been here.

His likeness to Mac is uncanny, except for his auburn hair and freckles. His area of expertise is interrogation and cryptanalysis, and he has a degree in finance. He's a valuable addition to the team.

"Things haven't been going well between us as of late. He's been cagey and not agreeable. I know very little about how long he's been with them and how far in he is." I pace the floor in the dining room.

"Based on the emails, the transport is happening tomorrow night." Peter's face glows with the light from his computer.

"The minute they leave the warehouse, we can hit them —" Dean shares his idea but gets cut off.

Sean's been listening quietly. "No. I want to see where this goes, who's involved, and how Wafiq fits into this." The wound of losing his longtime friend, Isaad, runs deep. He wants to see if we can save Wafiq.

Mac stands up. "What if we take it one step further? Is there a way to get undetectable trackers on the armored crates so we can see where they go?"

"When Beck and I were there, each crate had a high-tech padlock. It would take too much time to pick it and get a tracker in there," Pippa responds.

"There is something I've been toying with in the lab that may work. I brought some with me just in case we could use them." Peter's eyes light up like a kid with the secret code to get into a clubhouse.

He wheels away to get his invention and holds up what looks like a roll of tape. "I know. It looks like a roll of transparent tape, but it's not."

He takes the tape and rips off a piece at the perforation for each of us to examine. "What do you see?"

"I see a dot in the middle of the tape. What is it?" Declan holds the tape up to the light.

"That is a tracker. The back peels off, and you can stick it to anything. The tape is completely transparent, and the device is so small it's almost undetectable unless you know what you're looking for." Peter beams. "The best part is once the tracker is exposed to air, it dissolves within six hours. After that, if someone finds it, they'll only find a piece of tape."

"My God, I think you're better than Q." Mac grins. "What's the plan?"

"We need to get these on the crates with the diamonds and find out where they're being shipped. Peter, I need to pick your brain about the chemistry behind this." Declan's eyes haven't left the piece of tape.

"How the hell are we going to do that?" I ask.

"We need someone on that transport truck to stick these on the crates." Campbell rubs his chin.

"What if we get a crate, put someone in it, and then they can get out during the transport to put the trackers on the crates?" Sean smiles and turns toward Pippa. Everyone else's head turns in the same direction.

"No. Not going to happen. I'm not having her sit in a crate and put her life in danger." My low voice rumbles off the walls of a silent room.

Pippa stands up. "You don't have a say in whether or not I do this. This is my decision. I'm small enough to get in the crate, get out, put the trackers on, and then get off the truck. I'm in. What do you need me to do?"

Their eyes are on me as I say a few curse words under my breath. This is about her need to be part of the team. I don't want to relive what happened to Emilia, but Pippa is the obvious choice. I have to push my ego aside and trust her as an agent.

"I don't mean to get in the middle of a royal squabble, but if it were one of us, you wouldn't object. She's trained well for this, and we'll have her back." Dean gives his two cents, which is all it's worth.

"If this were Leigha, would you let her go?" I come back at him without thinking.

"As you recall, I had to let her go when she met with her Russian father, the mob boss. I couldn't even be there for Leigha until it was over. You have a choice to be there for Pippa."

"Hello, I'm right here. I haven't left the room." Pippa waves at me. "I know you're scared because of what happened to Emilia, but we have to do this. Otherwise, we will never get one step ahead of Deep 8."

I put my hands on my hips and stare at the floor. No one bats an eyelash because most of them are familiar with my story. Some of them were there when I lost Emilia.

This room is full of loss. We've each lost someone close to us, either a loved one, partner, family member, or friend. I haven't had to face this dilemma since being with Emilia, always controlling that I would never get a female partner again.

Neil blew that to shreds, sending me Pippa. He not only sent me a tough agent but an incredible woman who I'm falling in love with. He knew exactly what he was doing.

I scrub my face. "Okay, but we do this my way."

Pippa replies, "No. We do this together. Everyone here has a different expertise, and we need to listen to each other. This is a tight operation, and we need everyone on the same page."

My hands are up before she can finish. "All right, all right. I'm sorry. I'll get my shit together."

We spend the rest of the evening planning every single second of this operation. Precise timing is required to pull this off, and even then, there are no guarantees. I need to give myself the same speech I gave to Pippa and have faith in my team, trusting them with my most precious gift, who we are going to put in a box, literally.

Pippa and I exchange glances throughout the evening. She tries to give me reassuring looks, and I try not to have dread written on my face. She names it "Operation Queen in a Crate." I roll my eyes and laugh.

Everyone on the team calls Pippa "Red," referring to Peter and her as P&R. They need to hack into Wafiq's emails without tipping him off. We don't want him to run. They designated me to flip him to get information on Deep 8. I'm not sure how much success I'll have in getting him to play for our team. He seems entrenched in anger and bitterness, and I don't know where it's coming from.

We wrap things up late in the evening, and the team is tired. Dean and Mac leave to make calls home, and I can hear Sean talking to Jess. He hands the phone to Pippa for a chat and comes to sit down.

"You hangin' in there, buddy?"

Ever since Jess came back into his life, he's not been looking for the next assignment. He's looking to live life to the fullest.

"I didn't expect any of this. Right out of left field, as you Americans like to say," I mumble more to myself than to him.

"I thought I was living life but found out I was going through the motions. I've been on autopilot, following a routine that prevented me from feeling much of anything. Then I met the hurricane and got swept up in her whirlwind. She taught me what it means to live, and I can't go back to who I used to be. The coronation is in a couple of days when they acknowledge me as the king, and I've decided to hand it over to Sabeen, the rightful heir. But I want to leave here with my queen in one piece."

Sean laughs, "Yeah." He rubs his chin. "That's the way it happens. She'll be fine. She's a tough cookie and a survivor. I watched her work in Afghanistan, and she's got skills. Have faith, my friend. You should also know she's a lot to handle."

He pats me on the back, grabs the phone from Pippa, and heads upstairs. There's only the two of us in the dining room, and Pippa comes to sit on my lap, exactly where I want her.

She pulls my head onto her shoulder. "Operation Queen in a Crate is going to go fine. You have the best of the best, and they always come through for you. I trust you with my life, and if you trust them, then it's a win-win."

She strokes my head and whispers, "You can't control every event that happens. Just breathe and know you've done the best you can. Besides, do you honestly think you can get rid of me? Your queen isn't going anywhere."

I lift her under her legs and shoulders. "My queen is spending the night in my bed tonight. King's orders."

We make sweet love and have some rough and tumble, but with every touch, sigh, moan, and giggle, I lock it in my memory because I don't know what tomorrow will bring.

FORTY

Pippa

Dawn breaks, with a change in Beck's mood. Gone is the playful man who commands my body at every turn. He makes my body sing and sting, a skillful balance between rough and tender, knowing exactly what I like as if we've been lovers for years.

"Are you ready for today?" I need to soothe his nerves.

His body stiffens. "No, not really. Can't we put Dean in a crate with his smart mouth? If they capture him, they'll throw him back."

On the outside, I'm laughing, but inside, I give myself a high five. This man will do anything to protect me and make sure I'm safe. He's the only one to make me feel special. Nothing will stop me from completing the mission in the crate. My adrenaline kicks up a notch.

My legs hang off the side of the bed. "Let's get this party started. We have a lot of preparations to make before tonight."

He strokes my arm. "Can't we stay in bed a bit longer?" I look over my shoulder, and his eyes plead with me.

I crawl over to him and take his face in my hands. "You need to listen to me. I. am. coming. back. Besides, what good is a king without his queen? A king would be practically impotent."

He's quick as he flips me onto my back. "I'll show you impotent."

He grabs a condom and slides into me without effort. I'm always wet around this man. He only has to look at me, and I'm at his mercy. I've never been this compliant for any man, but I surrender to him because I know he'll catch me when I fall.

Once we're satisfied, we make it to the dining room, where the rowdy group from last night picks up where they left off. Declan entertains everyone with his ability to do any accent under the sun as we listen to his imitation of Sean Connery. I close my eyes, and sure enough, he sounds just like him.

"He also speaks fluent Chinese. That'll come in handy." Mac elbows Declan.

"Well, look who's all rosy-cheeked?" Dean announces from the other end of the table. "I'm not talking about you, Red, but your man, King."

Beck flips him the bird. "Jealous you're not getting some while you're here?"

"What I want is waiting for me at home," Dean replies.

The other guys laugh as Dean shrugs it off. Beck pulls out a chair for me next to him at the end of the table. Bacon, eggs, toast, fruit, and sausage fill the plates. These guys know how to cook and eat.

The table gets quiet as everyone eats, thinking about the night ahead. There are various discussions about logistics and the crate.

"Sabeen can help us with getting a crate," I say while

peeling an orange. "The crates at the other warehouse are the same as the crates at Wafiq's warehouse."

Heads nod in agreement.

"I'll contact her and see how we can get one over here to outfit it for tonight," Beck offers. This is his peace offering to let me know he's on board with the plan.

We spend the rest of the day accounting for the minute details and the contingency plans if things go sideways. The best part about this group is that they have an answer for everything. Their ability to think on their feet amazes me.

Beck arranges for Katoo and Jobi to bring the crate over, and Sabeen insists on coming with them.

They carry the crate into the living room and set it down. Katoo, Jobi, and Sabeen are introduced to the team as I hear Campbell say under his breath, "She's beautiful."

Beck snaps at him. "Don't get any ideas." Tensions are running high in anticipation of the mission ahead.

Campbell puts his hands on his hips. "I only said—" Mac puts his hand on his brother's arm.

"Okay, and we're done here. Let's focus on the task at hand," Mac redirects everyone's attention.

The guys decide to drill holes at the bottom where there's a small area of a forty-five-degree angle before it continues at ninety degrees for the base of the crate. Throughout this process, I'm in and out of the crate to see if I fit and to make sure I can breathe. Good thing I'm not claustrophobic because the darkness in here is all-consuming, but I have plenty of room.

I sit in there for about twenty minutes to get used to being in the space. Closing my eyes, I visualize math equations and codes, flowing in my zone when Peter opens the top to let me out. We rig the red light to stay on, so it appears locked, but I will be able to get in and out freely.

Beck hasn't left the room since we started the crate transformation. He sits next to the crate while I do my practice run and makes sure there's airflow.

The thought occurs to me that I'm sitting in a crate with holes in it in the middle of Africa, preparing for a mission that could go south, and yet, I've never felt more secure.

The meaning of the words "blood is thicker than water" never rang truer for this group of men. They run like a well-oiled machine and act like a family. I hope I can live up to their standards. If everything goes according to plan, who knows where Neil will send me next. I doubt if I'm with another team that they will match this one.

As the sun slides behind the hills, we get ready, dressed in our night gear, waiting for word to come. Peter has been monitoring Wafiq's emails and phone throughout the day, waiting for the final time frame for the transport.

Everyone has a very specific job, but mine is the most crucial to the operation. If I can't get those trackers on the crates, then this was for nothing. I'm aware the success or failure of this mission rests on my shoulders, and I'm okay with that because I know what I'm capable of under stress.

If Afghanistan taught me anything, it was to stay cool under pressure, use your head, and maybe use your assets and feminine ways when necessary. Each minute we wait adds to our anxiety. Mac and his brothers jab at each other for entertainment, but they're itching to get out and get the job done.

Beck takes my hand, and I follow him up to the triangle room. The window is pitch-black with twinkling stars. The warm light from a lamp in the corner is not enough to illuminate the room, leaving us in the shadows.

His arms are around my waist as he cups my butt in his hands. We've started little affections with each other, and I like it. "You're going to be fine. I've gone over the plan about thirty times. There is room for error, but it's marginal." I'm not sure if he's telling me this for my benefit or to quell his jittery nerves.

"The question is, are you going to be okay? You're very overprotective, and I kinda like it. No one has ever made me feel so secure." I rub my hands up and down his chest.

"I'll be fine. I'm surveilling Wafiq, so he doesn't go anywhere." They have him watching Wafiq so he doesn't get in the way and try to save me.

His eyes pierce mine, and he frowns like he is trying to find the words to say something.

There's a knock at the door, and Dean comes in. "It's showtime, lovebirds. Our stage awaits."

FORTY-ONE

Pippa

WE'RE DECKED out in camouflage gear from head to toe. I pulled on black leggings, a tight long-sleeve shirt, a ski mask, and gloves. The only things showing are my eyes.

They load me up in the crate and transport it onto a black Jeep Wrangler driven by Katoo and Jobi. We discovered my ear comm doesn't work inside the crate, so I'm dark until I slip out to place the trackers.

One thing we didn't account for was how hot it was going to be in the crate. A bead of sweat slips down my spine, followed by many more. I try to even out my breath and lower my heart rate to slow down the sweating. The African heat wins as my clothes get wetter by the minute.

Timing is crucial. Peter needs to send a text to their Chinese team leader using Wafiq's cell phone number after they've loaded the other crates.

The message informs them about another crate being added to their manifest for delivery. He's specific when he tells him Jobi will make the delivery. Peter is also in charge of the drone with artillery. This team is spot-on with every logistical move.

Katoo and Jobi will be the first to lay eyes on the men involved in Wafiq's operation. I bump around in the crate for a bit, and then the truck stops. I hear a door slam as Jobi gets out to approach the men. Voices get louder as they disagree with Jobi about the added crate.

"Do you have the text or not? I'll take it back, but my boss won't be happy," he says. There's silence, and then they agree to take the crate.

Katoo and Jobi lift my crate in place as the last crate in the truck. I hear the swoosh and then a bang as the back of the truck locks down.

I take a few deep breaths and count to thirty-one thousand before I climb out of the crate. This gives me a cushion of time to make sure everything is stable before phase three.

I open the lid to the crate and crawl out with the tape in my hand.

"I'm out. Over," I say, praying they can hear me.

Declan responds. "We read you. You have two minutes."

"Roger that."

Mac and Declan will drive up behind the last Jeep in the convoy, take out the drivers, and follow the truck. The wild card is what language we're dealing with, either Chinese or English. When they respond on the walkie-talkie, Mac will cover the British, and Declan can cover the Chinese.

I set the timer on my watch and use the small flashlight to scope out the truck. The crates are packed close together with a small space in between, forcing me to belly crawl along the tops.

Underneath the forty-five-degree angle at the bottom of the crate is a place to stick the tracker. I crawl over each one, reach between the crates, and place the tape with the tracker on the bottom.

I'm done with fifteen seconds to spare. "Trackers secure.

Going back in. Red, out." I crawl back into the security of the crate and wait for Mac and Declan to get me out of the truck. This is where things get tricky.

They won't try to shoot off the lock. The noise will draw too much attention. I can barely hear the clank as the lock gets cut and then the swoosh of the truck door opening.

I pop open the crate, crawl out, and close it again. Declan is there with his hand out while Mac drives the Jeep as close as he can get to the truck. I take Declan's hand, and something passes between us like he's having a memory of some sort. He smiles, and his eyes brighten. Maybe he remembers a moment with his sister.

I jump onto the hood of the Jeep, come around the passenger side door, and swing myself into the seat. No sooner do I sit down, when we hear gunshots ring out.

"We're taking fire," Mac says in the comm.

He decelerates, leaving Declan standing at the end of the truck. Declan gets the message and heaves himself to the top of the truck, closing the back with his foot as it speeds down the dirt road.

"I've got them in my sights," Peter says calmly.

The drone fires in the direction the bullets are coming from. Artillery lights up the night sky as the drone spins, turns, and fires with accuracy.

"What about Declan?" My heart feels like it's pumping out of my chest. I press my mic off, as does Mac.

Mac seems unaffected. "He can take care of himself. We need to get out of here. We've been made."

I can't wrap my head around the fact that we're leaving Declan behind. Isn't there a motto among soldiers about never leaving a man behind? Mac must read the worry on my face.

"He'll be fine. We planned for this. We figured they

would make us. Otherwise, it was too clean. Nothing ever goes according to plan. Besides, we got Sean and Dean on the ground at the airport with firepower. They'll get him out."

I nod, not sure I believe him. He takes us off-road and into the bush for cover. I hear bullets puncturing the Jeep. When we get far enough into the bush, the shots stop. Mac stops the Jeep under a huge bush for cover.

"Well, that's the most excitement I've had in a long time. Feels good to be back." He grins.

"The adrenaline rush was almost as good as one of Beck's orgasms," I say coyly.

"Not quite." Beck's dry voice comes through the comm. Oops, I guess my mic was on.

I hold my hand over my mouth and laugh. "I believe you mean queen."

Mac shakes his head and clicks his mic back on.

"Love, I'm so glad you're alive and well." A smile stretches across his face. His underlying meaning is that he'll be dishing out some rough and tumble later with an extra helping of rough.

"I'm sure you are," I smirk.

"We have incoming at two o'clock, and they are fired up, but there's no plane," Dean reports.

"Correction, there's a Harrier Jump Jet landing," Sean replies. "This is a quick in and out. It's dark blue with the Deep 8 insignia on it. This group has got funds."

The airwaves are silent. We're waiting for more information from Sean and Dean.

Sean's voice comes over the comm. "They've made a perimeter around the back of the truck, aimed and ready. They're off-loading." There are a couple of beats of silence. "They have the crates loaded, and the Harrier is up and out."

"I see no sign of —," Dean reports. "Wait, I take that back. He's topside."

"It's showtime. I need you to take out the Jeep at my six," Declan orders through the comm.

We hear something blow up through the comm. I look over at Mac.

"Rocket launchers." He stares out the front window as if he can visualize what's happening at the airport.

"We're taking fire," Sean says.

"Take out the rest of the Jeeps and get out of there," Mac orders.

I look over at Mac, who sits at the wheel calmly, waiting for something, but I'm not sure what.

"What direction is the truck headed?" Mac asks.

"South. Headed your way." Sean pauses.

We hear a series of explosions and the crunching of brush under their feet. "Jeeps are immobilized," Sean says.

"Is Declan a friggin' magician?" Dean asks.

"Magician? Is that the best you can do, Dean?" Declan says in his best Australian accent. I can hear the truck engine in the background.

"Dump the truck. We're on our way," Mac says.

"Nice work, Declan. You need to show me your moves," Dean says.

"I can't reveal my secrets. See you back at the house, mate." Declan laughs.

"The Dark Lord has many secrets." Mac chuckles.

We get out from under the bush and head back to the road. Up ahead, in the beam of the headlights, a man walks down the road. Mac stops the Jeep long enough for Declan to jump in.

I turn around in my seat. "Glad you could make it."

He shrugs. "There's always a Plan B. Operation Queen in a Crate is complete." He fist bumps me.

Beck breaks in, "Wafiq is on the move. I'm going to tail him and see where he goes. I'll report back when I have more info. King out."

My heart jumps to my throat. I put a tracker on Beck's phone without him knowing it and hold it up to Mac. He nods without a word, and we follow the red dot on the screen.

FORTY-TWO

Beck

THE TEAM CAME through with flying colors, getting Pippa out safely. Once we turn the trackers on, we'll be able to identify the crate locations.

I have the last phase of Operation Queen in a Crate. My assignment is to flip Wafiq and get answers to questions about Deep 8. He may be only one key to the complex organization, but he's better than anything we have so far.

Wafiq's Range Rover screams out of the driveway and races down the road, out of the city. He had to have gotten word that there was a shootout at the airport, and it wasn't the locals trying to ambush his loot. No, these foreigners were not the Chinese.

Given it's the middle of the night, I tail him from a distance. As we drive out of town and turn onto the dirt roads, the dust clouds from the road give me cover. He drives recklessly as he heads deeper into the mountains toward the mines. He's driving as if he's frantic to get to his location.

I speed up, not wanting to lose him as the car handles the curve of Mine 1, a yawning black hole waiting for its next victim. The mines give me the creeps, and the nighttime ambiance doesn't help.

He pulls in next to a trailer parked at the mine site and almost falls out of the car, leaving the door open and the engine running. Bypassing the trailer, he heads for the mine.

I exit my car and turn off the engine to his car. I pocket the keys and close the door. There's no hurry. I'll be able to see his flashlight easily in the black hole of the mine.

I walk around the corner and see he has lit a single torch one level below. I jog to the lower level as I hear him call out to Zahara.

"I take it you were supposed to meet Zahara here." I stand with my hands in my pockets, trying not to be confrontational.

He spins around. "What are you doing here? How did you find me?"

His tailored suit is wrinkled, and sweat soaks the front of his beige shirt. He is disheveled and harried.

"I followed you from your house." I let it hang there and see if he can put it together.

I lessen the distance between us to gauge his reaction. The amber glow of the torch lights half his face. His eyes narrow.

"Why are you following me?" He grits his teeth. "You need to leave."

I cut right to the chase. "We found your diamonds. You're right about one thing. We were in your warehouse."

He laughs. "You may have found them, but you have no clue as to what they can do." He puts his hands on his hips.

"You mean the lab-created diamonds with the chip in them. My queen found them and knows exactly how they work. How did you figure out how to make them?"

"Your queen? What a joke. You don't even know how to be king. A true king would never take a—"

My one step brings me face-to-face with him. "Be careful how you finish that sentence."

I tilt my head. "Stop focusing on what doesn't matter. How did you get that technology?"

His throat moves as he swallows. "That's none of your business."

"I'm going to guess Deep 8. Ring any bells?"

His eyes widen, and he looks at his watch. "Where is Zahara?" he mumbles.

"I don't think she's coming."

His head snaps up, and he lowers his wrist, then runs his hand over the top of his head.

"You need to tell us everything you know about Deep 8. We can protect you," I try to convince him.

"Trust me, you cannot protect me. No one can." He wipes the sweat from his forehead with the back of his hand as his other hand reaches behind him.

His sudden move triggers my instincts as he pulls a gun from behind his back. I grab his gun, twist his wrist, and knock his feet out from under him. I tuck the gun into my waistband.

My back is to the wall as he staggers to his feet with his back to the gaping hole of the mine. Dirt covers his suit, a far cry from the polished man he portrays. A scowl covers his face.

"You're always the friggin' hero. I've lived in your shadow my entire life, and I'm bloody sick of it. They talked about their dead son as if you were the second coming. What an outstanding leader you would have made, brother and son." He spits the words at me.

He steps closer to me with a sneer. "But then I had Katoo followed when he went on one of his trips to the UK, and lo and behold, look who's not dead after all. I had to put the pieces together, but it wasn't that hard. You were just out of university. Then you disappeared like a ghost. Poof." His fingers open and close.

"I went into the military and was picked up by MI-6, so I guess you could say I was a ghost." I let that hang in the air.

He gets millimeters from my face. "I know everything about you, and you know nothing about me, my brother."

"Why don't you enlighten me?" I don't move or back down.

"What's the point? You're going to be king." He steps back and spreads his arms wide. "The empire and power will be yours."

"You could have had the title if you weren't in bed with the wrong people or killed our parents to get there." I grit my teeth.

"I didn't kill my father!" he yells as his words echo off the walls.

Curiously, he used the word father and not mother. I frown, and he catches on.

"We're half brothers. My mother is from the rival tribe that went to war for the mines and lost. She got a job as a housekeeper and drugged our father to produce an heir. What she hadn't counted on was Aafia miscarrying her second pregnancy. When my mother presented me as their male heir, they struck a deal."

He reads my face. "Yes, she blackmailed them, threatening to expose me as the king's bastard. I was raised as a full-blooded Siwanda, the next heir to the throne, until you showed up."

His shoulders sag under the weight of his life. "I had big plans, and I was going to impress Father. Zahara came into my life and showed me a way I could take everything to the next level with Deep 8."

I have to know. "Do you know who killed our parents?"

He lets out a deep sigh. "I don't know for sure, but I think it was Zahara. She made many comments about speeding things up." His eyes glisten with unshed tears.

"Save your tears, Wafiq, because if you suspected her, you should have done something about it." My voice lacks sympathy. "Let me guess. She had the idea to assassinate me, not once but twice, but Sabeen got in the way."

"Yes. But it was only meant to scare you away. I would never harm Sabeen." Tears slip down his cheek, and he wipes them away.

"You had the opportunity to stop all of this."

"Don't get righteous with me. You haven't lived here long enough to make judgments about anyone. You drop from the sky like friggin' Batman, and everyone is kissing your ass. And for what? You know nothing. Deep 8 will improve the world for everyone by taking control of the necessities. We would get a piece of the pie." He's been drinking their Kool-Aid.

"You can come back to the States with me and start fresh. You can make this right. I'm handing the crown to Sabeen so it stays in the family." My voice shakes.

"You can't save me, hero." He takes a step back. "They are everywhere, and no one knows who they really are," he hisses. He takes another step back. "They are powerful and pull the strings no one sees."

"Don't, Wafiq. There's another way. There's always another way. Please, now that I found you, I don't want to lose you, too." My fingers curl into fists.

His foot skids, and I lunge to grab his hand as he spreads his arms wide and falls backward as the gaping mouth of the mine swallows him.

"Noooo!" I yell at the top of my lungs.

FORTY-THREE

Beck

MUBALA REEKS of death and sacrifice. Adding one more wasn't on my to-do list.

I stand at the edge of the black abyss that swallowed Wafiq, and I can feel Pippa watching me from the shadows. I've tuned into her energy, and I need her more than I've needed anyone. A dark figure stands behind her, probably one of our teammates.

She steps out from the darkness with her hands clutched in front of her. Mac comes up behind her. They stare at me with pity in their eyes.

"You put a tracker on my phone, didn't you?"

She nods.

My body feels tired and empty. I hold up my hand before they can speak. "Someone needs to get Wafiq's body from the bottom of the mine. We need a proper burial." My eyes stay fixed on the ground.

My hands shake, and Pippa rushes into my arms as my body slumps around her. There are no tears, only heartbreak for a brother I never really knew and who made a wrong turn somewhere along the way. Even with my training as an agent, surrounded by death on a regular basis, losing a life is never easy.

"Mac, if you don't mind, I'll take Pippa with me. See if the commissioner wants to come and take care of Wafiq's body. We'll meet you back at the house." My words sound far away.

"I'm sorry you couldn't save him. We can't save them all, but you gave it a damn good effort." He claps his hand on the back of my shoulder. "I'll take care of everything. Take your time. See you back at the house."

I need time alone with Pippa to process what happened here and discuss the coronation. My hand engulfs hers as we walk to the car. The Range Rover doors suction close cocoons us in our modern world.

We drive in the black of night that hides the mysteries of the Dark Continent, a beautiful yet primitive land trying to keep up-to-date with the modern world. No words were ever truer. The first explorers named it long ago for the land of unknown secrets and its unique rhythm.

We head toward the top of the small mountain over-looking where miners work in the river. The sun breaks on the horizon with a flare of golden rays of light, announcing the start of a new day. Down by the river, workers file in to start their panning for diamonds.

Pippa hasn't said a word but caresses my hand in comfort. I park the car and step out. She follows, coming around the front from the other side.

I lean against the car and pull her to me as I wrap my arms around her. My nose finds her scent, and I close my eyes. Breathing deeply, I try to calm my center. There have been very few moments of relaxation on this trip as tension invades my body.

"You were amazing out there tonight. I'm so proud of you." My words muffle in her hair.

"Thank you," she says and smiles.

We watch as daylight reveals the hidden secrets of the night across the land. The earth comes alive with rich greens, browns, and tan colors. Animals come out from hiding, switching places with their nocturnal counterparts.

This new day doesn't recognize what the night claimed. Time keeps going, lighting the path for daytime creatures to follow. Life keeps moving forward, whether or not I want it to.

"I want you to be part of the MBK team. How do you feel about that?" My heart races, waiting for her answer.

She turns in my arms. "What took you so long? I thought you'd never ask."

"I wanted to wait until our assignment was over. Besides, I can't have you roaming around the countryside without me. God knows where Neil would assign you next." I brush stray hairs away from her eyes, and the breeze whips around her face. "Is that a yes?"

"Yes," she says with a nod.

Her *yes* has more meaning than just joining the team. She wants to give us a chance. She trusts we both have been searching for this without ever knowing it. The last thing I was looking for was love, and it showed up at the craziest time. My need for routine has been shattered as I embrace a life that includes more freedom and a spark with a wild redhead.

"I'm going to have some demands that need to be met." She grabs my shirt collar.

She's doing a beautiful job of distracting me from my latest heartache. "Oh, really? I don't think you're in a position to make any demands."

"The queen's demands are always met, and she requires an office next to her king." Her hand strokes the outside of my pants because her demands make me as hard as diamonds. "He has needs only I can handle."

I smile. "You got that right."

My lips kiss her tenderly at first and then consume her mouth, wanting them to meld with mine and become one. She tastes like freedom, lust, and adventure wrapped in a pretty package I can't wait to unwrap every day. We kiss using our lips and tongues, heightening our passion and pushing away the conversation I don't want to have about Wafiq.

We pull away and touch foreheads. The emotions I put on ice bubble to the surface. "He could have been a good man, proud and strong. I think he would have made an outstanding leader." The older I get, the harder it is to hold back the pain of the fragility of life. Tears form in my eyes for the brother who was young, full of life, and who I will never truly know.

"I think you're right. He made some choices that didn't work in his favor. There were also choices made for him that didn't go as planned either." She strokes my face.

"You can't plan for everything in life." Her thumb wipes away my tears, tears for my brother and the parents who are ghosts in my memory. "How about we head back? You need some TLC, and we have plans to make," she says in a maternal voice. She'll make a wonderful mother someday for our children. *God, where did that come from?*

"About that. I want to honor Wafiq at the coronation as I hand the throne to Sabeen. The people of Mubala don't need to know the gory details, and I think they will embrace Sabeen as their leader." My words are more confident than I am.

We head back to the house full of support from my top-of-the-line team. I regret what I will have to tell Sabeen about her brother. Her loss is immeasurable.

There's a hush as we enter the house. One by one, my teammates enter the foyer and surround Pippa and me.

Peter rolls forward with sorrow in his eyes. "We're so sorry about Wafiq. Mac says you put up a good fight to bring him in. What can we do for you?"

This is why I treasure this team. We are wounded, and yet we stand together. 'When things get tough, the tough get going' is the motto we live by.

We circle Peter, arms across each other's shoulders, and take a moment of silence for everything lost and gained in only a few hours. There's an unbreakable bond that comes when you stand shoulder-to-shoulder with your brothers-in-arms.

"I want you to be at the coronation tomorrow. I wouldn't be here without each of you. It'll be a little different from the coronations you're used to," I say without breaking formation.

There's silence as I see heads turn to one another.

"Beck?" Dean says.

"Yeah?"

"The last coronation I attended was, let's see… oh, never."

I laugh. "My point exactly. I needed a little levity. By the way, I hired Pippa. She's part of the team."

From somewhere in the circle, I hear Declan say, "Yes."

There's a knock at the front door before it swings open, and Sabeen barrels in with a huge smile. As soon as she sees us, her smile slips away. I break from the group and put my arm around her, ushering her into the back room off the kitchen.

She turns toward me with her arms crossed in front of her.

"You don't have good news, do you?" Her eyes glisten with tears.

I shake my head. "No. I tried to convince Wafiq to come back with me where he would be safe." Tears stream down her face. "He took his life when he fell backward in the mine. I couldn't save him, and believe me, I tried." I leave out the information about his part in a world conspiracy group called Deep 8.

She grips her arms in front of her and curls into me as I wrap my arms around her. Her cries are gut-wrenching, like she's being ripped apart from the inside.

I can't imagine what it must be like to lose your parents and brother in the space of two months. Once she calms down, I'll have to tell her about Wafiq being her half-brother and that she's about to become queen. She has a lot to digest, but we're destined to follow a path we know very little about.

FORTY-FOUR

Pippa

WHAT WOULD ORDINARILY BE A CHEERFUL, upbeat day has turned into an event shadowed by Wafiq's death. Beck has dark circles under his eyes as he tossed and turned throughout the night, mumbling in his sleep.

The cloudy day adds to the mood as I turn over and see him lying on his back, staring at the ceiling.

"Are you okay?"

"I didn't think it would end this way. I thought I could bring him in." He turns his head to look at me through vacant eyes.

"He made a lot of choices that weren't in his best interest. You couldn't control the outcome." I nudge his arm up and slip under it with my head on his shoulder. "We need to get up and get dressed for the coronation, ready or not." My hands caress the ridges of his sculpted body. "You have so much beauty, inside and out. Don't focus only on the losses. Celebrate the gains and the future."

I roll on top of him, loving how our bodies fit together. I don't make any moves to get him aroused.

"Even though I'm not in the best mood, you could persuade me to have a quickie before we start the day."

I tuck my head under his chin and can feel him smile. "Maybe later, King, we don't have the time I want to spend on your body."

"You're going to make me wait all day? I think you have a mean streak."

Sitting up, I straddle him, laughing at his attempt to get what he wants as he moves around underneath me. "Yes, I'm going to make you wait. Waiting is good for the soul." I lean down and whisper in his ear, "It makes you want more."

I hop off and run for the bathroom as I feel a whiff of air as his hand misses my arm. My laughter echoes off the walls of the tile bathroom as I hear him say, "You'll pay for that, my queen." At least he's in a better mood.

My charge today is to get Sabeen ready for the coronation. I bypass the guys eating in the dining room as I wave to them with their mouths full of food. There is no rowdy celebration from them on the completed mission. The house is somber, but the tension has left it as if Tadashi and Aafia approve.

I hop in a car and head over to Sabeen's house. Her front door opens before I have a chance to knock. A beautiful young woman answers the door and, without saying a word, opens it wide enough to pull me in.

Her smile is innocent and infectious as her white teeth gleam and her eyes sparkle. I smile back and reach out my hand to her. Before I say a word, several other young women show up. At the same time, they kneel in front of me with their hand on their forehead and the other arm straight out.

The power of the moment hits me in the chest. In the time I've been here, the people have been less than welcoming. Many locals have made unflattering comments at my expense, but something has changed. I'm taken aback by the gesture and fiddle with my necklace.

"Please, stand up. I'm not sure what's going on, but you don't have to kneel."

Sabeen comes down the stairs. "I told them about you. Dacari shared with me how brave you were in getting your mission accomplished. You are a fierce warrior. They want to be like you, and they are honoring you as Dacari's queen."

"I'm not the queen. We aren't married, but thank you for the kind words." To say I'm humbled would be an understatement.

She is stunning in a sleeveless gold lace dress that fits her like a glove. The bottom flows around her like sparkling water. Her skin is brushed in fine gold shimmer. I stand in awe.

"You look like a queen, ready for the throne," I say breathlessly.

She blushes. "Thank you. We need to do my makeup."

She holds out her hand to me and guides me back upstairs. Her room is at the end of the hall, and she sits on a bench in front of the mirror.

Her beauty is one layer of a strong, smart, and kind woman. I think of the opportunities she would have outside of Mubala, but that's not where she's needed most. Her power and grace will come from leading her people to a better place.

"Are you ready to become queen?" I ask cautiously.

She picks up her makeup brush. "Is anyone ever ready to become a queen? Being in a royal family isn't always what it's cracked up to be. Ask Prince Harry and Meghan Markle."

"Good point." We laugh together.

She applies her makeup as I shave her, according to tribal tradition. She's even more stunning bald. I realize we are the same at our core as women, friends, and in strength. But we hold our power differently.

My power is obvious in the way I look and act. Her strength is internal in a quiet reverence. They have groomed her for this position since birth, whether she knows it or not.

I slip into the dress Sabeen has picked out for me for the evening. The gown is a deep ruby red that almost matches my hair. Sequins are patterned to have a likeness of flames. The cut of the gown is snug in the right places, and there's a slit up the side of the dress. This will tease Beck even more.

She hands me a box. "Open it. It's from Dacari."

I open the box to reveal the two stunning emerald and diamond earrings from her warehouse shop.

"Wow! These are beautiful. He went overboard."

I slip them on my ears and watch them shimmer in the mirror. I see a woman who's been transformed and accepted by her peers. In some ways, life is just getting started.

She grabs her *shuka* lying on the bed and drapes it over her arm. The young women stand at the bottom of the stairs and stare at her in awe. They kneel in a circle. She doesn't tell them to get up but walks through them to the door with her head held high.

They decorated the hall where the coronation will take place to the nines. The accent colors are red, black, and gold. Two long tables in the middle of the room are loaded with food. There's enough to feed the entire city, but they have limited this celebration to close family, friends, and town council members.

As before, we're asked to store our shoes and go barefoot. In honor of tonight, I've painted my toenails black and red, and Sabeen's are bright red. A man stops us at the entrance to the hall, and another man bangs his cane three times and announces us.

"Welcome, Princess Sabeen Ellen Siwanda and Pippa Stevens."

A hush comes over the room as Sabeen shakes hands with several people, and I make my escape to the huddle of men from my new team. I can't wait for our next adventure together. Family is who you make it.

They look uncomfortable. When I look down, I can see why. I laugh. "I guess you don't enjoy going barefoot."

Mac, Declan, and Dean are the only ones who wiggle their toes and smile. They are wearing black pants with some kind of red shirt, the standard dress code for this event.

"How's Sabeen doing?" Campbell asks. I think he's sweet on her.

"She's going to make a fine queen. Where's Beck?" I look around the room.

They raise their thumbs to the back of the hall. Behind the curtain, I can see him pacing and wringing his hands.

I peek behind the curtain. "Hey, whatcha doing?"

He's dressed in a special red and black *shuka* accented with gold beads. He shaved his head bald to show that nothing will come between him and the crown. The sight of him hits me right between my legs. He rushes toward me and holds me tight.

"I can't breathe. You need to let up a little," I wheeze.

"Sorry, I'm nervous. God, you look gorgeous. What do you say we skip out of here and go for a ride?" He lets me go but holds on to my arms.

I shake my head. "When you addressed the city council members, you were brilliant. You'll do fine, and I have faith in you. Lean down, please." I kiss him on the nose. "Thank you for the earrings. They are beautiful."

He breathes out. "You're welcome. They match your eyes. I've never been king before, even if it's only for a few seconds." He holds up a piece of paper. "There's a protocol I have to follow to make this official. I've only memorized half of it."

"Take the paper with you and read from it. Then you need to speak from your heart." I place my hand on his chest, feeling his heartbeat.

He nods, and his shoulders fall as he lets out a shallow breath. He's not relaxed, but he seems better.

"I reserved a table up front for you and the guys." His lips don't quite make it into a smile as his fingers grip the paper.

"We'll be there for you all the way. Now, go knock 'em dead."

His face falls.

My hands flutter in front of me. "It's an American expression meaning do your best."

I give him another kiss and find the table with the guys sitting around it with sodas in front of them. They're drinking soda instead of beer to support Declan. They look like fish out of water and get stares from other people attending the event. Some women have taken an interest.

I take a seat next to Declan, and he squeezes my hand and smiles. The Dark Lord seems to have shed his gloomy mood for a bit.

The ceremony begins, and Beck stands to deliver his speech, which he does brilliantly. He kneels as Katoo places the crown on his head and stands before the audience, beaming with pride. His crown has more bling than the Crown jewels.

The road to this event has been long and arduous, but the hurdles were worth it to see him at this moment. He makes the most of it, knowing it's fleeting. The audience gives him a standing ovation.

He sits on the throne, and Katoo hands him a red velvet

box. Sabeen enters the stage from the right side and sits next to him. He opens the box, takes out the crown, and stands. Sabeen kneels in front of him as he places the crown on her bald head. Her crown has enormous diamonds, rubies, and emeralds inlaid in gold. He hands his crown back to Katoo, who puts it back in a black velvet box. The transfer is complete.

Beck offers Sabeen his hand, and they stand together to a cheering crowd. Once the crowd calms down, Beck and Sabeen look at each other, ready to tell Wafiq's story.

"Our hearts are heavy as we stand before you without our brother, Wafiq. As you already know, he fell to his death in the mine." He pauses. "I tried to save him, but I wasn't fast enough to catch him before he fell. He was a brother and a leader you counted on. If it weren't for his death, he would be standing here instead of me." He takes Sabeen's hand. "We will celebrate his life and what he gave to this city."

The truth about Wafiq would serve no purpose and could hurt Sabeen's reign over Mubala. We don't know how far-reaching Deep 8's hands are, but we want to keep them guessing what we know and don't know. Beck has vowed to keep a close eye on Sabeen and any activity of Deep 8.

He nods as a screen comes down at the side of the hall, and a video cues up, starting with photos of Beck as a young boy. He stares at the photos in wonder about his time here in Mubala, a time he doesn't remember much of.

The audience laughs at funny photos of a little boy full of happiness. The photographs morph into pictures of Wafiq and Sabeen as children and travel through time to the two of them as adults.

When it's over, Beck shows Sabeen to the throne and leaves the stage to sit at our table. He shakes hands with each member of the team because, without them, we wouldn't be here.

He finds a chair and pulls it over next to me. My face hurts from smiling. His arm wraps around the back of my chair, and he leans over.

"What are you grinning about?"

"You. My lady parts are screaming right now because you are beyond hot as a bald man. Who knew? I think you should keep it like that. The queen has spoken."

He scoots around in his chair. "Maybe we should take that ride."

I take a sip of champagne, letting the sweet liquid coat my lips, and then lick them slowly. "I think I would love to go for a ride."

He breaks our gaze long enough to deliver his message to the team. "We're wheels up at oh eight hundred tomorrow. If you're not on the airfield, you'll get left behind, so don't stay up too late." He smiles.

He grabs my hand as we walk out of the hall and into the sultry night to discover all the ways we can ride.

Epilogue

BECK

Pippa and I ride into the night, never missing a moment of touching one another, marking our time here together. The alarm goes off way too soon as we pack our belongings in record time and get everything loaded up.

While everyone is out on the curb, I take a moment to walk around my parents' house one last time, inhaling the smells, running my fingers along the surfaces, and listening for voices from my past. The memories I had of being here as a child are fading, serving their purpose, and evaporating, replaced by memories made with Pippa.

I know I'll be back to visit, but there is a finality that rests here. My hope is the three of them are together and at peace. Jobi and Katoo will keep a watchful eye on Sabeen and any interference from Deep 8, but I think our message is clear. We know about you.

We take two Range Rovers to the airfield, where the corporate jet waits for us. The quiet in the car is one of contemplation about what's ahead for us where Deep 8 is concerned. We have only two pieces of a mystery that has more questions than answers.

The team throws their duffels in the cargo bay and shuffles up the stairs for the long trip ahead. Pippa walks ahead of me onto the plane as I enjoy the view.

"Whoa, nice ride. I'm glad I decided to join your team. Money is no object, and the possibilities are endless." She wiggles her brows.

I bend down and whisper, "Money is never an issue when it comes to you, but don't get any ideas about what this flight has to offer."

"But I'm full of creative ideas that could happen during the flight home, and I don't need your money," she scoffs.

I pinch her ass as a warning, and she giggles, swatting my hand away.

The team's time on this plane has been extensive, and it feels like home with its cream interior and saddle-colored leather seats. What Pippa doesn't know is that we got this for a song. This was a gift after a mission to take out a sheik who played both sides against the middle. Our client paid us very well for the job and threw in the plane.

We're settled in and have leveled off at cruising altitude when my secure line rings from Neil.

"Hello, Neil." Heads turn in my direction.

"Is everyone there?" Neil cuts right to the chase.

"Yes. I'm going to put you up on the screen." The touch-screen whiteboard does everything but make pancakes. I make Neil the co-host so he can share his screen.

"Hello, everyone. I hope you enjoyed your holiday because the fun is just getting started," Neil jokes, but everyone is silent. His head is about four feet tall, and we can see the pimple on his nose.

He clears his throat. "I see you have the woman extraordinaire you poached from me."

I give him my biggest smile. "She's mine to keep."

"I'm sure. I wanted to say how sorry I was to hear about your brother's death, especially when you were getting to know him. In case you're wondering, he had a long history of being involved with the wrong people. It doesn't make it hurt any less. I just thought you would want to know."

He shuffles papers on his desk, trying to make a graceful transition. "I have news about our friends at Deep 8, and the mineral Sean found in Afghanistan. Stellarium is a mineral that burns at a very high temperature for a long time. At the moment, we're burning a piece we've been burning for a month. That kind of burn rate is a powerful source of energy. I can see why Deep 8 wants it."

"What are we doing about the access to those mines in the sandbox?" Sean was in the Afghan mines that are worth over a trillion dollars.

"The Taliban has taken over the region again, and they have no idea what they're sitting on. Their takeover was well-orchestrated, but corruption runs wide and deep in Afghanistan. I doubt Deep 8 can get in there either. For now, it will sit in the mines untouched. What we don't know is how much they have already." Sean's face hardens as he nods.

Peter swings around from his laptop, a permanent extension of his body. "What about the trackers we planted on those crates with the chipped diamonds?"

"I'm glad you asked. Not all the trackers activated." Neil's lips pinch together.

"Damn it," Peter says under his breath. "I need to work on that. My guess is they dissolved before they got to their destination."

Neil waves his hand. "No worries. We have enough of them activated to know where they went."

Everyone shifts in their seat, waiting for Neil to tell us about the big reveal of the next puzzle piece.

"We tracked the crates to Qatar, Singapore, Luxemburg, Switzerland, and the United States. We have to dig through Wafiq's system to see if he was tracking them or if it's someone else. My guess is Deep 8 is tracking the individual diamonds. Based on the cities where they landed, those diamonds went to wealthy, prominent people in each country to gather intel or move large sums of money. We'll have more when we uncover the information on Wafiq's mainframe."

He hesitates. "I received a message from them via email, which is hard to do considering who I work for. My guess is they have people on the inside."

"Mate, are you going to share the message?" Dean asks.

He shares his screen. The quote is from Henry Kissinger.

Who controls the food supply controls the people; who controls the energy can control whole continents; who controls money can control the world. We're well on our way.

A hush comes over the team. "Do you think they know our firm is involved?" Sean asks.

"It's hard to say. I don't think so. Your firm is way off-book. No one in the agency is privy to what we are doing. You're safe for now, but that could change. Beck, any word on Zahara?"

"No. She's in the wind. I think she was the brains behind the operation, based on what Wafiq told me. Do you have a bead on her?"

"Yes, she went back to Germany to work for her former employer. Your blood work came back. There are some interesting components in the memory drug and other compounds we don't recognize. We think she's working to perfect the memory drug. She's a brilliant researcher and has been working on it for years. She seems to have come into a lot of money lately, and there may be ties to Deep 8. I need someone to infiltrate her company. Do you know anyone with a biochemistry background?" He sits back and rests his chin in his hand.

Our heads turn to Declan. "Oh, hell no. I just got out of the field and I'm still in recovery."

"The rules are different out here. You'll be able to do things you couldn't do before. You better study up. Once we debrief, you're on the next flight to Cologne, Germany. I'll give you the contact information when you get back to the office." Neil stares at Declan for a minute with sorrow in his eyes, an unusual reaction for him. "I'm sorry I have to send you back there, but we have no choice. You'll have a contact on the inside. There are too many lives on the line. Safe travels." Neil blips off the screen as it goes dark.

Silence falls over the cabin with the sound of jet engines whirling in the background as we race back home.

Mac turns to Declan. "What does he mean he's sorry to send you back there?"

Declan shrugs and stares at his hands. "It's nothing. You wouldn't understand."

Mac frowns at Declan's mysterious response. "I'm always here for you. Welcome aboard, big brother. You're about to have your first mission. Stay sharp." Mac doesn't press him.

The Dark Lord grumbles something, and panic washes across his face. His demons wait for him in Germany.

THE KEY *to unlocking a hidden love lies in the shadows of forgotten memories*. What demons wait for Declan in

Germany? Will he get answers about a past he can't remember?

Grab your copy of **BURN** in the Deep 8 series now!

FREE Book

I love staying in touch with my readers.
Sign up for my newsletter for updates, giveaways, and other exclusives, and receive **Silent Night** for **FREE** at

https://bit.ly/FREEKenzie

Caught between beauty's embrace and betrayal's kiss.

She must save her brother. He only sees her betrayal. Will they find love or fall prey to a deadly rescue plan?

Chloe's dream of becoming a journalist gets crushed when she can't secure a job. Forced to make ends meet, she takes a job at a J. Luc Gallery. But when her brother gets held for ransom, Chloe is thrust into a dangerous mission to save him, jeopardizing her budding romance.

Desperate to save her brother, Chloe makes a heart-wrenching decision, forcing her to betray Jean Luc. As MBK Global Security races against time to make the exchange, their plan teeters on the brink of failure, threatening to leave Chloe in danger and Jean Luc's heart in pieces.

Please consider leaving a review

If you enjoyed **KING,** I would love it if you let your friends know so they can experience the action-packed and suspense filled story of Beck and Pippa.

Reviews are so precious to writers. Writing a review helps other readers find my books and is helpful when deciding what to read next.
If you have a minute, please leave a review. Thank you in advance for taking the time to help others find KING.

Also by Kenzie Macallan

MBK Global Security

Truths

(Mac & Marbella's story)

Mara is hiding a terrible secret. He's on a dangerous mission. Can Mac protect the love of his life from a ruthless killer?

Edges

(Dean & Leigha's story)

Leigha is under threat. Dean is undercover. Will deadly family secrets ruin the romance of a lifetime?

Masks

(Michael & Raquelle's story)

Raquelle is investigating him. Misha is accused of fraud. Will a sinister conspiracy ruin their shot at unforgettable love?

Deep 8 series

Wild

(Sean & Jess's story)

Jess leaped into a war zone to get the story. Sean will endure hell to bring her home. Sparks fly, but will romance die on the wrong side of a bullet?

Burn

(Declan & Olivia's story)

Olivia is a scientist fighting to keep her secret hidden. Declan is an ex-soldier with a tragic past and lost memories. Will the chemistry between them ignite lost love?

Risk

(Campbell & Quinn's story)

She created a game-changing nuclear weapon. He must keep her safe from a powerful enemy. As embers ignite between them, will their passion lead to an explosive meltdown?

Torn

(Roger and Harlow's story)

Harlow is undercover to find her father's killer. Roger must find his father before Deep 8 kills him for the software that will change the world.

About the Author

Kenzie Macallan is an author who skillfully weaves intricate action-adventure romances as art imitates life. Not really, but her vivid imagination often finds solace within the pages of her books. Having explored the diverse landscapes of Africa, Greece, Switzerland, Holland, France, England, and Scotland, her travels have ignited a relentless wellspring of storytelling.

This fuels her artistic endeavors, from painting captivating portraits to capturing moments through her camera, all while nurturing her green thumb in the garden. While culinary mastery may elude her, she loves to bake, much to the gratitude of her husband.

Kenzie's true passion lies in transporting readers to captivating realms, where flawed yet endearing heroes emerge, intelligent and resilient women take center stage, and unexpected endings leave them in awe. With each new adventure, Kenzie eagerly anticipates the opportunity to further enchant her readers and embark on a shared journey of discovery.

She loves to hear from her fans.
Join her newsletter for cover reveals, new books, deals, and giveaways.
Website: www.kenziemacallan.com

Acknowledgments

A huge thank you goes out to the readers who took a chance on me and read this book. If you left a review, I'm forever grateful because they are like diamonds, so hard to find and yet shine brightly. Your support is greatly appreciated. You make it all worthwhile.

I want to thank my husband who doesn't see me for many hours on end and still gives me his unwavering support. He doesn't interrupt me except to show me a funny TikTok video. We seemed to have found a balance. You're wonderful!

To my mom, who is brave enough to read every one of my books.

Thanks to Karen, who gave me invaluable feedback and found the little things that make all the difference, making it sparkle like a diamond.